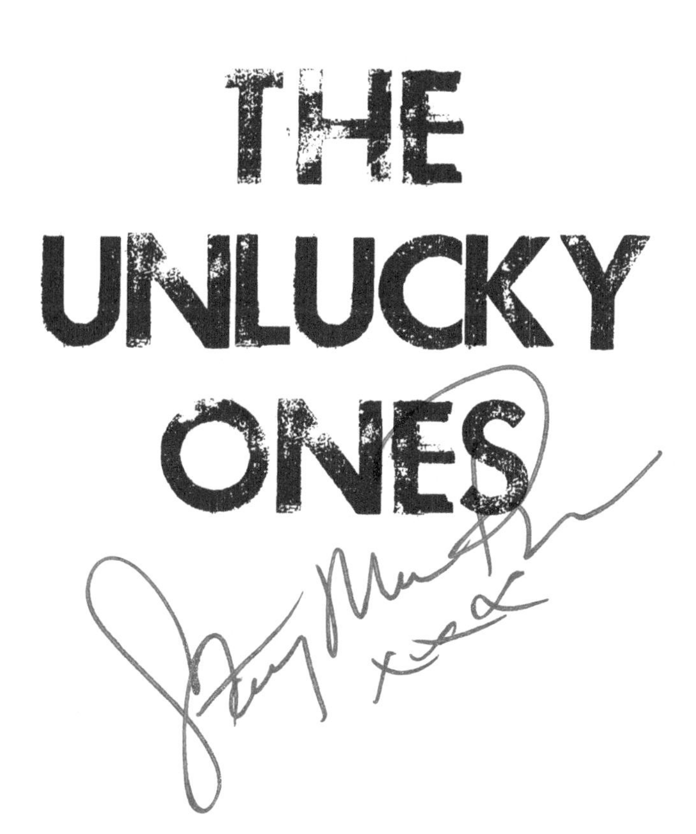

STACEY MARIE BROWN

Published by: Twisted Fairy Publishing Inc.

Cover by: Hang Le Designs (http://www.byhangle.com/)

Developmental Editor Jordan Rosenfeld (http://jordanrosenfeld.net)

Edited by Hollie (www.hollietheeditor.com)

ALSO BY STA

Contemporary Romance

Buried Alive

Shattered Love **(Blinded Love #1)**

Broken Love **(Blinded Love #2)**

Twisted Love **(Blinded Love #3)**

Paranormal Romance

Darkness of Light
(Darkness Series #1)

Fire in the Darkness
(Darkness Series #2)

Beast in the Darkness
(An Elighan Dragen Novelette)

Dwellers of Darkness
(Darkness Series #3)

Blood Beyond Darkness
(Darkness Series #4)

West
(A Darkness Series Novel)

City in Embers
(Collector Series #1)

The Barrier Between
(Collector Series #2)

Across the Divide
(Collector Series #3)

From Burning Ashes
(Collector Series #4)

The Crown of Light
(Lightness Saga #1)

Lightness Falling
(Lightness Saga #2)

The Fall of the King
(Lightness Saga #3)

Rise from the Embers
(Lightness Saga #4)

The Monster Ball:
(A Paranormal Romance Anthology)

"When the soul suffers too much, it develops a taste for misfortune."

—Albert Camus, The First Man

CHAPTER ONE

"There's nothing worse than meeting the perfect person at the wrong time."

Leaves brushed in deep crimson and brown floated and twirled to the ground. They kissed the earth in a gentle death, sighing in relief their time was up.

I wanted to be one of them. Floating away into a peaceful oblivion.

"Devon?" A woman's gentle voice tugged me back into the room where I sat, but I continued to stare out, not ready to let go of this last moment of serenity. Reality gnawed at my edges with a warning that it was about to run my ass over like a freight train. "Devon." A hand touched mine, and I jerked my head, busting the wall between me and the devastation I had held at arm's length. The shock and sorrow churned my mind into white noise.

"I know this must be a shock. But I am here for you. Don't be afraid to ask any questions."

I pinched my mouth together in resentment at the blonde woman I had known all my life. Her brown eyes closed with sympathy as she leaned nearer to me, her white doctor's coat brushing my knees. Jocelyn Walters, now Dr. Jocelyn Matheson, had graduated the same year as my mom and married the guy who ran the lone grocery store in town. My mom hadn't run in the same circle as Jocelyn, being more of a wild child, but everybody in this town knew each other. You couldn't piss without everyone knowing.

"Are you sure?" I croaked out in a whisper, though I knew in my gut it was true. I'd seen the signs for some time but brushed them off, making excuses for every episode. I tried not to think about how we lost my grandmother.

Dr. Matheson leaned back onto her desk, her eyebrows furrowed in sympathy.

"Yes. I'm sorry." She tugged at her doctor's coat. "It's extremely rare for someone so young, but not unprecedented, especially with your family history. We think it's a form of the disease called familial Alzheimer's. Most often someone has a grandparent or parent who was also diagnosed with it at an earlier age." She sighed, this being hard on her too. "She has early-onset, which is quite unusual. Only about five percent with Alzheimer's develop symptoms in their 40s and 50s."

I stared down at my hands, blinking back the tears, feeling the weight of taking this news alone. My older sister blamed her morning sickness and fatigue on why she couldn't make it. Bullshit. She wasn't throwing up. She just didn't want to come, leaving me to be the responsible one as usual.

"I have reading material for you, so you'll know what to look for. How to respond." Dr. Matheson grunted as she reached for the pamphlets behind her on the desk in her tiny white office. One framed picture of her family sat on the desk, and huge filing cabinets lined the wall behind the paper-cluttered desk.

She probably only used this office when she had to deliver bad news in private. When the nurse called me and walked me down the stark hallways to this room, my gut screamed I should run. Deep down, I knew what the results would be, but those few moments before…I could still live in denial. Hope.

My fingers wrapped around the brochures, filling my lungs with cement. By taking them, I felt as if I were agreeing to what was going to happen, to the devastation that would tug my small family further into hell.

My gaze wandered over the large bold letters at the top of the papers. *Dealing with Alzheimer's.* Tears burned my eyes.

"I know it seems scary right now, but your mother is in the beginning stages." Dr. Matheson tucked a strand of her shoulder-length hair back into her blunt-cut ponytail. "On average, a person with Alzheimer's lives eight to ten years after diagnosis, but there have been cases where they lived as short as three years but as long as twenty years. Usually, early-onset is a more aggressive form, which can lead to a more rapid decline. But, Devon, there are treatments now that can improve or slow its development and might be able to help her live longer."

Live? Is this what you call it when your own mind was being ripped from you.

I peered down at my hands, my long dark brown hair shielding my expression from her, a twitch of pain fluttering over my face. Those cases, we all knew, were the one percent of one percent. My family didn't have that kind of luck.

My father was not quite a year in the grave—shot in the line of duty. My sister barely made it through her first year of community college before getting knocked up by her abusive boyfriend and dropping out. My mom lost her job at the bakery a few months after losing my dad. Money was a constant problem; some months our cable and heat were turned off.

We had never been well off, but we'd never hurt like this. During the past year everything had declined for us, especially our financial situation. Chief Lee, the leader of the Native American tribe my father was raised in, took care of Dad's burial, his spirit and body back on tribal land up in the mountains, but the bills stretched far beyond his funeral. As generous as the residents of our town were, leaving meals on our porch for us couldn't pay the bills.

Almost eighteen and a senior in high school, it all fell on my shoulders to keep everything together.

After we lost my dad, I thought my mom's confusion and lack of memory were from grief. Why I had pushed away what I'd known in my gut. But no.

She had a disease that would slowly shred every memory and most of her bodily functions from her, tearing her apart along with us. Jocelyn told me the disease can go undiagnosed for several years.

"Your mom knows, but I wanted to talk to you alone." Jocelyn tilted her head, sympathy radiating from her. It was no secret I would be the one to help my mother. Amelia, though older, was never the responsible one. If she could get out of doing anything, she would. Responsibility fell to me as long as I could remember. "I can understand how devastating this news is. And you might have a lot of questions and concerns you'd rather your mother didn't hear. You can be yourself here. This disease affects everyone in your family. You might feel sad. Confused. Angry."

Silence.

"I'm here, Devon. Right now I can help with any concerns you have, but there will be a time when her disease will progress past what I am capable of dealing with."

Jocelyn was a family practice physician. Our miniscule town didn't have any specialized hospitals or doctors. For that we had to head to bigger cities.

The leaflets sat on my lap as I rolled over everything. I knew sadness, anger, fear, and a million other emotions were somewhere inside, but I didn't feel any of them. Just numb.

"I want to go home." The papers crunched in my hands as I stood up. Every bone seemed to have doubled in weight since I stepped in here.

"I understand." Jocelyn nodded, rising from her desk to her full height, her head barely reaching my nose. I was a little above average height, my five-foot-eight frame was muscular and lean from track. Running was my escape, where I could shut off the world and forget my life. "Process everything and if you need to talk, please call. Anytime. You have my cell. I know this must be so difficult for you and your sister…after your father." She placed a hand on her chest. "We all miss him so much."

My teeth thrust into my bottom lip. *So do I.* Sheriff Jason Thorpe had been the kind who volunteered on his days off, would stop for a duck and her ducklings crossing the road and block traffic to make sure they got safely to the river. Then return every day to feed them. He was fair and compassionate and didn't see every case as black or white. He took into account human mistakes and the situations causing them. He cared about everyone.

In this tiny town everyone had adored him, but sometimes I had resented it. I disliked all the weekends he chose doing his duty instead of spending time with his daughters. With me.

Now that he was gone, I saw him more for the man the town had. He'd been fit and handsome at fifty, which made his death even more cruel. He'd gone on a domestic abuse call, where the man had been high on PCP and shot him point-blank as my dad tried to get the abused wife safely away from him.

The role of head sheriff had gone to Dad's young brother, Gavin. My uncle, five years younger, followed in his big brother's footsteps. But Uncle Gavin was a stickler for the rules. To him, everything was completely black or white.

The door creaked open, and I turned toward the exit. Jody, the nurse, entered the room escorting my mom.

Mom had aged in this last year beyond her forty-seven years. Wearing baggy gray sweats and jacket, her once long silky blonde hair was now streaked with a few strands of gray and cut up to her shoulders. She was my height and curvy but had always kept herself fit…until my dad's death. Now the muscles were slowly dissolving away, her eyes and forehead lined with wrinkles, her eyes dull. She'd given up on everything except her several glasses of wine each night.

"Devon." Mom's face crumpled. "I am so sorry."

Her eyes flooded with heartbreak. She staggered to me, her arms wrapping around me. Her pale skin contrasted with my darker skin and hair. My mom looked every bit of her Norwegian origins. Amelia got the darker skin and eyes like Dad but seemed to try and be more like the Norwegian side, dyeing her hair a blondish color and complaining about her brown eyes. I liked being similar to my dad. I was proud of my Native heritage. The only things I got from Mom were her hazel eyes, freckles, and height.

Don't cry. Don't cry. She needs you to be strong.

"What do you have to be sorry for?" I crushed her to me, needing to comfort and be comforted. Even though she hadn't been present this last year, she was still my mom. She was supposed to take care of my sister and me, telling us everything would be all right.

No more.

It would probably land on me even more to keep this family going with Amelia pregnant. College would have to wait. My dreams of doing a semester abroad in Italy or South America crumbled into dust.

"Because. This is happening to you too." She pulled away, tears leaking down the corners of her eyes. "I am going to be such a weight on you. I can't do that to you." She gripped my face, her chest wracked with agony. "What about college? A job? Oh god…" She moved away, fear widening her huge eyes. "Will I know my own granddaughter when she's born? Will I be able to go to the park with her unsupervised? Witness my daughters getting married? I will drain you. Physically and emotionally. And the money? We don't have money for the care I'll need." Her arms waved around frantically, her feet pacing like a caged animal.

"Mom, stop." I swallowed. The nurse moved in behind her, trying to soothe her. "You are not a drain. We will figure it out."

"Figure it out? I'm slowly losing my mind. Soon I will not remember you, much less how to eat or breathe." She wailed, shoving the nurse away from her.

"Alyssa, let's sit down." Jocelyn swiftly cut in between us, taking Mom's hands.

"How would you feel, Jocelyn, if you knew you were going to lose everything that makes you, you?" Fear and anguish twisted her face. "I am forty-seven and I have Alzheimer's. How fair is that? Was it not enough I lost my husband, my heart? But I must lose my mind while my girls watch?" Jocelyn bundled up my mother as she crumpled to the floor, sobs wracking her body. Strings of saliva sprayed from her mouth as she yowled.

My throat swelled with torment, watching my mom fall apart. Inside I was walking close to the ledge, about to fall over with her, but I tried to push it away, knowing she needed me to hold it together. Be strong.

"She needs something to relax her." She stroked Mom's head as I watched the tension drift out of my mother's body. "I will send you home with something to help her sleep or relax when she starts to get like this." Jocelyn turned to glance at me. "This is a very normal response to this news. The pills will be temporary, until you all can start dealing with this."

Dealing with this? I think I need a bottle of the pills myself.

The drive home was silent. Mom stared vacantly out the window and walked like a zombie into her bedroom when we got to our small three-bedroom house. The house was built in the seventies. Dingy brown shag rug in the living room was so worn down it no longer looked like shag carpet, and the avocado-colored stove was with scuffed light-yellow laminate counters. Not much had changed since it was built, making it always feel grimy, no matter how much you cleaned.

Dirty dishes Amelia left in the sink were still there but, of course, she wasn't. I had tried calling and texting her a dozen times, but she was off in her own world. Probably at Zak's. Even though he made it clear he wanted nothing to do with the baby, she still clung to the idea she could change his mind. He was a massive dick. I hated him with every fiber of my being. My sister was self-centered but not cruel. He was the nasty kind of egotist.

My boyfriend was the opposite. Sweet, loving, romantic. Cory and I started dating in ninth grade, both captains of our track team. We spent a lot of time together, and eventually at an away competition he kissed me. We had been together ever since.

Tall, lean, with dark hair and eyes, big ears and smile, he was cute because of his personality, but by no means gorgeous. He was popular because he had a thing about him, a good nature which drew people in. Always happy, he had a smile that could make your day feel lighter. How many times his smile had taken away the sorrows of my life. All I wanted now was to feel his arms around me, hear his voice saying it would be okay, but he was four hours away at a track competition. My coach didn't even ask if I was participating. This last year, my extracurricular activities had been replaced by a waitressing job at the local diner. My friend Jasmine took my spot as captain.

"Do you need anything?" I helped lift my mom's limp form on the bed. She snuggled into her pillow as I covered her in blankets.

"No, I just want to sleep." Her voice sounded void of any emotion. "Did you talk to your sister?"

"I will try to call her again."

My mom nodded, sharing a look with me. She understood how Amelia was.

"Rest, Mom. I'll be right here."

"No." Mom's dull hazel eyes darted to me. "I know you were supposed to meet Skylar…please go."

"Mom, I am not leaving you."

"All I am going to do is sleep." She wrapped her hand around my fingers. "Please, Devon. I want you to. You need your best friend right now. I promise I will be fine." She held my gaze. "Go."

I hated the thought of leaving her, but the need to get away also tugged at my heels.

"I'll be upset if you don't. Make me happy and go have dinner with Skylar. Laugh, talk, cry. This will all be here waiting for you."

I blinked away the tears. The way she spoke, she was already treating herself like a burden.

"Mom…"

"Go. Devon. *Please*."

I nodded, leaned over and kissed her head. "Okay, but if you need me for anything, please text or call me."

"I will." She squeezed my hand, letting her lids flutter closed. Leaving her with a glass of water and her cell on the nightstand, I jumped into my run-down Toyota, the tires kicking the gravel as I zoomed for the other side of town. The evening wind swirling through the open window held a note of cooler weather to come. The late-autumn sun dipped toward the mountains.

A fleeting thought ran through my mind to keep driving. And never turn back. That was not who I was. I didn't run. But if I thought nothing more could happen to me today, or if I smartly assumed my bad luck had more in store for me, I would have kept driving.

CHAPTER TWO

I skidded my car to a stop next to Sue's compact pickup truck, which was coated in dust. She owned the restaurant, creatively named, *Sue's Diner*, so if the lights were on, she was there. I bit down on my lip, my gaze following the bodies moving around the restaurant. *This was a bad idea. I shouldn't be here.*

My cell dinged with a message from Skylar: *Too late. I see you sitting there debating.*

I shook my head with a snort. Ever since we became friends in preschool, I never could get away with anything. But I think if she knew what kind of news I was bringing, she'd want me to drive away now. My shock had kept me from texting her or Cory, and we told each other everything.

Well, in this town it was going to get out soon enough.

I blew out through my mouth and got out of the car, pointing my feet toward the entrance. The diner was full of the usual locals, with some tourists sprinkled in.

The lone thing keeping this town on any map was its close proximity to the Colorado border one way and skiing in the mountains the other. The diner also got rave reviews for its food, but we were neither a kitschy stop nor an interesting historical destination. Those were a few towns over.

The chime on the diner door announced my arrival. Working here, I had begun to respond to it like a dog expecting a bone, hoping for another big-tipping table to help pay the electricity bill.

Familiar heads swung my way, eyes burning into me. All chatter stopped as everyone froze in place. It took a moment for the tourists, who were looking around in confusion, to pick up on the silence.

"Oh my god…Devon," Skylar's choked voice sailed from our usual booth, her hazel eyes filled with tears. She hustled toward me on long legs and wrapped her outstretched arms around me, squeezing me tight. She wore one of the dresses she had painted herself, swirls of oranges, reds, purples, and blues spreading from her hip across her body as if a desert sunset exploded. It was so Skylar. Unique, vibrant, and beautiful. She was the child of two artists. They divorced when she was a kid. Her dad lived and worked in an artist shop in Santa Fe, where various artists rented out spots to sell their work in his shop. It helped pay rent while he painted canvas landscapes of New Mexico. Her mom sold jewelry she created from all kinds of recycled items to sell to vendors. "I am so sorry."

"How?" I whispered, my best friend's embrace melting the numbness, my lids fluttering with the currents of pain.

"Jody told her sister, who told Kelly, who told Alejandro."

My eyes darted through an opening to the kitchen, the chef's face popping through, his brown eyes soft with sorrow. Alejandro was an excellent cook, which was why we had so many tourists stopping on their way through. We might have been the only diner where the chef treated all his food as if it were a five-star restaurant.

It shouldn't have been a shock that everyone already knew about Mom. Most of the time I felt trapped by the smallness of this town, but today I appreciated I didn't have to talk. I could just nod as their apologies and promises of baked goods flooded in.

"I can't believe this." Skylar held on to me, her embrace soothing the icy walls I'd thrown up back at the doctor's office. "I-I can't...not your mom."

I stepped back, my throat tight, but I was not ready for sorrow to take me. If I let too much in, it would settle into every pore and drown me.

My best friend since we were three, she brushed the tears trickling down her face, her porcelain skin splotchy with grief, and tucked her long strawberry-blonde hair behind her ear. The moment her mother moved them here after a sticky divorce into the house down the street with her grandparents, we became immediate friends. My house was her house and vice versa.

We were both lean and about the same height, but that was where our similarities ended. Her pale skin and red-blonde hair were a beacon for the boys around here, even though she was only interested in the guys passing through town. She would wrinkle her nose at the prospect of dating any of those we grew up with. She was the ultimate trophy or treasure to date. Our other friend Jasmine was close behind, bringing more notice to our unique trio. Half Asian, half Caucasian, she was tiny with beautiful dark hair and eyes. The three of us caused a lot of attention, our differences standing out here.

Skylar had been there when my mom had a couple of her episodes after Dad died seeming to struggle in our conversations with finding the right words and being confused as to where she was. Skylar would always reassure me Mom was just grieving. I had held on to this belief so tightly, even when it felt I was trying to hold water.

"Oh, Devon, honey." Jennifer shuffled up to me, the material of her waitress's outfit stretching dangerously thin as she held her arms open to me. She was all of five feet with boobs the size of two toddlers playing hide-and-seek in her bra. In her early forties, she was the mother hen and always had a warm hug and smile waiting, no matter what was going on in her life.

I pressed my teeth into my bottom lip. If I let her hug me, I was done. Worse, a line of local well-wishers queued behind her. The oxygen twisted out of my lungs.

"Guys, she's had to process a lot today." Skylar stepped in, blocking their path, knowing without a word exactly what I felt. "Let's give her some breathing room."

The group of employees and townsfolk nodded, stepping back. Skylar had a way about her; she could pretty much get everything she wanted. Teachers, parents, peers—she had them all wrapped around her finger with a bat of her lashes.

Skylar grabbed my hand and pulled me into a booth.

"Thank you," I muttered, running my fingers through my tangled dark strands.

"Jesus, Dev." Skylar's eyes fluttered and she looked to the ceiling, presumably to halt her tears. "I can't believe this. Why didn't you call me? You know I would have gone with you."

"I know." I grabbed for the glass of water in front of me. "I appreciate it but…"

"But what?" Her attention returned to my face. "I know you were alone. I saw your sister and her dickwad boyfriend driving up to the mountain. What excuse did she give you this time?"

So that was why Amelia didn't answer her phone? Reception up there was spotty at best. You couldn't rely on her to show up in person, but she always picked up her phone. It was the one promise we kept, never to ignore each other.

"Does she even know?"

I shook my head and turned to stare out the large window, watching the sunset dye the mountains purple and red.

The thought of still having to tell my sister made my stomach clench painfully. She was going to flip out and the added pressure of her pregnancy shoved more weight onto my shoulders. It was up to me to hold everything together: keep the house functioning, pay the bills, make the doctors' appointments, fill the medications.

"Sorry, I didn't text you, but..."

"It's okay."

"I should have known the news would get to you first." I swallowed, tucking hair behind my ear. "Sorry you had to hear it that way."

"Are you seriously worried about my feelings right now?" Skylar grabbed my hands, pulling my attention to her. "I am worried about you. Your mom. I wish I had been there for you."

I squeezed her hands back, the knot in my throat expanding.

"Have you talked to Cory?" Skylar sat back, fiddling with her napkin.

"No." I sighed. I wished he was here. I didn't really want to talk to him over the phone about this, but I knew his mom would tell him if I didn't soon. "I'll wait until tonight. I don't want to ruin his meet today."

"You are too nice. Everyone before you."

I blew out air, knowing it was true. It wasn't as if I wanted to be. I wanted to say screw it and go to college, let everyone fend for themselves. But my family needed me. My mom couldn't work or handle the extra stress of paying our mortgage. I loved my sister, but in no way would I count on her to do any of it, and Dad was dead. We had no one else. My dad's parents were dead and only my mother's father was alive, whom she barely talked to. He was around ninety and living in a home in Denmark.

The weight of my responsibility felt crushing, my fingers rubbing at my forehead. *Breathe. Breathe.*

"Hey." At the sound of a familiar guy's voice, I tipped my head back.

"Hey, Ant." I nodded at my coworker. Anthony was also a senior and Jennifer's eldest son and worked here part-time. He was short with dark eyes and skin and a mop of black hair. Nice guy, but honestly, a terrible waiter. Sue kept him on because he was family.

"Hi." He shifted his weight on his heels, a pen pressed to a pad of paper, his eyes drifting from me to Skylar. He licked his dry lips. "Hey, Sky."

His tremendous crush on Skylar oozed from his every pore. Every class they shared, he stared at her with longing and a silly grin.

"Hey." She nodded back. Skylar was nice to everyone but had to keep her responses cool to keep guys from thinking she was flirting. At parties, guys regularly got into fights over her when she was just being herself.

"Uh, sorry about your mom," Anthony blurted out, not looking at me.

"Thanks."

"What do you girls want?"

"The bottle of the really good tequila Sue has stashed behind the bar." Skylar eyes darted to the spot near the soda machine. On special nights, like birthdays, she would pull it out and share it with the "of age" staff. One night soon after my father died, she snuck me a shot, understanding grief and stress had no age requirement. Sue was good like that, if you didn't abuse it.

I snorted as Anthony's eyes widened, glancing back nervously at the counter. "I can't do that. What if they catch me?"

"Come on, Ant." Skylar smiled at him. "You don't think on this kind of day she deserves it?"

"Just an iced tea." I handed back the menu, unable to even contemplate eating.

"Anthony…" Skylar fluttered her lashes. "Please."

"Sky, don't." I shook my head. That was just cruel; you could see the torment dividing the boy in half. Follow the rules or give in to his crush.

Her eyes flicked up. "Fine. An iced tea too. And a large sundae with extra chocolate."

"Healthy dinner." I fiddled with my napkin.

"Screw dinner. We need to go straight to dessert tonight."

Not even ice cream sounded good, but I could let it melt on my tongue instead of having to chew solid food.

Anthony nodded and hurried away.

"Man, you make the poor boy nervous." I shook my head.

"I've known him since kindergarten; you think he'd be used to me by now." She rolled her eyes. "Plus, I'm almost a foot taller than him."

"A lot of guys like that in a girl."

"Not me. I want them tall, built, with a sexy smirk…and slightly older." She sighed dreamily. "Where is that guy?"

"Not here."

"No kidding." She frowned, shifting back into her seat, her mood shifting. "I am here for you…"

"I know. But tonight I don't want to talk about it. Please, I can't."

She nodded. There would be plenty of nights ahead of me to talk, wallow, and lose it. I wasn't ready to break. Not yet.

Ant came back, setting down the sundae and iced teas.

"Enjoy your *tea,* ladies." Anthony cleared his throat, his eyes flicking to the drinks.

Sky's lids narrowed, and she took a swig from her drink then slammed a hand to her chest, coughs spasming through her.

"Oh, wow." Her eyes started to water, her hand tapping her throat as half the restaurant turned to stare at her. "Went down the wrong pipe." She composed herself. "But really good tea."

I took a sip already knowing Anthony had chosen his crush over the rules. Flames rained down my esophagus, shooting fireballs into my stomach. The large glass was almost all tequila with a splash of tea.

"Really. Good. Tea." My head already spun from the inferno in my belly.

"Thanks, Ant." Skylar looked at him, touching his hand, appreciation written over her face. His olive cheeks burned pink, unable to hold her gaze.

"Yeah. No worries." He skirted away, scurrying for the kitchen.

I guzzled more, loving the tingly feeling it flushed down my arms and legs. If Ant got in trouble, I would take the blame. But if I knew Sue, she'd frown and look the other way. Of all days, she had to know I needed something to help.

Skylar was being the perfect best friend, talking about nothing serious, while we drank our potent iced teas and used the ice cream as a chaser. An alcohol haze quickly padded my brain, my insides all warm and buzzing.

"Jas texted me earlier. Both she and Cory won first today."

"Really?" I couldn't help feeling a zing of jealousy. I wanted to be at the tournament. Doing what I loved. Winning first place, standing next to my boyfriend. "That's awesome."

"He hasn't texted you yet?"

I shook my head.

"Isn't it your anniversary today, too?"

"Yeah." I swallowed a heaping spoonful of ice cream. Three years ago, at this exact competition, he kissed me for the first time. The next year we celebrated our wins and anniversary by having sex for the first time. I can't say it was great, more bumbling and awkward, but over time it got better. He was always so sweet with me, and I loved him. "He said we'd celebrate it next weekend. You know how one-track-minded he gets when he's in full competition mode."

Skylar lifted her eyebrows and took another bite of dessert.

"Don't give me that look. I know you don't care for him…"

"I like him." She sat back.

I tilted my head, watching the room spin a little.

"I do! He's a *nice* guy."

"See." I pointed my spoon at her. "Right there, the word *nice*. I know you."

"What? He is nice."

"Not the way you mean it." I sucked at my straw. "Your nice means boring."

"Aren't they the same, really?" Her cheeks were pink with drink. "I still like him, though. But personally, I want someone who'd shove me against a wall and know exactly how to make me scream." With blurry eyes she leaned on the table. Skylar's mother was extremely open about sex. They talked all the time about Skylar having sex. The only restriction her mother gave her was to use protection and be in control of her own body. "Be honest, have you ever orgasmed? I mean really saw stars and cried out his name?"

Cory and I weren't that way. We were tender. Sweet. And if I was being truly honest, it wasn't something I encouraged; I often felt obligated. It was fine, but I didn't get what the huge fuss was.

"That's you. Not me."

"Pleeeeaassseee." She rolled her eyes. "There is not one woman here." She waved her arm around. "Who doesn't secretly want a guy to take charge and truly fuck her."

My head darted around, and I pressed my finger to my lips. Last thing I needed was everyone to hear what we were talking about. "I don't."

Skylar's laugh belted up like a bubble. "You are such a liar. I know you too, girl. And I know when you are lying your ass off."

A vibration knocked into my side, and I tugged my cell from my pocket, expecting to see Amelia or my mom's number on the screen.

"Speaking of." I wiggled my phone in front of her

face, displaying Cory's name written across. "He just texted me."

Cory could get sentimental, especially on our anniversary, and I didn't want to read his texts with Skylar reading over my shoulder. "I'm gonna go to the bathroom." The instant I stood, the alcohol rushed to my head, having no substance to hold on to in my stomach. I gripped the table, barely keeping myself from tipping over.

"You okay?"

"Yeah." I nodded, placing each foot in front of the other carefully. My cell buzzed again, another text.

I didn't want to appear drunk with so many eyes on me as I crossed the room. I concentrated on my screen, Cory's words blurred as I stumbled into the empty bathroom. I walked to the sink, leaning against it, trying to steady myself.

My eyes moved over his words as my brain couldn't fully comprehend them. The tone was strange. The words even stranger. He never talked to me like this. I blinked a few times, making sure it was actually his name on the text. Reading through again, my insides started to twist themselves together.

Cory: *"Shit, you don't know how bad I wanted to kiss you earlier when you won. All I could think was I want to lick every inch of you. It's been only hours but feels like forever since I was deep inside you. I can't wait to hear you scream out my name again, and pound you into the headboard."*

Vomit rose up my throat, spots twinkling in my vision as I tried and failed to take a deep breath, my chest trying to pump oxygen. *This must be a wrong number. A joke. Someone took his phone.* My fingers tapped at the second message.

Cory*: "I know it's wrong, neither one of us want to hurt Dev...but I can't stop thinking of you, Jasmine. I can't stop wanting to rip off your clothes every time I see you. I know you feel the same. Let's make tonight count. All night. Come to my room when you get this."*

Icy heat flushed up my spine, bile roiling in my stomach. I clutched the sink, head spinning, my legs dipping as I reread his words.

No.

No!

This couldn't be happening. Not Cory. He wouldn't do this. My boyfriend of three years. The boy who told me he loved me a couple times a day, kissed me all the time at school. Who everyone said was so whipped he would probably be proposing to me the moment we graduated high school. The one thing I counted on to be faithful. My rock. My friend. He was not the cheating type.

Since my father's death I'd barely been holding on, keeping everything together. Today, with Mom's diagnosis, my grip had become tenuous. Now Cory had stomped on my delicate fingers.

I was in free fall.

He was cheating on me. With one of my best friends. His declarations on my phone seared into my brain. He had never pounded *me* into the headboard. He had never licked every inch of *me*.

And Jasmine, *my friend,* who told me how cute we were together, was sleeping with him behind my back. She had taken my spot as captain and my spot as girlfriend. How long was this going on? How long had they been deceiving me?

Tears burned in my eyes, choking my throat, my lungs not getting full gulps of air. Today was *our* anniversary, and he was in a hotel room with someone else. Kissing someone else. Having sex with someone else.

I could almost hear the crack slicing through my heart. The wall that had been barely keeping me together shattered. Behind the numbness came waves of fury.

The unfairness of life picked at the dam. Anger radiated through every fiber. My father, my sister, my mother, my life, and now the deepest betrayal—my boyfriend cheating on me with one of my best friends. On our anniversary.

Sorrow retreated into the corners, hiding from the fury sizzling through my veins, rallying the tequila in my system into battle. The fight-or-fuck drink.

The reflection in the mirror didn't even look like me. Wild and savage, the girl there had a desire to rip everything off the walls, to destroy the world that was so cruel and kept kicking her and shredding her heart. My eyes widened, my cheeks flushed, and my ears pounded.

As I gave a wail of rage, I didn't even hear the door open.

CHAPTER THREE

"Ummm…" A guy's voice drifted in from behind me as he stepped into the restroom, looking back at the door then at me. "Think one of us is in the wrong bathroom."

I blinked, frozen by the stranger who gazed back at me, the side of his mouth hitched up in a cocky grin, his gray-blue eyes twinkling, screaming nothing but trouble.

And he was sexy as hell.

The guy shut the door. He held a backpack, his hand inside, and he peered into the few empty stalls, the short garbage can by my feet, then glanced at the tiny opaque window way up at the top of the room. "Shit," he muttered before glancing back at me, our eyes locking as he really took me in.

"Someone is in the wrong here." He smirked, pulling his hand out and zipping the bag.

In that instant, every feral instinct in me came alive. Tingles skated through my body, my heart thumping. My gaze tunneling on him. I sensed he was raw and dangerous.

He was everything Skylar would wish for and everything Cory wasn't. Older by at least five years. Tall, hinting at six-four, with broad shoulders, his corded arms and chest fitted his T-shirt perfectly. He filled out torn jeans and wore worn black combat boots. A light scruff lined his face, his dark-blondish hair sticking out of his black beanie.

"Just to let you know, that person isn't me," he rumbled.

"Huh?"

"In the wrong bathroom." His intense gaze pinned me to the spot as if he actually held me down. More heat flushed over my skin, the tequila flipping sides.

I had never had a visceral reaction to someone. Not even remotely. When Cory first kissed me, I felt tiny butterflies but nothing close to this. This guy emanated *bad.* Trouble. Everything that scared me. I was used to safe. Sweet. Nothing was nice about him. And in this moment, with Cory's horrible texts fresh in my mind, I liked that this stranger was everything opposite of Cory. Danger oozed out of his pores, dampening the rage and grief inside me.

Desire pricked at my belly, moving down my thighs.

Cory…the guy I was supposed to trust. Love. Betrayed me. He was in a hotel room at this moment, screwing my best friend, while my mother's mind was beginning to rot away. I wouldn't be going to college; I wouldn't be leaving this town. It was as if fabric wrapped around my throat, covering my mouth. Suffocated. Stuck. This town would be my life…

Resentment. Anger. Sadness. They swallowed me up in a gulp.

"Are you all right?" He took a step closer to me, one eyebrow curved in curiosity.

Was I all right? Far from it.

I couldn't shake images of Cory moaning as Jasmine rode him, her head tossed back as she cried out his name. I wanted the pain to go away. To disappear in pleasure. To drown in my anger and hate, not sadness and hurt.

Forget.

My heart pounded in my chest, but my hazy alcohol brain didn't let me think, only react. I swiveled around, staring at him.

"You okay?" His every syllable vibrated through me, slight confusion furrowing his eyebrows. Whatever I felt must have been written on my face. The cheeky smile slid off his face, turning to something else.

"No." I strode up to him, stopping a breath away from his body, tipping my head back to look at him. Cory was my size, so I never felt little or protected. This guy's frame dwarfed me, making me tremble. The heat from him slammed into me, demanding I get even closer. I placed my hand on his stomach. Rock hard abs rolled underneath my palm. "I'm not."

"What are you doing?" He tipped his head down, chest moving quicker as he took me in, his tongue sliding over his bottom lip.

I had no idea…but I liked the idea I didn't feel like me, as if all my anger became determination and purpose. I wanted him. To hurt Cory or take away the grief? I didn't care.

"Girlfriend?"

"Uh…no."

"Wife?"

A small burst of laugh came from him. "Definitely not."

"Good." My other hand pushed at his T-shirt, displaying his lean, toned torso.

"How old are you?" He tried to grab my wrist, but I easily tugged out of his grip. He didn't seem especially serious about stopping me.

"Old enough." Ish. He didn't need to know I wasn't quite legal. I stepped closer, shoving his shirt higher. His low-slung jeans displayed a deep V-line and a hint of hair, my heart now tripping over itself. A man's body. Not a boy's. My fingers trailed over the lines on his stomach, moving down.

"Are you drunk?" His voice came out in a rough whisper.

I sure was. This was not me. I was not forward like this. But something about him made me feel comfortable and wild at the same time. Probably because I didn't know what Underoos he used to wear as a child or what he got for Christmas in the third grade. I knew nothing about him.

My gaze caught on the huge bulge swelling his jeans. I had no idea who this girl was who took over my body, but she wanted nothing more than to touch him. Feel him.

"Shit," he hissed when I tugged at the top button, his hand firmly wrapping around my wrist. "You are hot as hell, but the timing of this really sucks. I'm in a bit of a hurr—" His words halted when my fingers brushed over his waiting hard flesh, his nose flaring.

"Girl, I don't think you want to do that." His eyes blazed into mine, full of warning and promise. I stared back at him. "I don't know what you're looking for or who you're trying to punish, but I assure you, I am not the answer."

"Why is that?"

"I am not the nice guy."

"Perfect."

"I am the one who takes." His eyes moved down my body. "Ruins."

"Too late." I laughed without humor. I shoved him back, his spine flattening against the wall. I licked my lips as he watched my mouth. "I need one moment of happiness before life consumes all of me."

I could feel the shift, the moment he sensed the truth in my declaration. Understanding. We stared at each other, breaths ragged, tension clawing at the air, filling every molecule.

Want. Need.

"Fuck it." He growled before his hands roughly grabbed the back of my head, knotting my hair in his fist. "You asked for it," he mumbled before his mouth slammed into mine, consuming me in one breath.

Desire shot up my thighs and through my stomach. I had kissed two boys in my life, and the first one was more of a peck. I was used to Cory, who never felt wild or that he couldn't get enough of me. Sometimes I felt when we made out or kissed at my locker, it was only because it was what couples did.

I was not prepared for raw desire to sprout in my veins, a pounding fierceness through my every fiber. His lips moved over mine viciously, far from gentle or sweet. And I loved it. Matching his intensity with my own, I kissed him back as hard.

His teeth tugged at my bottom lip, forcing a sound from my throat I had surely never made. The noise incited him more. He growled and grabbing my hips, he flipped us around, ramming my back into the tiled wall, his tongue slipping through my lips.

Holy shit. Logic dissolved as he pressed his body to mine. I could feel every inch of him. Hot. Needing. A deep moan escaped me, my hands moving frantically at his jeans. It scared me how desperate I was for him, to feel him slide inside me. My fingers trembled with intensity as I unbuttoned his pants, the tips of my fingers brushing the tip of him through his boxer-briefs.

He broke our kiss for a moment, groaning at my touch. "Was not expecting this when I stopped."

"No? A strange woman offering you sex in a bathroom isn't normal?"

"Oh no. That happens all the time." His fingers clutched the bottom of my shirt, ripping it over my head.

"Oh." I shouldn't have been surprised. For someone as hot as him, it probably happened more than I wanted to know.

"But never by someone like you."

"What do you mean?"

"Come on, Freckles. You are not this type." A sexy grin tugged at the side of his mouth, his hands moving down my body. My lids fluttered at his touch.

"Why would you say that?"

"Your cute cotton panties and white bra is one clue." He skimmed under the wire, pushing underneath the fabric, his hand cupping my breast. My head falling back into the wall with pleasure. "And you're the type a guy keeps, not fucks in the bathroom."

His words tickled at my conscience, stirring the part of my brain that might think this was wrong. But I was more afraid he'd stop and decide to be the moral one. The ache between my thighs and the anger blasting through my veins were unwilling to hear "no."

I unclasped the back of my bra, letting it fall to the floor. My breasts were small, always a source of insecurity, but he gazed at them as if they were perfect.

"Too much talking." I held my head high.

His steel eyes met mine, and he shook his head before his hands were back on me. He leaned over, his mouth taking in my nipple, flicking it with his tongue. I moaned.

"Oh god." I tugged off his beanie, raking my nails through his dark blond hair, pulling him in closer. In an instant he had me desperate and needy. I shoved him back, tugging out of my boots and pulling off my jeans, leaving me in my underwear. We didn't have time; any second someone could step into the bathroom, or Sky could come looking for me.

"Please say you have a condom." I was on birth control. I'd begun even before Cory and I started having sex, but I still didn't know this guy. He grabbed the backpack on the floor, clutching something from one of the pockets, and kicked it to the door. It wouldn't stop anyone from entering, but maybe it would slow them down a bit.

He strolled back to me, desire scorching his eyes. His mouth took mine again, slipping his tongue over my lips, nipping. Jesus. This guy could get me blistering hot in less than a second. Our kisses turned wild and deep, sucking all the oxygen from the room. Tearing off his shirt, we barely parted for a moment before we crashed back together.

Trailing down his hips, I shoved at his jeans, shoving his briefs with it. Boldly, my hand wrapped around his length, my heart fluttering at his size. He was all man. No boy left in him.

A deep growl came from him as his fingers shoved my underwear to the side, sliding into me. Air caught in my lungs, the sensation almost freezing me in place. It felt so good I closed my eyes; my breath staggered. He moved in deeper, adding another finger.

"Open your eyes, Freckles," he demanded, his voice making every nerve in me quake. "I want those eyes on me."

My lashes fluttered open, and I stared at him. His thumb found my clit as his fingers pumped harder into me, parting my lips in a gasp.

"Now. Please." My legs shook, feeling my spine burning. Did I just plead? I had never begged for sex. Ever.

He smirked, sliding his fingers from me, wrapping his mouth around them, sucking. He groaned in pleasure

"You taste so good. Too bad we don't have more time." He stepped into me, his erection scorching my hip. I wanted this so bad, my body actually hurt. With one arm, he grabbed my ass, picked me up, and I wrapped my legs around him. In a blink, he rolled the condom over his cock, shoved my underwear to the side, his tip sliding through my wetness. My teeth sawed into my bottom lip as he continued to tease me more.

"Please."

"Say it." His thumb found me again, twisting pleasure so intense through me, a sharp gasp pierced the air. My hips bucked against him. "If you want it dirty in the bathroom with a stranger, you need to ask for it." He dragged his fingers through me again. "If you're gonna live out the fantasy of being a bad girl, be it."

The way he had me rocking and wiggling against him, I would have said anything, but I knew what he wanted.

"Fuck me," I whispered hoarsely in his ear. "Hard."

In a blink, he crashed me back against the wall, his blue eyes burning thick with desire. "Damn, you don't know what you asked for."

My brain barely registered his words before he slid inside, slamming to the hilt. Air squeezed from my lungs, my muscles locking up as his huge size filled my body, trying quickly to adjust.

"Fuck." His grip on my hips tightened, the pain spiking more bliss down my nerves. "You feel so damn good."

I had never felt so full as I did while he moved out and thrust back in.

"Oh god." My toes curled with the onslaught of pleasure. He pumped faster and faster and then pushed upward, hitting a spot forcing a cry from my body, my hips buckling wildly against his, in search for more. The outside world disappeared; all I could feel was the bliss searing me. It made me desperate and greedy.

"Harder. Don't ever stop."

"Jesus, Freckles. The way you talk, I will gladly fuck you forever."

As if it were his mission to pleasure me, he drove in so deep, tears leaked from my eyes, but I only wanted more. I didn't think I had ever made much noise having sex, but loud cries propelled from me, feeling they came from some other girl.

"Believe me, I love hearing you." He grunted, regripping my hips, going even deeper. "But do you want the diners to as well?"

I almost didn't give a shit. But I clamped down on the curve of his neck, muffling my screams.

"Fuck." He roared as my teeth dug in. He pressed me harder against the wall with his body, seeming to forget what he'd warned me of, his hips moving in a faster rhythm against mine.

The burning inside me moved up and sizzled my brain and nerves. "Oh god." I chased the orgasm more desperately than air. Sadly, Skylar wasn't far off. I enjoyed sex with Cory, but my climaxes were quick and lackluster. I had honestly wondered if something was wrong with me or that was actually supposed to be the great thing people talked about.

This wasn't even on the same planet as the sex I'd had with Cory. My breath was clipped, my legs squeezing his hips as I felt myself start to clench around him.

A string of swear words hissed from him as he pounded me harder with so much intensity, I stopped breathing, my lips parting in a silent scream. I exploded, my vision blurring as my body spasmed around him. He grunted deeply, thrusting in so deep, I gasped. His dick throbbed inside me, stirring another orgasm through me. I heard him roar, but I was already far from earth, lost in utter bliss.

Slowly I sank back down, panting, sucking in gulps of oxygen. Every muscle and bone were putty, sagging with gratification.

His body was heavy on mine against the wall, like he could no longer hold himself up. Our breaths mixed as we both sank back to earth. His eyes met mine. Still inside me, we both stayed silent staring at each other.

Reality seeped in with every exhale, weighing me down to earth and to all the things I wanted to run from.

What do you say after something like this?

Thanks?

I didn't even want to think too much about how I'd just fucked some stranger in the bathroom at the diner because my heart and soul hurt.

With his forearms anchored next to my ears, we watched each other. Finally, he leaned back enough to force my legs to slide down his, touching the floor, as he pulled out of me. The wave of emotion I had been blocking all day surged down on me. For our brief, blissful encounter, I had felt happy. Weightless. But now, reality came back for me with a vengeance. I shut my lids with the painful realization of what I did.

Guilt. Embarrassment. Shock.

Cory was a fleeting thought, mainly because I knew this guy had ruined me. Not that I would ever go back to my cheating ex, but I couldn't anyway now. My body still quaked, buzzing with the high like it understood what it had been missing.

I heard him walk to the garbage can, toss the condom, then the rustling of clothes.

"You okay, Freckles?"

"Don't." I reached for my shirt, tugging it back on and quickly getting back in my pants. "Let's not talk. And you certainly don't get to call me some pet name."

"I don't know your real name."

"Let's keep it that way."

He buttoned his jeans, pulling back on his T-shirt. Amusement hinted on his lips. Snagging his beanie and his backpack off the floor, he nodded at me.

"Okay then. Bye, Freckles." He tugged the door. "It was a pleasure, but I really have to run."

I nodded back, watching him slip out of the room.

Don't think. Don't think.

I rushed to the sink, straightening myself out. What was the point? No matter how much I patted down my hair or straightened my shirt, I looked flushed and dazed. As if I had been fucked properly. Skylar was going to sense it on me before I even reached the table.

"Screw it." If anyone had reasons for acting out, it was me. Plus, he gave me exactly what I needed and more. But sadness skimmed my shoulders, reminding me of the true agony I was still trying to keep at bay. I knew he was only a diversion from my pain.

Mom still had Alzheimer's, like her mother. My father was still dead. My boyfriend was still a cheater.

I stared at my reflection, at the same hazel eyes as my mom's. What if it were my future too? What if it were sitting inside waiting to snatch all my memories and life until I had nothing left? Everything I did was erased like chalk? Jocelyn said there was genetic testing to show if you have a specific gene that puts you at high risk for developing Alzheimer's. Not sure I wanted to know now.

Flickering blue and red lights from outside the frosted glass window up high in the bathroom caught my attention and pulled me back into the present.

What the hell? Slipping my boots back on, I stepped out of the bathroom. The more I thought about it, the more I was shocked Skylar hadn't come searching for me or no one entered the restroom the whole time we were in there. I usually didn't have that kind of luck.

Nerves in my stomach coiled tightly, as if they were warning me something was off. I walked down the hallway, stepping back into the restaurant, my feet stopping dead.

A handful of cop cars were outside, their lights whirling as they circled a caramel, nondescript sedan, blocking it in from escaping.

Dread plummeted to my gut, my feet moving to the glass doors.

"Devon!" Skylar screeched, running to me. "Oh my god, where were you?"

"What's going on?"

"The cops pulled up about five minutes ago, surrounding the car." She pointed at it. "And this guy walked out from the bathrooms and stepped outside as if it were nothing, holding up his arms," she exclaimed, her eyes wide. "I was a moment away from going to look for you. What if I had run into him? I mean, the guy is super frickin' hot, but what if he's some serial killer? I could be dead!"

I moved to the doors, staring out at the scene with disbelief.

Brown eyes like my father's caught mine, doing a double take, motioning for me to move away from the door. But I ignored him, my gaze sliding to the guy they had pinned to the trunk of a police car instead, the cops pulling a gun from his backpack. Steel-blue eyes stared back at me. The sheriff roughly handcuffed him, jerking him back up, relocating him to the rear of the police cab. Before they tucked him into the back of the car, the stranger glanced over his shoulder and winked at me.

Shit. This was really happening. This was my life. A perfect end to a horrendous day.

The guy who'd fucked me against the bathroom wall had just been arrested…by my uncle.

I should have kept driving.

CHAPTER FOUR

5 years later

"Erin called again." Sue came next to me by the soda machine, sighing heavily. "It's the fourth time in an hour to say she needs to leave."

My teeth scraped my bottom lip as I replenished the Coke for one of my tables. The mother and father had already had three refills on their coffees, while the son was on his sixth refill of Coke. They were making sure they got their money's worth, I guess. My section was full, but this table was exceptionally demanding, asking for something every time I passed.

I told Erin I would be home by four. That was an hour ago. The restaurant was abnormally slammed for a Wednesday, everyone heading up to the mountains for Labor Day weekend, the last summer hurrah before all schools officially returned. Jennifer and I were on shift, splitting the diner in half.

"I'm sorry, Sue." I set the glass on my tray.

Sue leaned her hip into the counter, another sigh dropping her shoulders. "Devon, you know you are like a daughter to me. But this is still a business. *My* business. I can't have your mother's caregiver calling here more than customers do."

I bowed my head. Sue had let me go early or let me have the day off because of my situation so many times during the past five years. My mother's condition had worsened. Sue tried to be supportive, but everyone had a breaking point. Sympathy and understanding only went so far.

I had been a faithful employee for the last five-plus years. As servers, Jennifer and I had been here the longest. Jennifer would probably be here to the end. A lifer. At one time I hoped I could get out, explore the world, but I saw no escape in the near future. This full-time job felt more like a life sentence. Guilt quickly washed over me as I realized what the alternative would be. I shouldn't complain. The reason I was trapped was the one thing I held on to for dear life.

Almost everyone I knew was gone, having run off to college or to a job in a bigger town the moment we graduated. I had no such luxury. I needed the money, so I worked as much as I could, but it was getting harder to get through a whole shift now without a call from the caregiver or my mother.

My gaze returned to my demanding table where the wife sipped her coffee as though she had all the time in the world. I envied that feeling. To not have anywhere to be, no one wanting anything from you.

"Hey." Sue grabbed my tray, nodding at the door. "Go ahead and take off. I'll finish up your section."

"Sue…" My ponytail swung back and forth, brushing my back. "I can't leave you and Jennifer. It's crazy in here."

"We can handle it," she replied, her voice set with her decision. "Sadie and Travis are coming in at six anyway. Go, Devon. We'll be fine."

I knew better than to fight her when she got like this. Sue had the stubbornness and determination of a pit bull. This restaurant was her life, and she practically lived here. She had no kids or pets and even her husband only saw her if he came in for a meal. It said a lot that she was on her third husband and claimed the restaurant was her one true love.

Nodding, I watched her slip by me and effortlessly take over my tables. Another block of guilty weight settled down on my shoulders. Somedays it felt so heavy I could barely stand.

Waving at Alejandro and the rest of the kitchen staff, I grabbed my stuff out of my locker and darted out the back door to my car. The boiling sun from the late-summer day still pulsed off the asphalt, roasting my already overheated body. My car had no air-conditioning. I had to use a towel to sit so my skin didn't peel off every time I got out. The gas tank now had duct tape over it to keep it shut. Most mornings I had to cross my fingers in hopes it would start, but I was thankful it still ran. One of these days, in the near future, it would probably break down, and I had no idea what I'd do. We had no money for a new car, all of it going to bills and babysitting for both Mia and my mother.

I raced my Toyota across town, bouncing up to our tiny, worn house. The grass needed to be mowed, the roof redone, house painted, and the porch rebuilt, adding to the ever-growing to-do list. If we miraculously ever had extra money, I might check off something on the list. It always seemed when I did, something else went wrong or the health insurance went up.

The moment I shut off the car, my phone wailed like a baby wanting to be picked up. Seeing the name, I almost pretended I didn't see it.

"Hey, Amelia." I sighed, shoving the phone between my ear and shoulder.

"Devon, where the hell have you been? I've been calling you for the last two hours." I could hear the salon's music humming in the background. My sister got a part-time job at a hair salon. Her clients loved her, but she didn't have enough yet to really contribute to the bills, claiming any money she had went to take care of Mia.

Funny, I seemed to pay for the house where she lived, her pediatrician visits, and all the grocery bills, which were mainly Mia-approved foods. Strong-minded like the rest of the women in our family, Mia was in a stage where she only wanted chicken nuggets and fries.

"I took my private jet to Paris for a spa day. It's Wednesday. You know I go to Paris on Wednesdays." I climbed out of the car, slinging my bag over my shoulder. There was a beat before Amelia replied. She never seemed to get my dry humor.

"You're hilarious, Dev. Really." I swear I could hear her roll her eyes at me. "Erin kept calling me at the salon. You know how bad it looks to clients when your cell keeps ringing? I have to work. I can't have her doing that anymore."

A rush of irritation tightened my shoulders.

"I'm sorry, Amelia, that you had to deal with your *own mother*'s caregiver calling you. It must have been horrible." My teeth clenched as I turned away from the house, not wanting anyone inside to hear me. "You know I have a job too. One that actually pays our bills."

"That's not fair." Amelia's hissed at me. "I have Mia, my daughter, remember? And I am still somewhat new here, trying to grow my business. I have to make a good impression. They need to know they can depend on me, and they are my main priority right then and have my full attention. You wouldn't understand this. All you have to do is plop food in front of people."

Rage flushed over my body, my fingers gripping the phone painfully. Silence filled the phone line as I tried to contain my anger. This wasn't the first time Amelia and I fought about this. She didn't seem to think waiting tables was hard, though she had never done it. Those who have waited on the public know it is a thankless, exhausting job. Dealing with hungry people is similar to walking into an angry lion cage where the beasts haven't been fed in days. Lions that scream and complain and run you around without any gratitude.

"I'm sorry. That was mean." Amelia exhaled, her voice softening into butter. "I'm really on edge."

I knew my sister better than anyone; I knew by the tone of her voice when she needed something from me.

"The reason I really called?" Her voice dipped into a vault of sugar.

"What, Mel? Ask the favor." I switched the cell to my other ear, staring out at my neighbor's yard filled with rusting cars and parts, as the sun lowered below the houses, painting them in deep purples and browns.

"Zak called…"

Damn.

"You mean the lying, cheating douchebag? The pathetic excuse for a human? That Zak?"

"Dev," she warned. "He is still her father."

"Really? Just because one of his dumb-ass sperm helped create her doesn't make him a father."

When Mia was born, Amelia had hoped Zak would change his mind about being a parent. He hadn't. Nor did he want to be exclusive to Amelia, telling her a baby and a girlfriend were too constraining. Mel finally got wise and moved on, but she still tried to get her amazing little girl to spend time with her asshole father.

He mostly took Mia because the town judged everything you did here, and his mother didn't like her son being labeled a deadbeat dad, which he was. Most of his promises to take Mia for a night or a weekend were cancelled at the last minute, claiming his job at the garage needed him.

Sure… Strange how many people needed an oil change on a Saturday night.

"His job called him in again—"

My snorted laugh cut off her sentence. "Come on, you're not that dumb."

I could feel her defeat through the phone, the sorrow she carried. Sometimes my sister drove me nuts, but at the end of the day we were family and I loved her. And I loved that little girl so much my heart hurt to see her face fall when Amelia had to tell her Daddy wasn't coming.

"He's dropping her off. He should be there now." She cleared her throat. "And I have a date."

"Ah." I rubbed my face, the few strands escaping my ponytail were knotted and greasy. I felt sweaty and gross and was looking forward to a long bath. Amelia had one day, Wednesdays, to cook dinner and watch over Mom and Mia. I looked forward to it all week. I didn't ask for much; I didn't even leave the house. A glass of wine, a book, and a date with the tub. No responsibility for *one* night.

"Please, please, please, Devy?" Her tone took on what my father used to call the "snake charmer." Amelia played it so well no one was immune to it, not even me. When she would bat her lashes and use that voice, teachers, cops, parents would walk right into her web. "I really like this guy. He's different; I feel it." I tried to hold back from laughing. Every guy was "different," only proving later he was exactly the same. Amelia had terrible taste in men. Not that I should talk.

"I'll owe you. Please, Dev."

Right. She already owed me years' worth of IOUs.

"Yeah. Fine." I could never say no to my niece.

"Thank you! I love you!" Amelia cried out before hanging up.

Tires crunched across the gravel, spinning me around. Zak's souped-up, gleaming red truck pulled in, his spiky blond hairstyle still holding on to high school. He was such a stereotype. There were reasons stereotypes existed, and Zak made sure to continue their survival.

"Aunt Devy!" Mia's small voice called for me as she jumped out of the truck. I had to bite my tongue at the fact Zak shoved her booster seat out behind her, never getting out, rolling in the dirt, as if it disgusted him. Anything that ruined his "chick magnet truck" or his "single man status" was considered contemptable.

"Hey, Bean." I held out my arms and she flew into them, hugging me tight. Her long, soft, dark hair slid over my arms. She looked so similar to our father with her dark hair, eyes, and skin. It made me happy she looked nothing like Zak's blond, white ass. When she had been a baby, she was so long and thin she looked like a green bean, which is where her pet name came from.

"Hey." Zak clicked his chin at me, his jaw clenching with irritation. His eyes were hidden behind aviator sunglasses, and he wore his too-cool-for-emotion expression, grabbing Mia's overnight bag and holding it out to me from the car window as if it were some drug drop-off.

When Amelia first started dating him, he flirted with me, tried to grab my ass. I quickly set him straight with my fist. Ever since, we were like two warring countries which had to interact because of a peace treaty. But at any moment our hatred might win out and shred the barely hidden aggression.

One step away from reaching the bag, Zak dropped it in the dirt, his lips twitching smugly.

"Always a pleasure, *Devy*." He smirked, pulling out of the driveway, tossing up gravel in a mushroom of haze, spitting tiny chunks at me. I could hear his laughter as he drove away, his music pumping loudly enough to be heard blocks away.

"Asshole," I whispered, grabbing Mia's dusty bag and joining her on the porch. "So…what do you want for dinner?"

"Nuggets!"

"Shocker. And let me guess, French fries?" I unlocked the door, herding her inside.

"Loads of them. I'm so hungry." She ran in front of me as I grabbed the mail. Bills. Most with "urgent" or "final notice" written across the front. I sighed, adding them to the pile on the entry table from yesterday…and the day before…and the day before that.

I loved my family with every fiber of my being, but somedays it seemed I was repeating the same day over and over as my youth and life slipped away. Was it wrong to wish for something to change? To be more than this?

CHAPTER FIVE

"Erin?" I called out, shutting the door behind me, dumping my armload onto the table. Mia darted ahead into the family room. "I am so sorry I'm late."

I was shocked Erin hadn't come racing out the moment I drove up. And thinking about it, I didn't remember seeing her car.

"Erin?" Please, please tell me she didn't walk out, leaving my mom alone.

"Erin's gone," said a male voice from around the corner.

"Uncle Gavin?" As I stepped into the room, I saw he was dressed in his sheriff uniform. He stood over my mother, who was sleeping in her chair, and pulled a blanket to her chin. Even though it was hot, my mom was always cold.

"*Shinálí!*" *Grandfather*, Mia sang, reaching for my father's younger brother. My dad's side was Navajo. Though we weren't active with his tribe, my uncle wanted Mia to understand her heritage.

"Bitsóóké." Grandchild. A huge smile grew on my uncle's face as he swept Mia into his arms. He was not the same man with her as when I was growing up. At first, he felt uncomfortable being called "grandfather" he said it was taking the title away from my father, but Gavin was the only grandfather Mia knew. We told her about her biological grandpa, but Uncle Gavin deserved the respect of the title. He had been there for us, helping when I couldn't make the bills that month or watching Mom on a rare day off.

"Your mu-tash tickles." She giggled as he wiggled his graying scruff against her cheek. The stress of the job and the responsibility he must have felt for us showed on his lined face. He set Mia down and kissed her cheek.

"Can I watch something?" She peered up at me, using the same sweet "snake charmer" voice her mother had.

"Yes, but only until dinner. Then no more. Okay?"

She nodded, running over to the outdated TV, turning on the DVD faster than any kid her age should be able. We didn't have cable, so she watched the same handful of kids' DVDs over and over. She didn't seem to mind.

The instant she was settled, I turned back to my uncle. "Where is Erin?" My hand went to my hip. "She didn't call you at the station, did she?"

"Don't be upset with her, Dev. She didn't know what else to do. Her little boy came down with the flu. She was desperate."

I exhaled sharply as I peered down at Mom, sleeping soundly. Her once youthful appearance had diminished severely in the last five years. Fully gray now, her face lined with deep creases, and with a frail frame, she looked far older than her fifty-two years, especially having Norwegian genes.

At first she tried to keep up her appearance, but gradually as the disease took more and more of her mind, things like getting her hair colored no longer mattered. I knew we were lucky we still had moments when she knew us and recognized Mia. But they were getting further and further apart.

"Thank you for coming. It was crazy at work." I whirled around to the kitchen, getting a jug of lemonade out of the fridge.

"You never have to thank me. You are my family. I wish I could do more."

"You do enough." I poured two glasses, pushing one across the counter to him.

"No, I don't. And I hate how much you take on. You should be in college with your friends. Having fun."

"You mean my one friend." I snorted, taking a drink, the cool, tart liquid sliding deliciously down my dry throat. After the horrible moment when I found out my boyfriend and former best friend were screwing each other's brains out for over a month before he mistakenly sexted me, those "friendships" ended. They had stayed together the rest of the year, their gushy romance in my face every day. Sky told me they broke up soon after they got to college. Jasmine cheated on him with one of his frat brothers. No tears shed for either one.

The person I missed most was Skylar. Her dad got her a job with a local artist in Santa Fe, where she was loving life and "enjoying" the tortured-artist-type guy she now favored. We talked once a week, but it was mostly her telling me stories. Nothing new happened in this town, and it got depressing talking about my mother's decline.

"She was really agitated and scared when I came in. She was screaming at Erin that she didn't know who she was." His throat bobbed and he stared at his glass, twisting it in circles on the table. "She didn't know me at first. I had to give her a bit of her medicine in a small glass of water. She wouldn't let us give her a pill, saying we were trying to poison her. So I was lucky she drank the water."

I blinked back tears, my throat closing in.

"It might be time, Dev."

"To put her in a home? Where she knows no one? No. I won't do that. She still understands enough. I won't leave her in some institution." I swallowed. "Not yet."

"She's becoming too much to handle. You know it. Erin is not going to last long. She's not trained to deal with what your mom is going through."

He echoed what Dr. Matheson said at out last visit. *"You know when I said there will be a time when her disease will progress past what I am capable of dealing with? The time has come, Devon."*

"Your mother wanders away every time you blink." It was true. I'd spent several nights driving up and down the street when we found her bed empty. "She tried to steal the neighbor's car last week."

"A car with no engine," I pointed out, as if that justified it.

We had found her in one of the neighbor's parts car, thinking she was driving to the store. "The baby needs milk," she had said.

"What baby?" I asked her.

"Devon," she answered, and I had to choke back a sob. Her mind was always confusing memories with the present. Her knowledge of current events was almost gone now.

"Not the point, Devon." Uncle Gavin tipped his head to the side, one hand on his hip, reminding me so much of my father. "It could have been your car or Amelia's. She's becoming a danger to herself and to people in this town." He waved his hand outside the window. "There will be a time where the safety of others will override your choice."

I turned away and shoved the jug back in the fridge.

"At least think about it." He softened his voice. "You know I want the best for her. I love you guys so much. But I am also sheriff, and I can't turn a blind eye because we're family."

"I know." I stared at the pictures decorating our fridge. Images of a better time layered the wall, when death and disease hadn't touched our family yet. We wanted to surround Mom with familiar faces, even my dad's. Somedays he was the only one she knew. Other days she asked when he was coming home, where he was every day, forgetting he was no longer with us.

"I'll think about it." I pressed my back into the handle, gazing at my uncle. "But not today."

"Fair enough." A sad smile ghosted his mouth. He strolled over to me, widening his arms for a hug. "I hate putting this on you, but your mother had a reason she put you in charge and not Amelia. I love your sister like nothing else, but I can't stand how it all falls on you." He patted my back and stepped back. He would never outright say Amelia was selfish and overindulged, but we all knew it. Even she knew it. But if she didn't have to be responsible, she was okay with it.

"Thank you again for coming by."

"Yeah, of course." He adjusted his gun belt, but didn't move, clearing his throat.

"Is there something else?"

"No, not really." He glanced down at his black boots.

"What?" He seemed to be fighting back telling me something.

"Nothing." He swished his hand. "A case file came across my desk the other day, and it had me thinking about the time when that guy was arrested outside of the diner years ago? I'm sure you remember."

My body flushed with heat. Did I remember? You mean the guy who flooded my fantasies every time I closed my eyes? The countless times in the bathtub I pretended his fingers touched me instead of my own? Five years later, I still thought of the criminal. No matter how much I tried to force other images into my head, he was always the one my body responded to, desperate to feel him again.

"Uh. Yeah. Sort of." I grabbed the cool glass and turned away, hiding my pink cheeks.

Finn Montgomery.

I had learned his name later when I was called into the police station. Skylar found it so thrilling we had been so close to the sexy criminal, claiming it was the most exciting thing that had ever happened in this town. I wanted to run. I never told her what happened, wanting to forget my *huge* mistake. Thankfully, I never had to go to court, but we all had to pick him out of a lineup. It was the last time I saw him and his steel-blue eyes and full lips. I tried not to think about where his hands had been or how his mouth felt on my skin. But I could never forget the orgasm he gave me against the bathroom wall.

My uncle wanted to keep me mostly out of it, but I read Finn and his partner, who escaped, had robbed a hospital of drugs, probably to sell them on the street for triple the price, and held up the gift shop for cash at gunpoint. Though there were no prints on the gun, Finn had it on him at the time they caught him, which was enough to link him to the crime. My uncle always said possession of a weapon ticked up the sentence.

It was hard to accept the reality I had screwed a drug dealer in a bathroom. That wasn't me. Besides the countless times his image had made me come since then, I really did try to forget all about him.

"What brought this up?" I kept my voice even, even though the mere mention of Finn's name turned me into cellophane, and I was sure everyone would see what really happened between us.

"Oh." Gavin shifted on his feet, his mouth opening then closing, as if he were waging an internal battle.

I stared over my shoulder at him.

"Seriously, it's nothing." He shook his head. "I recently got an update on him, and it had me thinking about how strange the case was. Still don't understand what made him stop at the diner and why he stayed for so long. We didn't find any drugs or weapons in there."

Act normal, Devon. Do not react. Concentrating on keeping even breaths, I straightened Mia's artwork and magazines scattered across the table. "Have no idea. Remember? I only saw him through the window." I swallowed the ball of lies stuck in my throat.

I had heard the diner patrons informed the cops he had driven up, went to the back where the bathrooms were located, and stayed there for a good twenty minutes before returning outside, where he surrendered to the police. Because the gun and drugs were still in his backpack when they arrested him, the police were baffled to what he was doing in that period of time. I waited on pins and needles for weeks that Finn would give me up, confess to screwing some dark-haired freckled girl in the bathroom. By deduction, it would come back to me. But it never happened. My uncle's station now had a running joke that Finn Montgomery decided to take the world's most inconvenient shit.

"It's just so odd. Looking into his history, he and his partner had been thieving for a long time. Never got caught. Nearly uncatchable. Ghosts. Not one print left behind, not one step out of place. It doesn't make sense."

"Strange." I shrugged, moving to the sink, where I placed my dirty glass. Years of being a cop's daughter had taught me to keep calm under pressure, to keep my breathing and heart rate steady.

"Yeah…" Gav shook his head. "Anyway, I better get back to the station. I'll come by Sunday for brunch as usual." He took a step toward the hallway. "Bye, *Bitsóóké*."

"Bye, *Shinálí.*" Mia briefly looked up and waved back, then went right back to her movie. He gave me a last smile before disappearing around the corner. The door shut softly at his exit.

The moment he left, my heart pounded and I stared at the floor, feeling a delayed rush of guilt and fear. I didn't like lying, especially to my uncle, but after five years, I hadn't expected to revisit the topic of Finn Montgomery ever again.

My fingers curled around the sink, holding me up. My uncle saying his name out loud had only made him more real. Finn Montgomery was imprinted on my body. I couldn't stop his image from dominating my mind and couldn't forget the feel of him thrusting into me.

A ghost.

That was what he felt like. One who wouldn't stop haunting me.

CHAPTER SIX

"Mia, please eat your carrots." I jabbed my finger at the tiny portion I set on her plate, sweat trailing down my already sticky skin from the heat of the kitchen.

"No!" She huffed, folding her arms and kicking her heels angrily into the chair legs. Most of the time she was the sweetest girl, but she was still a Thorpe. We were incredibly stubborn.

"Mia, please. Just one."

"Nooooo!" She kicked harder into the chair.

"What is this?" My mom stabbed at a tiny piece of chicken nugget with a deep frown on her face. I had been so tired all I could muster was baking nuggets, fries, and canned carrots for all.

"It's a chicken nugget, Mom. You've had them before." I rubbed my temple, sliding the plate of carrots toward Mia. She shoved it back, turning her head away from me in an angry huff.

"I don't want this." Mom dropped her fork, her shoulders slouching like a pouting child.

Great. It was going to be one of those nights.

"Mom, you need to eat." She would live off M&M's if she could, but the last few times she snuck them, she ended up choking. Like an infant, we had to cut her food into tiny pieces. Most of the time I made her mashed potatoes and soft, finely diced chicken breasts, but tonight I was too exhausted.

"No." She rammed the plate back, her forehead wrinkling. "You're trying to poison me. I am no fool. You are trying to kill me." She hissed. Then she stood and heaved the plate of nuggets at the fridge.

"Mom!" I watched the plate with the rest of Mia's dinner crash into the refrigerator. The plastic platter clattered to the floor, the nuggets tumbling over the ground.

A blimp of shocked silence twisted in the room before Mia burst into scared wails, which only agitated my mother. She covered her ears, wailing even louder than Mia.

Sweeping Mia up in my arms, I rocked her on my hip, curling her head into my shoulder.

"Mom, stop." I tried to keep my voice calm, but my nerves were raw and frail, feeling as if my chest was about to crack open.

Both continued to cry before exhaustion got a hold of my mother and she dropped back into the chair. Her chest heaved, and she stared around as if she had no idea where she was.

"Mia, shhh, sweetheart." I bounced her in my arms, kissing her head. She quieted, peeking out toward her grandmother.

"W-what's wrong with *Enisi*?" Mia sniffed in my ear. "What did I do?"

"Nothing, Bean. You did nothing. She gets confused, remember? We've talked about this before."

Mia nodded, curling deeper into my neck, her body finally going lax.

"Okay, I think it's early bed for everyone tonight."

Normally, Mia would fight me, but she didn't even twitch as I pointed us toward the room she shared with Amelia.

"Mom, do not move. I'm putting Mia to bed." I touched her arm, readjusting my niece on my hip.

"Mia?" Mom's head jerked up. In the present moment. "Oh *barnebarn*, good night." Mom used her Norwegian nickname for "grandchild" and with her shaky hand touched Mia's back.

Mia wiped away her salty tears. "Night, *Enisi*," she said in a small voice, still unsure of her.

"Stay here," I ordered Mom again before I went down the hall and got Mia into her PJs. Quick as I could, I brushed her teeth, read her a story, and turned on her star nightlight.

"Sweet dreams, Bean." I kissed her head as she snuggled into her tiny bed, cuddling up with her many stuffed animals.

"Love you, Auntie Dev."

"Love you more." I shut the door behind me, my shoulders sagging with sorrow.

Thankfully Mom was still in her seat, her face streaked with tears, sobbing so hard she barely breathed.

"Mom." I rushed to her side, crouching next to her. "Shhh…it's okay." It was getting harder and harder to pretend the good nights outweighed the bad.

"No." She shook her head. "No—I—don..." She struggled with her thoughts, letting them drift off into space. I wrapped my arms around her, rocking her as I had Mia. Biting my lip to keep my heartache and anger back. How was this fair for her to go through after my father? Why did life always have to bring you to your knees, then kick you while you were down? It took everything I had not to lose it with her, but she depended on me to keep this family together and surviving.

After she calmed, I stood up, gripping her arm softly to get her attention. "You need to take your pills, Mom."

She shook her head.

"Please." My voice wobbled, the fight to not break into pieces, barely hanging on. "Do it for me."

Her hazel eyes met mine, taking me in. For a second, she looked like my mother, not the shell of a person stolen by the disease. She blinked, and my familiar mom was gone, life shutting down in her eyes. She held out her hand silently as I placed the pills in her palm, downing them with water. Detached. Lifeless. Sometimes I hated this side of her more than when she was feral, scared, and wild. The robotic mannequin was the opposite of who she'd been in life, and it crushed me to see her like this.

She didn't say a word or struggle when I got her in her pajamas. She curled up robotically on her bed as I laid the comforter over her.

"Night, Mom." I kissed her temple.

Silence echoed my sentiment, but I no longer took it personally. My mother was no longer "home."

I fell back against the door after I closed it, staring down the short hallway, where a dim light revealed the chipped paint and dingy rugs.

At twenty-two, I felt three times older. The weight was too much to bear today.

My chest heaved with a silent sob, and I could feel a million following behind it. Not wanting to wake anyone, I ran into the bathroom and started the bath water. Hiding my tears in a stream of water was not unusual for me. My bones craved more than a shower and decided because everyone was in bed early, I could still have bath night.

The instant I sank into the warm water, sobs wracked my body. The tears weren't just for me or my mother or our money woes, but for everything. I knew why Mia acted up and went to bed early every time Zak took her. She understood deep down he didn't want her. She tried so hard to please him, and no matter how good or quiet she was…she never would.

I cried until I had nothing left.

My head tipped back onto the ledge, my lids shut, and I exhaled, letting everything go.

Sleep wrapped me up in its warm embrace and stole me away before I even realized it.

CHAPTER SEVEN

A loud wail rang through the air. My eyes bolted open, and my heart leaped into my throat. *What the hell?*

Confusion plucked me from a deep sleep and jogged my thoughts. The cold water in the bathtub splashed around me as I jerked in response. Awareness stabbed my chest like an adrenaline shot. I'd fallen asleep in the bathtub.

The alarm continued to screech within the house, piercing my ears. I clambered out of the tub, grabbing my robe. The instant the door swung open, my eyes clouded, my nose filling with smoke. Burning oil and grease singed my senses.

"Oh. God. No." My stomach bottomed out as I darted toward the kitchen, where the haze grew thicker with each step. I whipped around the corner, seeing flames sprouting high from the stove, black billows curled up into the range hood. My mother stood over the stove batting at the fire with a burning towel, flinging ash and flames around the room every time she flung it back. With the other hand she poured water, igniting the flames higher. The last thing you did was throw water on a grease fire.

"Mom! No!" I screamed, as magazines on the table went up in flames. The fire quickly spread over the table to the fabric chairs. "Stop!"

She continued to strike at the stove, unaware I was there. I slammed into her, shoving her to the side. I reached for the knobs, my skin sizzling with heat. I grasped the potholders hanging nearby, trying to turn off the knobs. My heart thumped wildly in my chest as I nudged the pan she had on the stove to the side.

The wails from the alarm shredded at my nerves. I was vaguely aware of Mom moaning in fear and Mia's terrified voice calling out for me. The fire was spreading behind me. I had to stop it now or we would lose the house and possibly our lives.

"Mia," I yelled over my shoulder, waving away acrid smoke. "Go stand on the front lawn and call 911. You remember how, right?" I hoped my constant drilling it into her head would override her fear. "Mom, go with her!"

In my periphery I saw Mia dart to where my phone charged in the living room and sprint for the doorway. "*Enisi*," she called out to her grandmother through her hacking coughs, but my mother was locked on the flames in a different world than ours. "*Enisi!*" More panic dripped from Mia, her hand reaching out to Mom.

"Go, Mia! I need you to call 911 for me. Now!"

She nodded and disappeared, zooming out of the house.

My five-year-old niece was the only one I could depend on to help. She understood how dire this was and acted. Behind me, my mother rocked back and forth in fear and confusion, coughing and moaning but not moving away from the scorching flames, forcing me to bump her back with force.

From my time working in the restaurant, I knew grease fires were not easy to put out and spread quickly. Baking soda and a fire extinguisher were the best bets.

Spinning around, I rushed into the hall closet, grabbing the extinguisher and covering my mouth as my lungs tried to fight against the smoke as I ran back in. I squirted everything in sight. Thick white foam coated the stove, table, and chairs, the fire sizzling under the suffocating weight of the spray, not wanting to give up its fight. I unloaded the entire contents, smothering every bit of the fire as tears streamed down my face from terror and smoke.

When the last of the foam trickled out and the cylinder blew only air, I dropped my arms, scanning the room. The crackle of the dying flames and the smoke filled the room with an eerie feeling of death, as if the fire had burned out my last thread of hope and left me hollow inside.

In the distance I heard the fire engines heading our way.

"Mom, come on," I choked, grabbing her under my arm and rushing us out into the clean night air, my skin caked in soot and sweat. Stepping outside, I spotted Mia standing by the tree, running for us the moment we stepped off the porch.

"I d-don't know what happened." Mom's voice was small and rough as she leaned into me. "I-I just wanted to make breakfast for my baby girls. Thought it would be fun for them to give their daddy breakfast in bed for Father's Day."

Fresh tears zigzagged down my face, blurring in the red and white lights zooming up our road, followed by police cars.

The had fire gutted our kitchen, but her words gutted my heart.

The fire brigade stomped in and out of our house, the lights from all the trucks, ambulance, and police driving our neighbors out, staring at us as if we were on a TV show.

I sat in the back of an ambulance, Mia on my lap wrapped in a heavy blanket, as the EMTs checked us all out. Mom screamed and fought, forcing them to sedate her. She eventually curled up on the cot in the back and fell asleep, never aware the events were of her doing.

My face was streaked with soot, and my white robe looked as if I'd rolled in mud. My lungs burned, and my throat felt as if it had been rototilled. Otherwise I was fine. Thankfully both Mia and Mom checked out too, though we all looked like dirty street urchins.

"Devon." Uncle Gavin strode toward me, his expression pinched in a frown. He had made sure we were all right before pursuing his duties.

I watched him silently while holding Mia's sleepy body close to mine. He stopped a few feet from me; scratching his head, he glanced back at the house.

"That could have been really bad."

"I know," I croaked out.

"Really bad." His head snapped back to me. "Do you understand what could have happened here tonight?"

"Yes," I gritted out. I hadn't even closed my eyes and the nightmare of the worst outcome looped over and over in my head. I gripped Mia even tighter to me, needing to feel her solid little presence and know she was okay.

"Do you?" Gavin barked before taking a deep breath, letting his panicked anger settle down. "This has solidified my decision. When my granddaughter is put in danger, when *you* are put in danger, there is no choice anymore. For my family. For the town. I will do my duty to keep you all safe."

My lashes fluttered, staring back at the house. I knew this was coming, had known it for a long time. But there had always been tomorrow. A tomorrow when I would deal with it.

Tomorrow was today.

"This is not something that will get better, Devon. You know that. She will continue to get worse. I've stood by too long now, waiting for you to get to this decision yourself. No more. She has to go into a facility. Where people know how to take care of her."

The lump in my throat coiled tighter. Understanding his point didn't make it easier to accept. She was my mother. I had such little time left with her anyway. And my soul understood the moment I put her into a home it would feel like the end. I would have to say goodbye soon.

My lips rolled together, forcing the tears back. "Okay," I whispered.

Gavin's face softened with empathy, and he bent down and rubbed my shoulder.

"I know how hard this is. Believe me. I love her too. She's been in my life for the last thirty years. But she is no longer the woman she was. You know in her right mind she would want you to do this. She wouldn't want to be a danger to her own grandchild or daughters. This is the best." He drew his hand away. "I will help any way I can."

I could only nod, my vision blurring with heartache.

"Mia!" A screech tore through the air. I jerked my head back to see a jeep pull into the driveway. My sister jumped out of the passenger side, her face riddled with panic and horror. "Oh my god! Where is my little girl? Mia!"

Mia lurched awake the same time Uncle Gavin yelled out to Amelia, my throat unable to speak above a whisper.

"Amelia! Over here. She's fine." Gavin waved her over.

"Mia?" Amelia spotted her sitting on my lap and sprinted to us.

"Mommy!" Mia scrambled off my lap, running with open arms to her mother. Amelia swept her up, a pained-joyous cry breaking from her lips as she wrapped her daughter tightly against her, stroking her head. Her eyes closed, the love of a mother exploding out of every pore of her body at seeing her child was okay. Amelia could be a pain and very shallow, but when I saw the love she had for Mia, how she would flip the world upside down for her, those things were easy to forget.

Amelia set her down, taking inventory over her little girl's body. Alarm widened her eyes when Mia started coughing.

"Fine, Mommy," Mia's voice squeaked.

Amelia's head snapped to me, our gazes locking. "What happened?" She stomped up to me, peering around at the commotion. "Where's Mom? Are you okay?"

"They're fine. Alyssa is sleeping in there." Gavin answered for me, pointing inside the ambulance. "There was a little accident. A fire. But everyone is okay."

"Little accident?" Amelia's voice rose. "Doesn't look little to me." She waved at all the trucks and emergency crew taking over our front yard. "Why didn't anyone call me?"

"I tried." Gavin folded his arms, curving up an eyebrow at her. "Maybe if you actually kept your phone on."

At the sight of her messy hair and puffed lips, I had no doubt what she had been doing instead of answering her cell.

I could see a deep blush forming, humiliation abruptly turning to anger. My father had also been incredibly sweet, until he was angry. We all had hot tempers, but Amelia came with even a shorter fuse than the rest of us.

"Tell me what the hell happened." Amelia's face twisted into anger. "You were supposed to be watching my little girl. I trusted you to keep her safe."

"Seriously, Amelia?" A burst of sardonic laughter popped out of my mouth, burning my throat. "You really are judging me right now?"

"I leave for *one night,* and my daughter almost dies in a fire. Yes, I am judging you, Devon." She moved up into my face.

Fury flushed over my skin, making me stand up. "One night? Please, you are home *one* night. I am the one home with your daughter and Mom. Me. You're trying so hard to find a man who will take care of you, do you even bother with names anymore or just bank account statements?"

"How dare you?" Amelia shrilled, shoving me.

"Whoa! Whoa!" Uncle Gavin stepped in, tearing us apart. "Stop it now! This is not helping."

Amelia got in one more shove before Gavin pulled her back farther.

"Stop it, Amelia! Your sister is not to blame here. It was an accident. Don't turn your guilt and fear into anger at your sister. She is doing the best she can."

Amelia stepped back, crossing her arms, looking at the ground and taking deep breaths.

"If you want to blame anyone, it should be yourself."

"Why? What did I do?" Her head popped up, her lids narrowed on our uncle.

"Because Mia is *your* kid, and the woman in there is *your* mother too." He pointed at the body sound asleep in the ambulance. "I'm not stupid or blind, Amelia. I'm well aware of who pays the bills and keeps a roof over your head."

"I work! I have an actual career I'm working toward. I work hard."

"Amelia." Gavin touched her arm, giving her his warning look. "Stop."

She huffed, dropping her head again.

"The situation is different now, and you two are going to need each other even more. Everything is going to change, and you girls need to depend on each other and not fight."

"What do you mean?" All anger drained from Amelia, her throat bobbing with alarm.

"I mean, as a family member, as the sheriff, I can't allow Alyssa to stay here. She needs to go into a home. Someplace safe for her. And everyone else."

We all knew no such place existed in this town. This meant Mom had to go to a bigger city where they had facilities which could deal with her disease. I wouldn't abandon her.

It was time.

"What are you saying?" Amelia turned to me as if I were the parent making the decision. "Devy?"

It hit me like a thunderbolt. What would happen? Something I wanted for so long, maybe not this way, but it still led to the same conclusion.

I gulped, meeting my sister's gaze.

"We're leaving."

CHAPTER EIGHT

"Mia, please come help." My sister's voice rang out behind me as I stared out the window of our new apartment, the city alive with activity below. The minuscule two-bedroom place wasn't much and wasn't in the best part of town, but I couldn't stop the smile from engulfing my face. I was living in Albuquerque, which to me was everything. It felt like a giant leap from the town we came from.

Uncle Gavin was helping us financially until Amelia and I got jobs; the rent was almost the same as the mortgage we used to pay. Gavin took over our house. He had been subletting a converted garage because his divorce from his "bitch wife," Lisa, two years ago, and he jumped at the chance to make the house his own.

So he got his own place, and we got out from an unsellable house and a mortgage we couldn't keep paying. Granted, it came with a shitload of repairs, especially the kitchen, but he didn't seem to mind. It was all his.

With the little he had left, he paid for our first month's rent on our apartment, while the sale of Amelia's car covered the last. I hated feeling the weight of his kindness. He couldn't afford it any more than we could. I would pay him back the moment I could, but the facility mom was at would take most of my paycheck. Mom qualified for some Social Security disability benefits because she worked long enough to pay into the system. She received a small monthly payment, which helped some. But first thing tomorrow, I was looking for a job.

"Mia!" Amelia yelled again, wiping the sweat from her brow. "Damn, it's hot here."

We'd grown up in the mountains of northeast New Mexico. Albuquerque was a high desert area, and mid-September felt like a sauna to us.

I swiveled around to see the small kitchen/living room chock full of boxes, which showed how small it was because we didn't have a lot of stuff. Uncle Gavin had kept all the family photos and memorable items in the garage at the old house. I had filled a few boxes of clothes, books, shoes, and personal items. Ninety-five percent of these boxes were full of Amelia's and Mia's stuff.

Mia bounded into the space from the bedroom she would share with her mom. Thankfully I got my own room. Technically, I had my own room in the old house, but for the last six months, when mom's wandering got bad, I ended up sleeping in her room, making sure she stayed there. I hadn't really had my own space for a while.

"Take this box to our room." Amelia handed her a small one stuffed with toys. My sister had fought leaving for a week, saying she couldn't leave her clients and job, but when she realized I was going with or without her, she changed course. She understood she couldn't afford a place on her own and also take care of Mia. Uncle Gavin was nice and invited her to stay in the house with him, but she admitted she was more terrified of being without me than the need to stay. I knew she liked the built-in babysitter attached. Uncle Gavin worked too much for him to watch Mia.

"You have an interview tomorrow?" I pulled dishes out of a box, loading them onto a shelf.

"Yeah. Can you take Mia to her new daycare? I really want to be ready for this interview."

The daycare was an elderly woman two floors below us who sweetly said she'd love to watch Mia sometime. My sister jumped on that, and before the woman could blink, she had obligated herself to watching Mia during the week.

The "interview" was with one of Amelia's previous clients' daughters who had a salon here. It was more like Amelia stopping by and hinting at wanting a job while dropping the mother's name and telling the daughter she did her mom's hair every week than an actual professional interview.

I pinched my lips together, holding back my true response. "Sure."

My resumes were printed out, in my bag, ready for me to pound the pavement. Tomorrow I would go to every restaurant downtown. I would not leave without getting a job or at least an interview. I had no other choice.

"After we're done here, let's take Mom dinner." I set the last plate on the pile, glancing at Amelia.

Mom was probably so scared. She had been fine on our initial walk-through, but when she really comprehended the facility was her new home, and we would be leaving her there, things went bad fast. She had thrown tantrums before, but this was violent and feral.

I jumped in, but the nurses scooted me away, telling me to let them do their job. Their natures were soothing and efficient.

I expected to feel relief, the responsibility no longer mine, but instead I felt odd. Useless. Guilty. Like she was a pet we were cruelly dumping off at the pound.

Abandoning her.

Breaking me into even smaller pieces.

My shoes pinched my feet, my teeth digging into my bottom lip as I pretended I wasn't a moment away from tugging them off and going barefoot. The sun pounded against my temples, wilting my put-together appearance like ice cream left in a hot car.

It was four thirty in the afternoon, the sun still high in the sky. For the last two hours I had walked everywhere and heard enough "Not right now" or "We'll keep it on file" to fill the Rio Grande. College had started a few weeks earlier and summer was ending, so either the college kids already nabbed the serving jobs or the restaurants were cutting back until the holiday season.

Whatever the reason, I was getting noes all the way around. It didn't help I had only served in one place.

While five years showed I was faithful, a single line on my resume wasn't helping me. I tried to fluff and fill it with all things I had done at Sue's, but it wasn't hard to see I didn't have a lot of outside-of-the-diner experience.

I peered down at my phone to a text from my sister boasting about getting a job at the salon. I pinched back a wave of aggravation at myself.

"I can't go home yet. Next one," I gave myself a pep talk.

Tired, thirsty, hungry, and cranky, I pushed myself through the last bit of Old Town, daring myself one more place before I gave up for the day.

The last restaurant was a sophisticated, elegant steakhouse I had walked by three times, because it looked too fancy for my pathetic resume. But desperation forced my hand.

It was quiet, the lunchtime crowd long gone. One thing I knew in the restaurant business was never, ever, drop off an application in the middle of lunch or dinner rush. I already felt I was walking the fringes of the dinner crowd.

I stepped in, the cool air-conditioning soothing my overheated skin. The dark, sexy ambiance with dim crystal chandeliers hanging from the tall ceilings, dark wood, and soft leather seating, lured me in with the possibilities of how much money I could make here. I was a hard worker and learned fast. If they'd give me a chance.

"Hi." I forced a bright smile on my face, flashing it at the hostess. She stared down at her phone, looking bored. "I was wondering if you guys were hiring."

She glanced up at me through eyes lined heavily in black liner and a thick smear of pink gloss on her lips. The girl couldn't have been older than eighteen.

"Maybe."

It was the first "maybe" I'd had all day.

"Really? Can I speak to your manager?" I pulled out my resume.

"He's busy." She sighed, scrolling through her phone again.

"Can you get this to him?" I shoved the paper to her, covering her phone. Annoyance filtered over her face, but she took the paper, scanning it.

"Are you serious?"

"What do you mean?"

"You have one other job on here." She snorted. "I have more experience than you do." She handed the paper back to me.

"Can you please give it to your manager?" I tried to keep my tone pleasant while anger crawled up the back of my neck.

"I'm being nice here. Save your paper. And your time."

"Excuse me?" I could feel my face cheeks flaming with heat.

"I'm just saying maybe you should get more experience. At a small bistro or possibly McDonald's." She lifted an eyebrow mockingly. "My manager will throw this out with the leftovers."

Her words hit every raw nerve. Suddenly all I could feel were my aching feet, pounding head, dry throat, and growling stomach. I wasn't some coed looking for extra cash to blow on shoes and makeup. This was survival. The way I could help my mother stay in her facility. How Mia could remain clothed and fed. With a roof over our heads.

My hand started to crunch the paper in my hand but halted instantly. Another drill of resentment shot through me. I couldn't afford to ruin a resume; I didn't have a printer at home. I had to get them printed, which cost money.

This little teenybopper had the nerve to belittle me? Life came up and punched me in the face; with my pinched toes and sweaty blouse, this girl was looking down at me. Bitterness nibbled at my bones.

"Actually, thank you," I gritted out. "You saved me from working with assholes like you." I spun around and stomped out of the place, the heat blasting me the instant I shoved through the door. The sun seemed even more malicious. I wanted to slip back inside into the dark, cool space and lie down on the benches for waiting customers.

"Screw them," I muttered to myself, my feet moving without destination. Rage still locked my neck muscles tight, making my aching feet feel like cement bricks.

My cell pinged with a text, my hand pulling it from my bag.

Amelia: "Crissy from the salon called, saying she wants to start me right away. My trial starts Thursday. Taking Mia to park. See you later. Celebrate?"

I was happy for my sister, but her victory highlighted my failure. Leave it to Amelia to get a job on the first day being in Albuquerque. She had that kind of charisma people loved.

It had been a shitty day, and I was nowhere closer to a job than when I left this morning. While she wanted to celebrate, I wanted to drown in my bad mood. I wanted a drink, to escape the downward spiral of my mood.

Normally I would run straight home. My mother had always been a reason to go home instead of going out with friends. Not that I had many of those left other than Skylar. Sometimes the gang at the diner would go out to a bar after closing and hang out, but I never could.

Realization came over me, halting me in my tracks. "Holy shit." I blinked.

I had no reason to go home. No one needed me tonight. Visiting mom would be the right thing to do. I should see if she was all right. For the first time in years I didn't want to do the right thing, and I didn't want to go home. I didn't want to fake excitement for my sister.

I glanced up at the rustic sign above my head. Engraved in wood by a branding torch was the name *Brothers & Thieves Saloon.*

There were a ton of bars in this area but only one on this strip. I needed a drink and *ta-da*, my wish was granted.

Without hesitation, I tugged at the large wood-and-iron doors, stepping into the darkly lit, cool space. The homey design made me feel comfortable. It walked the line between a dive and stylish, welcoming all walks of life. A few patrons sat at the bar and at tables, a mix of ages and types.

Stepping deeper into the space, I looked around. The saloon had the same rustic iron and wood as outside but was trimmed with refurbished lights and funky art. Recycled barrels and oil containers were reshaped into tables and lighting fixtures.

"Hey there," a woman called from behind the bar. She was a few inches shorter than me, curvy, Latina, and probably in her early thirties. She wore bright red lipstick and winged eyeliner, similar to an old-fashioned pinup model. A tight black tank showed off the tattoos down her arms, her long, dark hair pulled up in a bun. Beautiful but intimidating, she seemed sure of herself. Strong. To someone like me, who was floating with no solid footing, this woman was like ramming a mirror up to my face and revealing me to be weak and insecure.

"What can I get you, sweetie?" Her red lips parted into a warm smile, dissolving her scary demeanor in a flash. Suddenly I wanted to run up to her and cry on her shoulder.

Slipping onto a barstool, my mind came up blank with what to order. I didn't go to bars. I didn't have a drink.

"I don't know." I secured my bag on the bar hook, peering at the rows of bottles, overwhelmed by the choices.

The bartender leaned on the bar, her eyes staring straight into me. "What do you like?"

"Tequila." It was the one thing I'd ever really had besides beer. And beer was not strong enough for the day I had.

"My kind of girl." She grinned with a proud nod. "You want a shot or maybe a margarita? I make the best in town."

"Screw it." I stared back at her. "Both."

She laughed, pushing off the bar. "That kind of day, huh?"

"That kind of life."

"You don't look old enough to have that kind of life."

"Looks can be deceiving."

"I hear ya, girl." She bobbed her head. After checking my ID, she got to work on my order, waving at one of the customers leaving. "See you tomorrow, Rick."

The older gentleman grinned, winking at her before stepping out into the evening. As he exited five more patrons came in, settling on the sofas in the far corner.

"Here you go." She set the drinks on a napkin in front of me.

"Thanks." I wrapped my hand around the shot glass, pressed the other to my temple.

"They say bartenders are good listeners." She tipped her hip into the bar, laying down limes next to my glass. "And a lot cheaper than therapists."

"Depends on how long I stay tonight." I tipped the alcohol into my mouth, biting down on the lime right after, which cut the burning down my throat.

"Look, I understand having a rough life, believe me. I didn't have it easy, but…"

"I don't look like the kind who had it *all* that rough?" I filled in. I had heard it before. I swear it was the freckles. Freckles seemed to equal wholesome and sweet. If you had them, then your life had to be carefree and easy.

"I've seen all walks of life here. There's an innocence to you, as if there's still hope, but at the same time, a heaviness. As if you are trying to hold up the world."

Snorting, I took a gulp of my margarita. "Wow, this really is good."

"Thanks." Her shoulders went back with pride. "Now, talk, uhhh…?"

"Devon."

"Natalia, but call me Nat." She shook my hand.

"Well, Nat. Do you really want to hear this story?"

"Do you want another drink?" she challenged.

"Not fair."

"Bartenders hold all the power." She winked playfully.

I leaned on the bar with a sigh.

"The gist of it is…six years ago my father was killed in the line of duty, five years ago my mother was diagnosed with Alzheimer's, and my sister became pregnant by an abusive asshole who is now a deadbeat dad to her five-year-old. We had to move here since my mother tried to burn down the house, and I can't get a job to support the facility she's at."

"Holy. Shit." Nat's mouth parted. "I am so sorry."

I shrugged, trying to not let my confession turn to tears. Some days it really hit me.

"Shit. You really have been dealt a bad hand." She patted my arm, her eyes drifting over to the customers making their way to the bar.

"Is there table service?" The guy thumbed back to the sofas holding his friends.

"Do you see anyone else but me?" she retorted.

"No."

"Then probably not." She winked, putting a blushing grin on his face. Damn, she was good. Flirting and slighting him at the same time. "What would you like?"

He ordered a mix of cocktails and beers. She completed his order, refilling my shot glass at the same time. Gulping it back, my insides started to warm, shrugging off the weight of the bad day.

The door swung open and another group of people came in, taking up the entire corner section. The place was filling up and as far as I could see, she was the sole bartender on duty.

"When does the restaurant open?" A woman waved a menu at the bartender.

"Six." She brushed a bead of sweat from her brow, setting up the glasses for her next order.

"You have someone else coming in, don't you?" I peered around, feeling compassion for her. I still had recurring nightmares about getting too many tables and not being able to get to them all. I think most servers did.

"The owner is coming in later, but for now it's just me. The other bartender is off tonight, and Lincoln doesn't seem keen on hiring another server to handle the floor. We only have one on the weekends."

My head jerked to her, the tequila in my system warming my cheeks, words sprouting from my mouth without thought.

"I can do it." I swallowed. "It's what I was doing all day. Going to every restaurant practically begging for a server job."

"You have experience?" She lifted a perfectly sculpted eyebrow.

"Five years." I nodded. "At a busy diner."

She wiped her forehead again, putting her hands on her hips, her lips twitching in thought.

"We really do need an extra hand. Weekends are crazy here, and weekdays are getting too busy for me to handle on my own," she considered out loud.

"Please. I will do anything." I sat higher in my chair, my eagerness dripping all over the bar. "I'm a hard worker and dependable." More so now that I didn't have to run right home to Mom.

"You know what?" She tilted her head to me, the door swinging open with more people coming in, the crowd at the bar deepening with impatient customers. "Screw him. He made me assistant manager, and I say we need a server on the floor. He can bitch and fight all he wants, but tough."

I tried to swallow over the nervous lump in my throat. "What are you saying?"

"I'm going with my gut. You're hired, Devon. You can start tomorrow."

"Really?" I squeaked.

"Really," she replied flatly, flicking her eyes at the throng lining the bar. People called out for her as she danced in a whirl behind the bar, trying to get the drink orders ready. "I need you."

"You don't want to look at my resume or anything?"

"Leave it so I can contact you, but really…I don't care. We need help, and you need a job."

"Thank you." I pressed my fingers to my lips, trying not to cry, flattening the slightly crumpled resume on the counter. "You don't know how important this is to me."

"I think I do. And it's why I want you here even more." She grabbed six beers out of the fridge, wrapped her fingers around the necks like octopus's legs, and plopped them in front of a guest. "Come in tomorrow around three and we can start training. You can meet the owner, Lincoln Kessler, then. That work for you?"

"Yes. Thank you." I popped off my seat, feeling the need to get home and tell my sister the great news. Also, it felt strange drinking as a patron when I would be working here tomorrow. I laid some bills down.

"No." Nat shook her head. "Those are on the house."

"I can't—"

"Think of them as 'welcome, new employee' drinks."

Nodding gratefully, I slung my bag over my shoulder. "See you tomorrow, Nat. And again, thank you."

"Don't thank me yet. You haven't met the owner."

"Why? What do you mean?"

"Lincoln is a real son of a bitch." She twirled a shaker in her hand. "Just warning you."

If money went into my bank account, helping my mother, I could handle anything.

Even an asshole boss.

CHAPTER NINE

Two hours into my first shift, my head spun trying to keep all the information from floating out. This place ran so differently than Sue's. I had grown accustomed to the diner and didn't even have to think about the effortless flow. Now, I was back at ground zero, learning the computer system and the location of all the items, trying to absorb everything as fast as I could.

The skeleton kitchen staff was prepping when I arrived, but it didn't open until six at night and only served hors d'oeuvres and snacks.

"We used to have a full kitchen, but when Lincoln took over, he revamped it and cut back. He wanted it to be more of a bar than a restaurant, to focus on having the best drinks. And I have to say he saved us. We didn't have enough tables to really turn a profit for dinner. The food cost more than we made off it."

"When did he take over?"

"About five months ago, I guess." Nat strolled behind the bar, greeting a customer I recalled from the night before, Rick, I think, then turned back to me. "His brother owned it before, but let's say he wasn't the best business person. The bar was about to go under."

"Is the brother around?" I shoved my hands into my apron, twirling the few pens I found there. We had no real uniform here. Denim bottoms—shorts, skirt, jeans—it didn't matter, and a black tank with the bar logo on the back. It was so much better than the button-up polyester blouse and skirt at Sue's.

"No." Nat shook her head, pouring a beer for the gentleman without even asking, a sign of a true regular. It was after five o'clock and the place was filling up. "I don't know what happened, but one day James was gone and Lincoln was here. And a warning for you. Do not mention James. Actually, forget I told you at all."

"Why?" I eyed the new group entering, grabbing a tray.

Nat's mouth opened then snapped shut, her head whirling behind me, the sound of the back door slamming closed.

Maybe it was Nat's warning or something else, but nerves jumped around my stomach. I knew my new boss was behind me. A prickling awareness crawled up my back, coating my skin in goosebumps. It was strange, but without even seeing him, I could sense him fill the room.

My head whipped around, and I beheld the man holding two cases of beers. His eyes snapped to mine.

Everything stopped. The tray in my hands clattered loudly to the floor. I sucked in air sharply, like I had been punched in the stomach, a strange *déjà vu* spinning my head. I took a step back.

The man stood about six-four with brown hair, tattooed ripped arms, and a chest bulging through his T-shirt as if he lived at the gym…making him intimidating as hell. He looked to be in his late twenties. His full beard defined his sculpted jaw and rugged face. Sexy didn't even describe him, but the icy-hot sensation burning my body in opposite ways screamed with fear and familiarity.

He stopped dead in his tracks, his jaw locked down, his face expressionless, but his lids lowered, his nose flaring. A muscle along his neck twitched, displaying a tattoo on the side of it. Brown eyes bore into mine.

"Hey, Lincoln." Nat grinned, popping a hand on her hip, as if she waited for his disapproval.

"Who the hell is she?" he growled. His voice vibrated through me, clenching my thighs at the same time it made my heart pound with fear. I had a handful of one-night stands in the last five years, but only one man had ever made my body react with desire instantly like this. One I tried to forget.

"Devon Thorpe. She's our new hire." Nat's voice was strong and defiant. No matter what she said about him, she certainly wasn't scared of him.

I couldn't stop staring at him, moving over every inch. My chest clenched at the little air my lungs were drawing in. Sweat beaded at the back of my neck and began to drip down my lower back.

"No. She's not." His voice was gravelly, deep. Sexy as hell. So was the man, but also terrifying. He unsettled me.

"Yes, she is. I need help. You made me assistant manager for a reason. And I made the decision."

He finally tore his intense gaze off me, softening a bit as he turned to Nat. "And I can unmake you an assistant manager." He set the boxes down on the corner.

"Please." She rolled her eyes, going back to mixing a cocktail. "You couldn't function without me."

"You want to try me?" he rumbled, his fists clenching.

"You think you scare me?" Nat tipped her head back like she was talking to a toddler. "*Cabron,* please. I grew up with five brothers. Three of them in gangs." She shook her head. "This place is growing in popularity. You have one weekend server and two bartenders total. We're drowning here."

His jaw went back and forth, flexing his hands. "I do the hiring. Not you."

"From now on you can hire." Nat winked at me.

"No. From before her. Did you even ask if she's worked in a bar before?"

"Here's her resume. Interview away, but she's already hired." Nat grabbed my resume from behind the bar and flattened it in front of him.

His jaw locked while his eyes scanned the page. For a second, I saw his lids squeeze together, his fingers pinching his nose, before he shook it off.

"Fire her. She doesn't have enough experience."

"What? No. She's perfect. She's caught on faster than anyone I've ever trained before."

"You're fired," Lincoln threw out. This time I realized he was talking to me. Rage coiled in his shoulders. *What the hell?* "I'll find someone next week."

"No." My mouth parted, dread filling my stomach. I couldn't lose this job.

"No?" His head jerked to me so quickly, I tipped back on my heels. "Excuse me?"

"Please, I need this job. I will do anything." I hated the desperation laced through my words. Getting this job was a fluke, but I couldn't lose it. The first bill for my mother's facility was already sitting on the kitchen counter, waiting to be paid.

"You can't stay." He sucked in, shaking his head almost desperately.

"She *stays*, Lincoln." Nat folded her arms, her jaw set. "Or you lose me too."

"What?" Lincoln's mouth dropped. "You don't even know her, and you're willing to risk your job?"

"Yes." Her gaze shot to me for just a moment, but I felt every word she didn't say. She was doing it for my mom. For my niece. She understood how desperately I needed this job. The warmth bursting in my chest as she laid down her own position for a stranger made my eyes burn with emotion. "Now what will it be? Keep two extraordinary women working here, kicking ass and bringing in money for this bar, or you find yourself down two employees in a day?"

"Nat," he snarled.

She tilted her head, a grin spreading across her face like he saw something in his demeanor I hadn't.

"That's what I thought." She winked at me again, turning back to the bar.

Rage flickered over his face, but he only looked at her, then stomped down the hall and slammed his office door.

I stared blinking at his vacant spot. Nat stood there, a smile engulfing her face.

"I can't believe you did that. What if you lost your job?"

"He can't do without me. I know how to run this place better than he does." She grabbed a bottle off the shelf, pouring the contents into the glasses. "I know it. He knows it."

"You put your job on the line for me." I touched my chest, shaking my head slightly in awe. No one had ever done something like that for me.

"I like you, Devon, and I know how badly you need this job. I understand having to pay bills to survive. I'm a single mom and up until last year I was taking care of my dying grandmother." Her brown eyes met mine, sympathy deeply entrenched in them. She shrugged, letting the moment go. "Plus, I love pissing him off. Though, I'm at a total loss as to why he wouldn't want you here. You are *gorgeous*; the customers, mainly guys, will love you, and you are a hard worker. Seems a no-brainer to me."

Maybe I was imagining things, but Lincoln didn't just not want me to *work* here; he seemed to *dislike* me. He didn't even know me. I mean, most people at least waited to get to know me before they hated me.

"Did I not warn you he's a real son of a bitch?" She chuckled. "Sexy as hell, but from experience, I've learned to stay far away from that type. Always bad news. Especially for the heart." Nat flicked her chin toward the front door. "Now get back to work. We just had more people walk in."

Still flushed, I swiped up the dropped tray and headed toward the tables. Lincoln was an asshole, but unnervingly hot, reminding me a little of the one guy who had completely made me lose my mind.

I had my experience with a bad boy. I learned my lesson, and I vowed I would never do that again.

By the time the bar closed, my feet throbbed in my shoes and my body was sticky from sweat and smelled like booze. But I felt fortunate I had a job.

"Sorry, this ended up less a training day and more of a throw-you-in-and-see-if-you-can-swim day." Nat wiped down the bar then planted her butt on one of the stools with a groan.

Cleaning the last table, I dragged myself to the stool beside her, flopping onto it. I worked hard at the diner. I was used to hustling, but this was like a crazy day at the diner on ten shots of espresso. I could barely keep up with the drink and food orders.

"How did you guys do this without a server?" I rolled my shoulders back, stiff from carrying trays loaded with drinks and appetizers.

"I have no idea now." Nat smoothed back her hair. "Tonight seemed extra crazy. That's why I kept telling Linc we needed to hire more people. Since we've reopened this place, it keeps gaining in popularity. Eventually he'll give in and add another bartender to the roster. At least on the weekends."

My eyes drifted to the office door at the end of the hallway, knowing he was behind it. Earlier it had gotten so busy he jumped behind the bar with Nat, turning orders out to customers standing at the bar while Nat made ones for my table orders. He never once looked at me or acted as if I were even there. I, on the other hand, had the opposite problem; I couldn't seem to stop watching him. He was cordial and joked with customers he knew but was guarded with anyone else. There wasn't a woman who didn't flirt with him. He was sexy and mysterious, and it drove women in hordes up to the bar to see if they could be the one to get him to smile or flirt back or take them home.

Did he have someone? Wife? Girlfriend? "What's his story?" I stirred in my seat, still staring at the door as if I would get x-ray vision.

"I don't really know. As I said, he surfaced one day. I didn't even know James had a brother until Lincoln showed up. He's tight-lipped about himself, but he's a cool guy once you get past the first couple of layers."

"What do you mean?"

"James was the same way, so I'm thinking they had an awful childhood or something, and he has serious trust issues. Once he lets you in…and when I say that I still don't mean you're suddenly buddies. Far from it. But you see glimpses of this other side of him. It took me four months to get anything even remotely personal out of him."

"And what was that?" I lifted my eyebrows, craving any information about him. He was my boss and a real jerk, but something drew me to him. A feeling of familiarity, real or imagined, compelled my curiosity to understand him. Why did I feel this strange pull to him? Especially because he was such a dick. I was no different from those girls at the bar who were flirting with him, hoping to be the one who cracked the stoic armor.

Nat raised an eyebrow at me. "Uh-oh. Not you too."

"What?" Embarrassment coated my cheeks like paint. "What are you talking about?"

Nat's lashes fluttered. "Please. I'm not stupid. Hell, even with my past, I couldn't fight wanting him at first too."

"Really?" A zing of jealousy darted up my spine. "Did you guys?"

"No." She shook her head. "Though I wanted to. But he didn't even give me a sideways glance."

"He has a girlfriend?" A lump formed in my throat. "A wife?"

"Look at you…fishing for details." She nudged my arm, my cheeks reddening more. "As far as I'm aware, no to both. But who knows? He doesn't talk about anything outside this bar. If he does, whatever woman has claimed him has never stepped foot in here. I tried asking him once, but he never answered. Lincoln Kessler is a man full of secrets." She sighed, her attention shooting to the door then back to me. "Over the weeks working with him, I realized it was for the best nothing happened. Men like him are quicksand. And I'm done with that type. Isaiah's father, *pinche cabron*, was the ultimate bad boy. Leader of a gang. And the reason I will only date nice guys now. Need a good role model for my boy."

"Is he still involved with Isaiah?"

"He's dead." She shrugged.

"I'm sorry."

"Don't be. He was an idiot, and I was even dumber for falling for him. Not long after I got pregnant, I realized I was attracted more to the danger and prestige of his title than the man. I didn't want my son anywhere near the gang life, and Carlos would never leave. Not unless it was in a body bag."

"Damn," I whispered.

"You're not the only one with a messed-up past." She smiled. "You did awesome tonight. I'm glad I trusted my gut. I think you will work out fine here."

"Even with him?" My head nodded to the door at the end of the hall.

"I got a feeling he'll come around." She tightened her ponytail, a funny smile playing on her lips.

"I doubt it." I slid off the stool, my feet screaming in agony.

"Show up, work hard, and prove him wrong."

"I plan on doing precisely that." I would be the best employee he could ever dream of because a lot of people needed me.

And I would fight tooth and nail for them.

CHAPTER TEN

The weekend passed in a blur—days spent with Mom, nights at the saloon. I finally met Julie and Miguel, the other employees. Julie was a cute blonde, who went to UNM during the week, making the bar a perfect place for her to work on weekends. Miguel was in his early twenties, good-looking, and fit. The moment he locked eyes on me, he flirted relentlessly. It didn't take me long to realize his conversation was elementary at best, not much deeper than working out, women, his diet, and how awesome he was. The customers ate up his cheeky, flirty vibe. He was the perfect bartender, but my tolerance for his unsubtle quips about getting me in bed had reached its limit by Sunday night.

I barely saw Lincoln the whole weekend. When he did venture from his office to help stock or get a count of inventory, I was no more than a ghost to him, his frostiness toward me not lifting an inch. It frustrated me beyond belief, especially because I worked my ass off. I stocked, cleaned, and did side work before I was asked, covered more tables than Julie, had customers laughing, bartenders in awe, and the kitchen staff blowing me kisses.

I was the frickin' model employee.

Did he even utter one word of "good job" or "I'm sorry I was a total douchebag. Forgive me, I'm so glad we hired you"? No, not once.

When I grabbed stuff out of my locker Sunday night, I heard Miguel tell Lincoln how good I was. Though I wasn't sure I felt flattered.

"Hey, man." I heard Miguel's voice stream from Lincoln's office near where I stood, dreaming about a shower and bed. Sunday had been almost as busy as Saturday, and I looked forward to the next two days off. "Here's the till and report."

Lincoln only grunted in response.

"Can I say thank you for hiring that girl? Damn, she's good. Surprised me. Had all her tickets in order and was on every drink the moment I finished making them." Miguel scoffed, as if he were shocked I was capable of being good. "And doesn't hurt she's fucking hot. Nice eye candy for the bar."

A noise rolled out of the room, a feral growl, and my skin rose in goosebumps.

"Just sayin'. She's smokin'. And you know my standards."

"And if you want to keep your job, you will keep from ever speaking like that about *any* woman at this bar again." A sound of a chair screeched across the wood floor, Lincoln's voice a rumble. "Especially her."

"Relax, Linc. It was a *compliment*."

"Miguel, you are an average bartender with an overinflated ego." Lincoln's voice vibrated with cold anger. “And I warn you, if I hear you make one more sexual comment to her, about her, or even *look* at her…you’re fired. She may not be easy to replace, but you are. Now go home before I change my mind.”

“Someone needs to get laid. Jesus, what is your problem tonight?” Miguel shot back. “And you wouldn’t fire me; you need me. I’m one of the best and you know it.” With a huff, Miguel stomped out of the office, passing me without a glance, and slamming the back door.

What the hell happened? Did Lincoln actually stand up for me? When did he notice Miguel’s attention on me? He didn’t act like I were even here.

Boots hitting the wood floor snapped me out of my trance. I looked at the doorway as Lincoln strode out, his brown eyes catching mine. His expression went taut, his jaw twitching with irritation.

“What are you still doing here?”

“I was finishing side work.” I forced my feet to stay planted on the floor. He was not going to scare me.

He rubbed the spot between his eyes, his nose flaring. “Go home.”

“Yeah, I was. Thanks for your permission,” I snapped, my temper flaring out of my mouth before I could think.

He swung back around, his expression detached, but his jaw tightened with aggravation. His stare latched on to me like a trap, locking me in place. Thick tension sprouted between us, tangling my lungs in its web and slinking around my body.

He took a step closer, stopping a few feet from me, looming over me.

I couldn't move or look away. The air in my lungs skimmed the surface as his eyes moved over me. Slowly. Meticulously. Heat bloomed inside, flowing through my veins, and tightening my thighs.

This man was a jerk. Had been nothing but rude to me, but I still couldn't fight the desire to touch him. See if he was real. Understand why my heart thumped when he was close, and why my body responded the way it did to him.

"*Devon*." He said my name like he was finding how it tasted on his tongue, the rumble of his voice vibrating through me.

"What?" My voice came out a whisper.

Lincoln took another step closer, the heat from his physique feathering my skin. My heart thudded against my ribs. He leaned down, his mouth close to my ear.

"Get the fuck out of my bar. Now." His voice rumbled in my ear, sending frissons down my spine. Until his words sank in. I jerked back, my teeth crunching.

Screw you! I screamed in my head, but silently I held my chin up, swiveled around, and stomped out of the saloon. The crisp evening air stabbed my heated cheeks.

Nat was wrong; not only was there no good guy under any layer, but he was worse than quicksand, which you didn't willingly step into it.

If he was trying to get me to quit, he would quickly find I didn't break so easily. Life had tried over and over. Lincoln Kessler would not even make a dent.

Three weeks passed with very little interaction with Lincoln, for which I was grateful. Miguel backed off openly making passes in public, but he made up for it in private to annoy me. I didn't subscribe to the notion that boys will be boys, so women should let them get away with being assholes. But Miguel was harmless. It wasn't long before I realized he didn't know any other way to interact with women. Sexual comments were his pleasantries. I still called him on it, but I wouldn't tattle on him to the boss. Not yet.

Home life was in a routine. Amelia worked four days a week, and Mia had started school down the road. We had barely enough money to pay bills and get food, so not for a lot of extras. I pleaded with my car every day to keep going. I actually had time to pick up running again, helping to relieve some of the stress. I was nowhere near my track days, but it felt good, just me, my music, and the pavement under my feet.

Mom was another story. She lost more weight and could no longer go to the bathroom on her own. She had become petulant toward people and stared out her window for hours. Having early-onset, the disease was more aggressive and progressing fast.

The doctor warned us as the disease progressed, patients lose the ability to coordinate basic motor skills such as swallowing, walking, or controlling bladder and bowel. These could understandably cause confusion and frustration.

"Mom, you need to eat." I scooped up some yogurt on a spoon, her face turned toward the window, lost in her world. "Mom."

"Mom, please?" Amelia scooted Mia onto her other leg, leaning into Mom's eyeline. "Mia said she'll eat with you."

Mom's head rotated enough to glance at us, her face blank of recognition.

"*Enisi?*" Mia said her grandmother's nickname softly, timid and shy around the strange woman who had possessed her loving grandmother. "Look. I love yo-gert." She licked her own Go-Gurt package. "Yummy."

Mom stared at her as if she were an alien, then went back gazing out the window.

I dropped the spoon in defeat, sharing a look with Amelia. Frustration lined Amelia's forehead, her patience with Mom getting shorter with every visit.

"Mom. Eat. Now," she demanded.

"Not helping, Mel." I shook my head at my sister. "Mom, you have to keep up your strength." I leaned over, touching her arm. Wrong move.

With a strangled cry, she whirled around, her arms flayed out, whipping and thrashing at anything close. The tray of food flew off the counter, crashing onto the linoleum with a loud clatter, yogurt spraying over us. Her howls of anger and irritation pierced the air.

My niece's face crumpled and wails zipped up her throat, clashing against my mother's moans of frustration.

"That's it. I'm getting Mia out of here." Amelia grasped Mia's hand and stomped out.

"It's okay…Mom…shhh." I tried to calm her down, but her moans only rose to shrieks. Nurses scuttled into the room, moving around her, speaking in low, calm voices, pushing me out of the way. At first she fought against them, her body flopped to the floor, taking one down with her. Bethany, my mom's main caregiver, sat down with her and talked slowly and calmly to her. Mom struggled and cried until her body sagged into Bethany.

"We'll take her back to her room now. She can rest for a bit," Bethany said to me.

I nodded, staring at the nearly unrecognizable face of the woman who used to braid my hair, and make me tea when I had a bad day. The nurses helped lift her up, her feet moving like a zombie back to her room.

"I'm sorry, Devon." Bethany touched my arm, her light brown eyes soft with sympathy. "I wish I could tell you it will get better or easier."

"I know." I blinked back the emotions. To watch someone you love die a slow, horrific death, stripping them until they were broken, was worse than anything I could fathom. Losing my dad had been terrible, but it was fast. He didn't suffer.

Bethany squeezed my shoulder, then took off toward my mother's room.

I wiped at the yogurt on my face, straightening my shoulders, then I moved outside to where my sister waited on the steps.

"I can't do this anymore," Amelia spurted the moment I stepped out. "I can't keep seeing her like this. And I won't let Mia remember her that way." She motioned to where Mia played on the grass.

"Mel…"

"No, Dev. You may be fine seeing our mother fade away into nothing, but I can't." She stabbed at her chest. "I don't have the strength to watch Mom slowly die. Not after Daddy. I won't do this to myself anymore."

Frustration at our situation, at my sister, flamed up my spine, I rolled my hands into fists. "What *other* choice do we have?" I screamed back at her. "Just because you don't like it, Amelia, doesn't make the problem go away."

Amelia bit down on her lip, anger reddening her skin. "Get off your high horse, Devon. You're not the only one going through this."

A snort huffed from my nose. My patience reached its limit.

"Yeah, but I'm the one handling it. Taking care of everything," I gritted through my teeth. "Have you ever once paid a bill or watched Mom for more than an afternoon or gotten the medication she needed? You couldn't even be bothered to come with us when she was diagnosed. Couldn't even answer your phone. So excuse me and my high horse. I feel alone in this."

Amelia narrowed her eyes. "You are such an uppity bitch. All you can see is yourself. I have given up so much for you and Mom."

"Oh my god." I shook my head in disbelief, taking a step back. "What? What have you given up, Amelia?

"School, opportunities. I moved here for you."

"School? The one you flunked out of? And what opportunities? A hairdressing career in a dead-end town? Yeah, I'm so sorry you sacrificed it coming here." Rage tightened my throat as another bout of anger was ready to burst. "You can tell yourself anything you want, Amelia, but you are selfish, lazy, and spoiled. You didn't move here for me…but because of me. You were afraid. You couldn't handle the real world on your own."

I knew I should walk away before I said too much. I turned away from my sister, her mouth parted, her face a deep purple, and I marched to Mia, kissing her on the head, then continued toward the car.

"Wh-what are you doing? You can't leave us here. What are we supposed to do?"

"It's called a bus. Use it." I slammed my door, the hinges groaning with effort. "Or walk."

"Devon!"

"I have to be at work." I fought against the voice telling me not to leave them, to give in to Amelia again. The facility wasn't far from our apartment, and the bus went straight by it. My fury overrode my guilt. I pulled out of the parking lot with a squeal of tires.

Deep autumn darkened the sky early, shadows creeping over my car as I rolled into the parking lot behind the bar. The anger had quickly turned to grief and guilt, my hands shaking. I'd meant what I said to her, but I shouldn't have said it in front of Mia.

"Get it together," I demanded of myself. I had a full shift to make it through before I could properly lose it. I twisted the key to pull it out of the ignition.

Snap. I blinked, staring at the half key pinched between my fingers, the rest still stuck in the ignition.

The key was the last drop of rain that broke the dam. A sob heaved from my chest, tears burning my lids until I could no longer hold them in. My will to fight my grief fell away. Putting my face to my palms, I let out my heartache. The pain, guilt, responsibility, and fear felt bottomless. I covered it up, hid it from those around me; I didn't realize how heavy it had become.

My body shook as my cries filled the car. Drowning in my own tears, I didn't even hear someone open my door, the night air nipping my bare legs.

"Hey." A deep voice spoke in my ear, large warm hands cupping the sides of my face, turning my head. I lifted my eyes, heavy with tears, to find Lincoln crouched next to the driver's seat, his brows furrowed in concern. "Are you okay?"

Part of me wanted to burst out with laughter, asking why he should care, but I didn't have the energy. Shutting my eyes, I let out a leaden sigh. He let go of my face, not speaking, letting me breathe in and out until I could compose myself. Of all people, I should hate he was the one to see me this way, but when you were covered in crap, pride took the last seat in the bus.

I wiped at my eyes, flinging the broken car key onto the dashboard. Not as if anyone could steal it. Nor would they want to. Probably couldn't pay a thief to take it.

His gaze landed on the item, standing up. "Is this why you're upset? A broken car key?"

"Yeah." I shoved past him, grabbing my bag, and slamming the door. "That's why I'm sobbing in my car like someone gutted my soul…because I snapped my key." Annoyance rubbed out my grief like a windshield wiper.

"Then what happened?" He touched my arm and I spun to face him. "Devon?"

"Why do you care?" I glared at him. His mouth snapped shut as if he had no idea why he cared. "Now let me go before my asshole boss tries to fire me, *again,* for being late."

Lincoln's eyebrow curved up, his fingers tightening around my wrist.

I shouldn't have said those kinds of things to the owner, but I was all out of fuck yous today.

"Maybe you should tell your boss to go fuck himself." He took a step closer, his voice so soft, it took me a moment to comprehend his words, keeping my surprise locked down.

"Believe me." I mirrored his step, our figures only a few inches apart, "I dream of saying that to him every day."

"Sounds like a real asshole."

"He is."

We watched each other, not looking away, his touch spreading fire through every nerve.

Finally, he jerked his head away, dropping my arm as if it stung him, his tone icy. "Get to work, Devon. You don't want your asshole boss getting on your case. *Again*."

My lids narrowed on him. I shook my head, spinning around, trudging through the back door, trying to ignore the part that wanted to stay and wanted my boss *on* my case.

As if I didn't have enough going on in my life, I didn't need to add my attraction to the jerk to the pile.

CHAPTER ELEVEN

The night was quiet for a Wednesday, and by ten, Nat told me to head home. Even though I was pretty sure Lincoln was somewhere around—I didn't see him once during my shift—my head still chewed over the strange interaction. Nat shrugged off his absence, and we spent most of the night cleaning and chatting between customers.

Nat and I got each other. She understood the pain of loss, growing up fast, being the kid responsible for taking care of the family. It was nice to have a friend here. Skylar and I talked and texted, but I still hadn't seen her since the move. The gallery where she worked kept her occupied, and my life kept me from doing anything past work, Mom, and watching Mia. I missed Skylar so much and hoped we could see each other soon.

As I stepped out the back door, stars danced above my head, their true brightness tempered by the city lights, but it was still one of my most favorite views. No tall buildings blocked the vast desert sky.

Two steps from my car, I stopped, swearing under my breath. Crap, I totally forgot it was undriveable, and it was too late for a mechanic to fix it.

My gaze roamed over the dashboard, my head crumpling in confusion. My keys were gone.

"Seriously?" I exclaimed, reaching for the door. "They steal a broken key, but not the car? Come on, help me out here." The door squealed on its hinges as I swung open the door, leaning in.

My breath caught, reversing down my throat as my eyes locked on a sparkly new key sitting in my cupholder. My fingers went to the ignition, realizing it was new as well.

"What the hell?" I dropped into the seat, my mouth still parted in disbelief. It was fixed. My attention darted to my rearview mirror where Lincoln's black 1970s blazer sat on the other side of the lot.

He had to have done it. No one else would play fairy grandmother and fix my car. I rubbed my head, letting it fall back onto the headrest. What was I supposed to do with that? Why did he do it? He hated me. Wanted me fired.

Growling in frustration, I inserted my new key, turning on the car, which sounded better than it had before. I searched for the usual lighted symbols around my fuel gauge telling me it needed help. I pinched my nose. They were gone too.

He changed my oil as well? What else had he fixed?

Part of me wanted to march back in and demand his reasoning, grasp why he helped a girl he despised. But instead I pulled out of the parking lot and drove home, fleeing from the temptation of his nearness.

My sister was still up, sitting on the sofa reading a magazine, when I entered the apartment. Mia would have been put to bed long ago.

"Devy?" She dropped her reading material and leaned over the back of the couch, her expression soft. "You're home early."

"Yeah," I whispered, setting down my bag, leaning my hip against the counter. "It was slow."

"Oh." She licked her lips, her regard going to a spot on our worn sofa. "Look, I'm sorry for what I said earlier… I didn't mean it."

"I'm sorry too." Though I meant what I said, I didn't have to be so cruel in my delivery. I flopped on the sofa next to her. "It's only going to get worse. We can't turn on each other."

Her long lashes fluttered, and she wiped her eye. "How do you do it? How are you so strong? I can't even be in the same room with her anymore without wanting to roll into a ball."

"You don't think I want to also?" I peered over at her. "But we can't. Mom needs us. She would not give up on us, not for a second, and I don't plan on giving up on her."

"Jesus, Dev." Amelia dropped her head on the sofa, close to my shoulder. "You're like a frickin' saint."

"Yeah…that's me," I snorted.

"Sometimes I forget you are younger." Amelia cupped my hand, snuggling into me, dropping her head on my shoulder. "You take on so much. And even if I don't say it, I do appreciate it. And I love you so much."

My sister was selfish and a pain, but in moments like

this, it was easy to forget all of it. "I love you too." I let my head fall on hers.

"I'm going to try harder," she said softly.

I had heard it many times before, but I wanted to believe this time she really meant it.

Friday night of Halloween weekend was insane, with customers in costumes of superheroes, sexy cops, slutty rabbits, and a lot of men as women. The place was filled with young coeds dancing everywhere they could, including a few getting up on the tables. Two hours into my shift and I already felt as if I had been here ten—sweaty, tired, and unable to keep up with the drink orders. Julie was slower and struggling even more, and I tried to cover some of her tables too.

The crowds drove Lincoln from his office. He jumped behind the bar. Miguel and Nat tried to make a dent in the hordes at the bar, while Lincoln tried to catch up with the endless drink tickets popping up from Julie and me.

As I waited at the bar while he mixed my five mojitos and eight shots, I tried not to stare at the muscles rippling down his arms as he worked, to little avail.

Damn it. What was wrong with me? And what was it about him? Every day I craved to be near him more and more, especially since he fixed my car, which neither of us had mentioned. It was more than wanting to break the stoic, sexy bartender of his aloof walls. I felt a strange pull, a feeling I had known him in a past life or some crazy shit like that. I couldn't explain it, but I felt it deep in my bones.

I knew there was no point denying I was attracted to him. I mean, crazy, unreasonably attracted. To the point he was starting to replace the last bad boy who'd occupied my fantasies. This angered and embarrassed me, but he was the reason I climaxed, whether I wanted to admit it or not.

My gaze drifted to his fingers wrapped around the muddler crushing the mint and brown sugar cubes. My gaze darted to the side. I looked down unable to meet his gaze, feeling the heat crawl up my neck, my lids shutting with the fantasy I'd had last night and where I'd imagined those fingers. How they had made me cry out.

"Why are you suddenly blushing?" His raspy voice snapped me back to him, my eyes wide. He had a slight smirk on his face, a glint in his eyes.

"What?"

"Right there." He flicked his chin at my face. "What were you thinking about?"

"Nothing." *Liar*. "It's hot in here." I fanned my face, my skin burning hotter. My skin was a light olive color but still showed my emotions.

"Yeah, it is." He set the mojitos on my tray, lining up the shots to pour, not looking as if he believed my story.

Not able to hold his gaze, I peered over my shoulder to my tables, nibbling my lip.

"That's what I thought," he all but whispered, then placed the rest of my order on my tray. "Go."

Get it together, girl, I ordered myself, turning around and running right into a familiar face. "Amelia? What are you doing here?"

"Hey!" Her grin engulfed her face. "Thought I'd finally check out where you work."

"Where's Mia?"

"Oh, I tossed her a candy bar and remote. I'm sure she'll be fine."

My mouth dropped open.

"See, you're not the only one with a sense of humor in the family." She winked. "Jeez, Dev. Relax. Lucia from downstairs is watching her. I needed a night off. I haven't really been out since we moved here. I took a taxi, so don't worry."

"You go out every week with the girls from the salon."

"Doesn't count."

"I'm busy, Mel." I tried to cut around her, more people joining the tables in my section.

"Don't worry about me…oh my god…who is that sexy beast of a man?" She pointed over my shoulder. I didn't need to turn to know who she was looking at, but I still hoped she'd spotted Miguel instead.

No such luck.

Her wide brown eyes were directed straight at Lincoln.

"He's the owner. Leave it, Amelia. All men who work here are off limits."

"Sorry, Dev… He is sexy as shit. And so my type."

"Mel…"

"What do you care? He's not your type. I'm only going to say hi."

"No. Don't." My words went unheeded. Amelia's radar was set on Lincoln, and nothing could stop her.

She swung her hips a little more as she made her way to the bar, shedding her jacket.

She wore tight jeans and heels. Neither of us had big boobs, but she knew how to use a push-up bra and a sexy, low-cut top to her advantage.

Amelia leaned on the bar, and Lincoln's head popped up at the sight of her. I couldn't hear them, but I watched Amelia's body language turn into femme fatale. She pushed out her boobs, moving her body deliberately, touching her chest and constantly biting or licking her lower lip.

She was gorgeous; there was no doubt about it. Men loved her. She was easy to flirt with and talk to, and she was not shy about going after what she wanted.

I envied that. I was awkward and cautious. Cory had been so easy because we'd been friends for so long before. After him, I didn't have time to flirt or go out and act my age. I stayed home. Flirting was foreign to me; a language I didn't know how to speak. And now a burning anger tumbled around my stomach. My hands curled with the desire to grab her arms and yank her away from Lincoln.

"Waitress! Hey," a man's voice boomed, drawing me back to my tables. "We need drinks here?"

I rushed to the table and took their order before moving to other tables. Every time I neared any of them, someone needed a new drink, even if I had just been there. Normally, it wouldn't bother me. Busy meant money.

Tonight my attention was emaciated and my patience even thinner, my head constantly glancing over my shoulder to see what was going on between

Amelia and Lincoln, but all I could make out was the top of Lincoln's head.

"Can you take my table four?" Julie pranced up to me, her face sweaty, her eyes swirled with panic. "I am so in the weeds."

I really couldn't. I was in the weeds myself. But for some reason my tongue struggled to form the word no. Taking on more responsibility to lessen others' stress was what I did.

"Sure." I nodded

"Oh my god, thank you." She touched my arm before running off.

Twisting my body to table four, I saw it was full of college-aged guys. Already drunk and rowdy.

Great.

"What can I get you guys?" I asked sternly, not in the mood to deal with bullshit.

"Well, hello there." A dark-haired guy slurred, his glossy eyes running down my short jean skirt to my legs. "Damn, you're fucking hot."

"Thank you. What can I get you?" I showed no emotion. Drunk men were disobedient toddlers. You couldn't show fear or give them any leeway, otherwise they'd soon be running with scissors and hanging you from the inch of rope you gave them.

"How about your number?" A blond guy leaned over, licking his lips.

"How about your drink order?" My patience was cracking.

"Smile, sweetheart, we're nice guys." The first dark-haired guy grabbed my arm. "We only bite if you ask."

Anger sizzled up my neck. I ground my teeth to keep from saying something that would cost me tips. This came with waiting tables, part of the territory you had to learn to handle, but it never became less degrading or irritating.

"Come sit with us." The dark-haired guy tugged on my arm, pulling me into his lap.

"Let go." I gritted. Fighting against his tug, I ripped my arm free.

"Oooooh, feisty. I like it."

I groaned and turned to walk away.

"Whoa-whoa… Where do you think you're going?" The guy leaned out of his chair, his arm wrapping around my waist, yanking me back. "Get your sexy ass back here. Aren't you going to take our drink order?"

"No." I wiggled against his hold, my rage stinging down my arms and legs. "You guys have had enough."

"Excuse me?" Dark Hair's smile dropped, anger twitching the side of his mouth as he got up, standing an inch or two above me. "Listen, sweetheart. We're the customers. You're the waitress. *You* take *our* order."

"No! I said I think you've had enough." Rage burned from my eyes into his.

"No?" He pressed himself into me, rubbing against my hip, making my skin crawl. "I like you."

"Let go of me. The feeling's not mutual." I shoved at his chest and he stumbled back. In a blink his expression went from slightly irritated to full-blown fury. His body hunched over, barreling for me.

Fear stabbed my lungs. Without thought, my arm swung, my fist smashing into his cheekbone, pain exploding up my arm in a rush. He stumbled back, his hand going to his face, rage blistering his eyes.

Suddenly hands were on my hips, shoving me to the side, and Lincoln's form bounded past me, ramming into the college guy and shoving him over his chair onto his back. Lincoln sprang on him, clutching the fabric around his throat, his teeth bared.

"You will get the fuck out of my bar before I call the cops." He drew the boy's face close to his own, his grip so tight, the guy's face turned deep red as he gasped for air. "If I ever see you in here again or even in the vicinity, I will not hesitate to beat the shit out of you." Lincoln's shoulders stretched out, and his face twisted in a feral expression, his muscles twitching. "You speak to any woman like that again, or touch them without consent, and you will find yourself a eunuch. If you *ever* get within five miles of her?" Lincoln tilted his head toward me, his body heaving with wrath. "Even look in her direction, I will hunt you down and *kill* you. Don't think I won't. I've killed for a lot less."

He dropped the boy, whose head clanked on the floor. The guy grabbed his throat, gasping for air.

"GET. OUT. NOW!" Lincoln roared, making everyone, including me, jump. The group hurriedly grabbed their friend and scurried out of the bar, fear and resentment clouding their expressions.

Music still played, but the crowd around was silent, watching in awe and probably a little fear.

I felt the same, holding my throbbing hand to my chest. I couldn't seem to move, my eyes fastened to the back of Lincoln, not sure what to do. His power and rage were nothing I'd seen before. It was on my behalf.

Hands on his hips, his head down, Lincoln took several deep breaths, trying to calm himself. Then abruptly, he swung to me.

"Lincoln, I'm sor—"

"Come on." He softly touched my lower back, herding me toward his office. His shoulders were tight and hunched as he moved us through, every step a thump, which matched the beat of my heart. He strode into the room, flicking on the light, motioning for me to sit down.

Nervously, I followed his unspoken command.

He shut the door, muffling the loud music and crowded bar, and in that instant, I felt we were in a different world. Alone.

He rubbed roughly at his head, then perched himself on the edge of his desk in front of me.

"I'm so sorry. Those guys—"

"Stop."

My mouth shut. I couldn't think how to finish the sentence, but he leaped in, "Why are you apologizing?" He peered down at me, his forehead creased.

"Because I caused a fight in your bar. I *punched* a customer."

"He deserved it. You've got a mean right hook, by the way. But next time go straight for the balls. Quicker and less painful for you."

"You're okay with it?" I blinked at him in surprise.

"He was a slimy asshole who wanted something you weren't willing to give. Don't ever be sorry for standing up for yourself. Sometimes you might be the only person who will."

I stared at him, sensing a deeper meaning to his statement.

He exhaled, pushing off the desk. "Stay here. I'll be right back."

"What about my tables?"

"What about them?"

"I need to get back to work. It's crazy tonight."

He stared at me so intensely I stirred in my seat. "You might have broken your hand, and you're worried about your tables?"

"Yeah. Julie needs me out there. She can't handle them all."

He waggled his head in disbelief. "Fuck them, Devon. You are staying right there." He pointed at the chair. "They will survive without you, I promise."

"But—"

"They *will* survive." He leaned over, getting an inch away from my face. "Don't. Move. Got it?"

My throat constricted around itself, and I nodded, looking down at my throbbing red-and-purple knuckles.

He slipped out the door, leaving me with a pounding heart and the urge to vomit. Though, that might have been from the pain in my hand.

Less than two minutes later, he stalked through the door again, a bag of ice in one hand, a Coke in the other. "Put this on your hand, and drink this. Sugar helps with shock." He popped the tab of the Coke, handing it to me.

"Shock?" I took a gulp and exchanged it for the bag of ice, cringing as I placed it on my knuckles.

"You might not think it was a big deal, but when your body goes into fight-or-flight mode, defending itself, adrenaline flows through your system. When it comes down, you may crash. Sugar helps counter that."

"You've had experience in this."

"More than you know," he muttered, leaning back over his desk, opening a drawer, and grabbing two items out of it. The white one rattled with pills. "Ibuprofen." He lifted the other bottle. "And whiskey. Two of my favorite painkillers."

I didn't realize I was studying him until he cocked his head.

"What? Why are you looking at me like that?"

"You're not being an asshole." I continued to scrutinize him. "I'm not sure how to handle it."

His mouth twitched, a ghost of a smile tugging one side of his mouth, squeezing my heart and reconfirming the feeling I was sinking in quicksand.

"Take these." He handed me a couple of pills and the whiskey. I tossed both back, the alcohol hitting the back of my throat in a smoky burn, trailing into my stomach. Whiskey had never been my first choice, but this skated smoothly down, warming my chest and cutting some of the pain almost instantly.

Taking another swig, I handed it back to him. He put it up to his lips and took a drink. The idea our lips had touched the same bottle moved the heat from my stomach down between my thighs. I could not look at him. I glanced around the room. There was not one single picture or decoration to give any insight to him.

He set down the container and wiggled closer. "May I?" He motioned to my hand.

My mouth refused to open, but he took my non-response as a yes, his warm fingers wrapping around my knuckles. His touch was careful, but it still sent waves of electricity through me. Did he not feel it? Was I alone in this?

"It seems okay. For one, you're not screaming when I press on it. For another, it doesn't feel broken. Just bruised." His head was pointed down, but his gaze flicked up to mine. He was so close; air evaporated in my lungs, and I froze.

Desire. Yearning. My pulse thumped between his fingers.

For a second, his eyes flicked down to my mouth, the action drawing attention to his eyes. I blinked, taking in the color.

"You wear contacts."

Lincoln jerked back, his expression shifting to a wall of stone in a blink.

"Yeah." He stood up, tossing the whiskey bottle back into his desk. "Nearsighted."

"Oh." It was no big deal, lots of people wore contacts, but his abruptness took me off guard.

"Go home. Take some more painkillers before you go to bed and keep ice on it." His fingers tapped at the paperwork on his desk, his voice detached and aloof. "I've got work to do."

I licked my bottom lip, rising from the chair, feeling confused, embarrassed, and rejected in some strange way.

"Okay." I headed for the door, stopping when my good hand was on it. "Thank you, Lincoln."

His only response was a grunt.

Stepping back into the loud, crowded bar was as jarring as being awakened by a fire alarm in the middle of a *really* good dream.

"Devon!" My sister's voice rang down the hall, reaching me. "Where have you been?" She ran down, taking in my hand. "Are you okay? I was so worried. I heard from that bartender, Miguel, another hottie by the way, you had been in some bar brawl. What the hell happened?"

It had felt like the entire bar had seen or heard us, but obviously it only felt that way. It was too loud and busy, the other half clueless to the drama. For once I was grateful for a crowd.

So how did Lincoln know I was in trouble? He had been the farthest away. I shook my head, not ready for any more riddles I wouldn't be able to solve.

"Let's go home. I'll tell you everything there."

"Yeah, okay." She nodded, following me out to my car. It actually sounded perfect to curl up on the couch with my sister, watch movies, and not think about anything.

Especially my extremely hot and confusing boss.

CHAPTER TWELVE

I tossed and turned most of the night, so the next morning my blurry eyes stared at the coffee maker willing it to go faster. My mind was exhausted, but something kept revisiting the night before, trying to figure out an equation that had no answer. Rolling it around and around, trying to find missing evidence of something. I was like my father, unable to let go until I figured it out, to the point of obsession.

While my head kept replaying the scene, my hormones kept reliving the moment with Lincoln, stirring almost painful restlessness through me. My aching hand only added to the vibrancy of the memory. The way he could threaten the guy but touch me so gently. He was extremely guarded and on the edge of violence, but he had this other side. The guy who fixed my car and shared his whiskey with me. The one who joked. Worried about my welfare. Smiled.

Damn. His grin almost had me falling out of my chair. It wasn't fair a tiny tug of his lips made the ground heave from under me.

It didn't make sense. *He* didn't make sense. Amelia was right; he wasn't my type. I had never been drawn to the muscular alpha male. Sweet, funny, down-to-earth Cory had always been my type. So why was I so drawn to Lincoln?

"Hey, Devy. How are you feeling this morning?" Amelia dragged herself up beside me, ogling the coffee maker. Her hair was messy, eyes half-lidded.

"Okay," I lied, wiggling my hand, sucking through my teeth. It hurt worse this morning than last night, the bones voicing their opinions of the impact.

"Oh my god, I had the best sex dream." Mel grabbed a cup from the cupboard, yanked the coffee pot out, putting her cup straight underneath the drip.

Or you could do it Amelia's way and not wait.

"Really?" I exhaled.

"I didn't want to wake up, but now it's got me all hot and bothered. Definitely time to get laid."

"You go, girl," I said flatly, watching her cup fill.

"I will. You know me, once I set my mind on something, I will get him. Shit, he's probably *amazing* in bed. Like blackout kind of orgasm."

My head jerked to her, nerves twisted in my stomach, knowing I didn't want to ask but couldn't stop myself. "Who?"

"Lincoln. Duh." She grabbed her full cup, shoving the pot back under and taking a long sip. "He's so frickin' hot."

As if hands dug into my chest strangling my lungs, frost formed around my bones.

"What?"

"You know, *your* boss?" She lifted an eyebrow at me. "He has the sexiest voice. Like, I was instantly wet."

"You talked to him?"

"Yeah." A carnal smile curved her mouth as she took another drink. "We chatted for *a while*." She stressed the part as if it meant a lot more than she was letting on.

"Oh?" I tried to swallow over the lump in my throat. "What about?"

"This and that." A secretive beam lit up her eyes.

Oxygen barely grazed my lungs. "I thought Miguel would be more your type."

"Miguel?" She stuck out her tongue and shook her head. "He's cute, but Lincoln is ten times better. Miguel is a boy compared to Lincoln."

"Do you think he likes you?" I grabbed the ready coffee and poured the rest into my cup.

"Definitely." Her mouth spread into a full grin.

Searing heat poured over the ice in my veins. Amelia was an expert in men. There wasn't one guy she wanted whom she hadn't been able to get. She was gorgeous, fun, flirty, and direct.

"H-how do you know?"

"Jeez, Dev, what are we in, grammar school? I can tell when a man is interested." She rolled her eyes, walking over to the sink, depositing her empty cup. "It won't be weird, right? Dating your boss?"

My mouth parted to answer—scream—yes.

"Oh shit, I'm running late," she said. "I need to get ready for work. Lucia's keeping Mia until I get off."

By the time we got home last night, Lucia said Mia was sound asleep and to leave her because she was watching her the next day anyway. Lucia was probably one of the best things that came with moving into this run-down building. She was kind, loving, patient, and always willing to watch Mia, as if she were in need of a grandchild as much as Mia was in need of a grandma figure. They spent a lot of time playing games, coloring, and making cookies. A few times I wanted to ask if she would babysit me.

"Maybe Lucia will continue to watch Mia for a few more hours so I can stop by the bar again tonight." Amelia tipped her shoulder playfully, sauntering back down the hall to her room.

No.

No. No. No.

It was the only thing rolling through my head while my guts screwed up into a ball. Amelia and I had such different taste in men, there had never been a worry we'd be attracted to the same one.

Until now.

I was drawn to Lincoln, but I didn't know how I felt past that. All I could think was *not him. Anybody but him.* But if he liked her too, I had no right to be upset. The thought of watching them kiss or seeing them together darkened my already temperamental mood.

Perhaps I read him all wrong last night, and he didn't experience the sparks flaming between us or want to kiss me. Maybe he was just being a nice guy and aiding a hurt employee. That was it. Amelia usually had awful taste in men, but her instincts about them being interested in her were typically on point.

With Cory, Finn, and every awful one-night stand, I had proved I had no radar.

"I'm out!" Amelia poked her head in, dressed in cute, snug, torn jeans, brown booties, and an off-the-shoulder blouse. "You're seeing Mom today?"

I nodded.

"Okay. There's a good chance you'll see me tonight. Have a good day." She waved and whirled out the door like a tornado, clueless to the reason I still stood in the same place feeling as if I were going to vomit.

It was another bad day visiting Mom, which was becoming the norm. For one brief moment she remembered my name, but then something else would capture her attention. She looked back at me as if I were a stranger who sat down next to her.

There were days I could handle it better than others, turning off my heartache and trying to be there for her.

Today was not one of those days.

My mood was sour before I got there. Exhaustion and the constant throbbing in my hand kept my temper on the edge. Seeing my mom left me full of sadness and anger.

Strangely, it gave me determination to talk to Lincoln. Confront him. Even if I embarrassed myself, I wanted to know what was going on. Why he was so hot and cold with me, and I needed to know if he was interested in Amelia. If they dated, it could make things a bit awkward for me, especially if they broke up.

Nat's head popped up when I burst through the door. She watched me stomp into the bar, her eyebrows curving in curiosity.

"Is Lincoln here." It was more a statement than a question, my resolve set. "I need to talk to him." I turned for the office.

"Devon, no. Not right now." Nat shook her head, her gaze darting to the back room. "It's not a good time."

"Why?"

"He's with someone…"

"What?" A knife stabbed straight into my torso, stealing my breath. He was with someone? Was he dating someone? Was she in there? Were they having sex? What was wrong with me?

Nat apprehensively gazed down the hall, then walked over to me, keeping her attention fully on the office door. "James is here," she said quietly, nodding to the back.

James. His brother. Not a girl. The relief that washed over me triggered electricity down my arms. *Oh shit.* I shouldn't care if he was with another girl.

"James looked totally drugged out." She clicked her tongue. "Let's say it was not a warm welcome between brothers."

At the click of the door, I swung around. A blond man with glassy blue eyes stepped out of Lincoln's office, wearing ripped jeans and a black T-shirt. He was a few inches shorter than Lincoln and thinner, but they had the same jaw and facial structure. James appeared older. His skin was leathery in places, as if he spent too much time in the sun, his lips dry and split. His hair was shaggy, his scuff uneven, as if he couldn't care less what he looked like. You could tell if he showered and took care of himself, he would have been incredibly handsome. Looks ran strong in their family.

"Well, well, well…" James staggered toward me, his eyes wandering up and down my figure. "You're new."

"Leave, James." Lincoln stood behind him, his arms folded, his jaw ticking with anger.

"Don't tell me you aren't tapping this one." James nudged his brother and stumbled. "I know your type."

"Leave. Now." Venom filled every syllable. "I will not ask you again."

"Oh, the almighty *Lincoln*…has spoken." James pointed at him with a wink. "I'm quivering in my boots."

"You're wearing flip-flops." I tipped my head toward his feet.

Lincoln's gaze snapped to me; the briefest flick of humor wiggled his mouth before he looked back to his brother.

"Oh, I like her." James wiggled his finger at me. "Funny. Smart. I can see why you hired her. Quite different from your last one." He snapped his fingers. "Kim, right? What a bitch."

Lincoln dove for his brother, grabbing his arms. "Stop talking now," he growled, his voice vibrating the ground. "I'm not changing my mind. Get someone else to help, James. I'm done helping you."

James's easygoing expression dropped, his eyes narrowing with resentment. "Fuck you." He shoved his brother away. "You think you're so much better than me? You're not. Pretend all you want. I know the truth. You haven't changed. You're just a fraud pretending to be a king sitting on your throne here." James threw up his arms, gesturing to the saloon. "It was mine first. You're benefiting from what I started."

"You mean the one you ran into the ground?" Lincoln snarled, stepping back to him. "I saved it. It's still here because of me."

"With one call all that could go away." James smiled deviously.

Fury quivered through Lincoln, his temper settling into a chilling calm. "What do you want?"

"You know what I want." James didn't waver from Lincoln's deadly gaze. "*Brothers & Thieves*… My name is still on the paperwork."

Lincoln's jaw rolled, his nose flaring. "Get out."

"Is that a yes?"

"Get out now." Lincoln folded his arms, his chest heaving up and down.

"I will be back. You can't get rid of me so easily." James gripped Lincoln's corded arm. "Wow, getting a little scrawny there. Time to hit the gym," he mocked and turned to Nat, reaching for her hand. "Always a pleasure, *mi bellezza*."

Nat tucked her hand away.

James whirled toward me. "I don't know you, but I would very much like to."

"I'll pass."

He snorted, walking backward. "I really like her." His playfulness dropped as he spoke to his brother. "You can't fight it, brother. You'll come back. Can't argue with nature." Then he walked out of the door.

The three of us stood in silence for a few beats, my head trying to wrap around everything that happened.

Lincoln cleared his throat.

"I'm sure you girls have work to do." He swiveled

around and strode back to his office, slamming the door.

Slowly turning to Nat, my mouth parted. "What the hell happened?"

"James." She sighed, rubbing her forehead. "He's a piece of work."

"He was your boss? Really?"

"Honestly, I don't know how he kept this place going as long as he did. I grew up with brothers in gangs. I know when things are crooked, and some shady shit was going on. Our books were always in the red, but somehow, he always got more booze, drugs, and money from somewhere." Nat pulled glasses from the washer, wiping them down. "Makes me think there's more to the *Thieves* part in the name."

"And you didn't mind working for him?"

"Who in the hell am I to judge?" She chuckled. "I had a child with an infamous gang leader."

Fair enough.

"See, this is where you and I differ and where your innocence comes into play. You may have been through some crappy stuff, but you have never had to live on the other side of the law. Things aren't black and white when they're about survival."

"When your father was the head sheriff and now your uncle is, you could live on one side of the law," I sighed.

"Oh shit, your family is law enforcement?"

"My dad died in the line of duty."

"Right, you told me." She picked up another wet glass. "I didn't put it together he was a cop. Thought you meant the military." She rolled her bright red lips together. "*Pinche*, all the stuff I told you and you're a cop's daughter."

"So?"

"You don't understand. It's instinctual. People like me stay quiet and as far from the law as we can get."

"But you haven't done anything."

"Doesn't matter; the color of my skin can be enough." She set the clean glasses on the shelf. "And I'm not so innocent. There are things in my past far from legal."

"Really? What?" I was not shocked but curious.

"I'm not going to go into it," she responded evasively. "But let's say when a loved one is in need, there is nothing you won't do."

Saturday night was even crazier than the night before, and once again Lincoln emerged from the office to tend bar. I expected him to be in a foul mood, but he seemed more introspective. Lost in thoughts, while his hands automatically worked. Strangely, my impulse was not to pull him out of it but touch him—connect eyes—let him know I was there in some way. Not sure why I felt so protective of him, but I couldn't stop the instinct from overwhelming me, twitching my hands.

He set an order on my tray, already grabbing for the next ticket.

"Thank you, Lincoln."

At the sound of my voice, his head jolted up, as if I'd broken him out of a trance, his eyes landing on mine with a penetrating focus. Flames flared in my stomach, burning down the world around us. Nothing else existed, his brown eyes swallowing me whole. Ferocious and brutal, his stare consumed me. Held me in place, flipping the switch that didn't think. Only wanted.

Neither of us moved or breathed.

"It's packed in here tonight." A hand hit my arm, jolting me. "Took me ages to get here." My sister's voice infiltrated my ear.

"Amelia?" I waggled my head in confusion as if I just woke up. "What are you doing here?"

A flirty grin bowed her lips, her eyes sliding to Lincoln. "I told you I'd stop by, remember?"

Right. She did.

"I was hoping to see you tonight." She leaned on the bar, a coy expression coloring her cheeks, her full force centered on Lincoln.

Damn, she was good.

Lincoln dipped his head at her, his gaze going to me.

"Better get those to your table." He waved me off.

What happened? Was he trying to get rid of me? Did he want to be alone with my sister? I gritted my teeth and grabbed my tray, the weight making my bruised hand ache. Spinning around, I shoved through the crowd, reaching my section, slapping the beverages on the table so hard they spilled onto the table.

"Hey!" a couple cried, moving away from the spill. I went to my next table, ignoring their calls for me to come back.

"What do you want?" I clipped out, impatient for the group to spit out their order, my attention drawn behind me, trying to observe my sister.

I felt punched in the chest. Arrows shot into my torso, forcing me to gasp for air. Amelia had moved to the end of the bar closer to Lincoln, her hands on his arms, up on her tiptoes, pressing into his solid form, whispering in his ear. What hurt even worse was he leaned down into her, an odd grin on his face, listening to whatever she said to him.

Oh. God. I was an idiot. This was what it looked like when a guy liked you. A lump strangled my throat and embarrassed tears blurred my eyes.

I prided myself on always being a good employee. Never taking my personal mood out on the customers, but in this moment I lost my head. My attention constantly slipped back to the bar.

"Devon! Your orders are piling up here. Get them off my counter." The kitchen staff kept yipping at me every time I came in.

I heard the complaints, but I couldn't seem to get my shit together. Whenever my gaze snuck over my shoulder, my sister was all over Lincoln, touching him. Her face was bright and smiling as she cupped one hand to his face, dragging his head to her lips, her lids heavy, murmuring something in his ear.

Lincoln blinked and then his lips parted in a laugh I could hear all the way from my table. The sound, usually delighted me in the rare times I heard it, now filled me with jealousy. I had never felt this way over a guy, not even when I found out Cory was cheating on me with my best friend.

Amelia had made him laugh when I could barely get a smile out of him. My throat choked with emotion, my eyes suddenly moist. I couldn't believe it; I was going to cry. In the middle of an order, I spun away, with the urge to hide from the blast of irregular emotion.

"Hey? Where are you going? Miss, we didn't finish our order yet." I didn't respond. I needed oxygen before the room strangled me to death. Propelling through the crowd, my elbow knocked over a tray of Julie's drinks. Her mouth dropped open, but I didn't stop, jetting out the back door, sucking in gulps of night air.

What the hell was wrong with me? I was being stupid. This was probably more about what was going on with Mom than him. I mean, nothing was going on between us. Nada. He wasn't worth the hurt. Still, the brick of pain sat on my chest, not budging no matter what excuse I claimed.

I wasn't the girl who cried over boys, who wasted time on drama. I had too much going on at home to have time for anything else. Yet, since I moved here and started working at this bar, things had changed. My patience had grown short, and my temper ready to flare at a moment's notice. I hated feeling out of control.

Gathering myself together, I sucked in a few more gulps and went back inside. Ten steps were all I got before a hand wrapped firmly around my bicep, pulling me back toward the office.

"Are you *trying* to get fired now?" Lincoln growled, his huge frame coiled like a snake, plodding us down the hall. "In a matter of minutes, you spilled ten drinks and left three tables complaining of crappy service." He swung open his door, practically throwing me in, and slammed it behind him. "You want to tell me what's going on with you?"

"Not especially." I glared at him, my arms folding over each other.

He took two steps, his frame dwarfing mine, his jaw rolling back and forth. He didn't speak, staring down at me, a vein in his neck bulging with tension.

His nearness only aggravated me because of his intoxicating smell and warmth. "You don't scare me."

"Really?" He regained the space I put between us.

"No." I craned my head back, challenging him. "Are you trying to intimidate me?"

"Trying?"

"No one likes a bully, Lincoln."

His mouth twitched. Amusement touched his face.

"What happened?"

You. My sister. Life.

I pinned my lips together.

"Devon," he warned.

"Are you dating my sister?"

His eyes went wide, his boots shifting back. "What?"

Shit. Why did I ask that? It was too late now; I opened the can.

"I think I have a right to know." I clicked up my chin. "I don't want it to interfere with my job."

His gaze ran over me, dropping my righteousness down to the floor. I dug my toe into the wood slats.

"Is that what's wrong?" His voice held a note of surprise. "You thought I was interested in your sister?"

Now I felt stupid. But she made him laugh and flirt back. Why wouldn't I think that?

Lincoln moved closer, the heat from his body blasting into mine. "Are you jealous?"

"What? No!" I spurted out. "Get over yourself… I just know my sister. And if you guys broke up, I wouldn't want it to affect my job."

"So…without my knowledge, I've already dated and broken up with your sister?"

"Yes. No..." I shoved at his chest. Damn, why was he so close? "You know what I mean."

"No. I don't. Please, I'd love to hear this."

An aggravated groan crawled out of my throat, my fingers pinching my nose. This guy tied me in knots, losing all sense of up or down.

"Damn, you are infuriating."

A low chuckle vibrated from his chest, and I was lost in the deep timbre of it. He stared down at me, all humor dying away, the room filling with tension.

"I'm not the only one." His hand lifted, looking as if he were going to touch my face, but it dropped, picking up my arm instead. "How's your hand?"

"Hurts," I croaked.

"It will for a while. Bruises can be worse than breaks." His thumb brushed over my knuckles, my heart knocking so hard against my ribs I was sure he could hear it. He lifted his head and peered back at me.

Kiss me. The thought practically screamed at him.

As if he heard it, he took a large step back, tipping his head forward. "You better get back to work. Julie's probably rocking in the corner by now."

"Yeah." I swallowed with a nod, stepping around him. "I should. Sorry."

"Before you have me married with children, give me a heads-up." He turned to face me.

"Shut up," I snorted, shaking my head.

"And no more spilling drinks tonight, okay, Freckles? I'm trying to stay out of the red."

Scorching heat zipped down my spine, whirling me around. "What did you call me?"

Lincoln's expression went neutral, his eyes boring back into mine with no emotion. "Nothing."

"No." My lungs struggled to get enough air, my voice low and severe. "What did you call me?"

His head dropped, his fingers grazing his files a little too nonchalantly. "Did I overstep the employer/employee line? I apologize."

My gaze ran over him, my chest heaving. "Why did you call me that?"

"Because you have a lot of freckles. I'm sure I'm not the first." He shifted on his feet, his impassive regard going back to me. "Again, I apologize for crossing the line. Won't happen again." He pulled out his chair, dismissing me.

My feet seemed locked in place, the nickname slamming into my gut like a bullet.

"Get back to work, Miss Thorpe."

It still took me a few moments before I opened the door and left, my legs shaky.

Of all things to call me.

Freckles.

It may not have been unique or original. Many people have called me it. It was a nickname I got teased with a lot as a child. I did have a lot of freckles. But I couldn't get over the way it slid from his mouth, melting my bones.

"Open your eyes, Freckles. Want those eyes on me."

"Jesus, Freckles. The way you feel? I will gladly fuck you forever."

In this memory I could still feel the cool wall of the bathroom stall against my back, pressed up against the guy I'd recreated in my head for so many years. The way his tongue wrapped around the pet name…and me.

Get a grip, Devon. Stop turning every guy into him.

The nickname was a trigger to me, similar to when you heard an old song or smelled something that would place you back to another time and place. I became restless and quite frankly, horny.

Maybe my sister wasn't the only one who needed to get laid.

CHAPTER THIRTEEN

Weeks skated by and Lincoln kept his distance from me. When we did interact, he was professional, calling me "Miss Thorpe," irritating me beyond belief.

Thanksgiving break was a little quieter, with people spending time with their families, but we still had a crowd the night before and after. I guess bonding with family on Thanksgiving made everyone want to drink.

Mine was spent helping Mom eat some mashed potatoes, which she choked on. Mia played in the corner, and Amelia chatted nervously at Mom, filling her in on Mia's latest milestones and news from Uncle Gavin. Mom seemed more content now and less combative, which was encouraging, although she mostly stared at the TV, saying little. When she did speak, her words were getting harder to understand. It often sounded like nonsense.

"Devon, can I talk to you?" The head nurse, Bethany, pulled me to the side as my sister, the escape artist, glided by me, taking Mia to the car.

My shoulders dropped, "Yeah, of course."

"This is the worst part of my job, especially during the holidays." Bethany shifted her weight, gripping her clipboard. "But I wanted us to be on the same page. Your mother is showing signs of entering the final stage. She is having difficulty swallowing as you noticed, but also she's unable to control her bladder or bowels. She seems to be losing the ability to coordinate her basic motor skills. Unfortunately, this is when it gets really tough."

It wasn't before?

Bethany pressed her lips together sympathetically. "Your mom is young. Strong. She might not slide as fast as others. There is always hope. And luck." *Nope, we didn't have that.* "She will become increasingly harder to communicate with. It will get to a point she can no longer eat…and then."

"Yeah, I know. She will forget how to breathe." I had read everything I could on each stage of Alzheimer's.

"When you're ready, sooner than later, you need to look over the paperwork your mom set up when first diagnosed. I noticed you and your mom signed a durable power of attorney for both the financial and health care, along with a living will. It will help tremendously."

My nails dug into my palms, trying to hold myself together. "Mom told me when she first found out she would not want to prolong her life. She would come back and haunt my ass if I did. She definitely signed a DNR."

"Sounds like the Alyssa I met when she first came in." Bethany chuckled, a sad smile on her mouth. "We still need you to come in and go over all the paperwork."

I nodded in agreement, but my heart screamed like a child throwing a tantrum. It didn't matter I had the last five years to come to terms with her disease, it wasn't enough to get used to losing her.

Between the ages of seventeen and twenty-two, I'd carried the responsibility of knowing my mother would die young. Guilt weeded and grew inside me because there were days I had even wished it for her, wished the pain and heartache away for her, for all of us. But now death was running up the road, and I sought to shield her, hide her from its finality. I wanted to be selfish. To keep her. Without her, Amelia and I would be orphans. No matter how old you were, it never felt okay.

The drive home was quiet. Amelia also seemed aware we'd crossed another line. And this one was final.

Walking up the stairs to our apartment, a figure sitting at our front door stopped me short. My eyes widened on the person, making sure she was real.

"Skylar?"

"Oh girl, it looks like I came just in time." She stood, opening her arms. She was tall and lean, though curvier than in high school, her long strawberry-blonde hair woven in an intricate braid over one shoulder. She wore paint-covered jeans and a white V-neck T-shirt under a long bright yellow cardigan.

I rushed the last few steps, crashing into her. No matter how long since we had talked or seen each other, we picked up as if we had seen each other hours earlier. She was the remedy to my heartache.

"I've missed you so much, Dev." She squeezed me to her.

"You have no idea how much I've missed you." I pulled back, trying to take in the reality of her presence.

"Aunty Sky!" Mia wiggled on Amelia's hip, her arms stretched out for Skylar. Mia was two when Skylar left, but she came to visit us enough Mia never forgot her. I think Mia had a "girl crush" on Skylar, looking at her as if she were a rock star.

"Mia-bean!" Skylar reached out taking Mia from my sister. Mia wrapped herself around Skylar like an octopus, both of them squealing with joy.

"Hey, Amelia." Skylar smiled cordially at my sister, who gave her a quick hug around Mia. They liked each other okay, but Skylar had seen too much of Amelia's selfish nature to really be close to her. She had been there too many times when Amelia had run off to do her own thing, Skylar taking on the role of the sister I needed.

"What are you doing here?" My head waggled in disbelief. "Don't get me wrong, I am so happy, but you said you couldn't get away."

"Christophe told me to get my ass to Albuquerque and see my friend. And while I'm here to check out this artist who wants to show in his boutique." She lifted her eyebrow. "A little business and pleasure."

I didn't care. I was happy she was here.

"Come in!" I grabbed her bag, her arms still full of Mia, and walked into our tiny place.

"It's just for the weekend, and I'll try not to be in your way."

"No! Stay forever." Mia hugged her again before Sky deposited her on the floor, rubbing her head.

"I wish, Bean, but I love my job and where I live."

"And if I remember correctly, your boss too," I muttered with a wink.

Pink washed into Skylar's cheeks, and a smile exploded over her face. This was the face of a woman besotted. She had told me enough to Google him. He was the opposite of everything Skylar claimed she wanted. He was ten years older, nicely built but average, and the same height as her, a trait she had once declared made a man "undateable." Most of all, he was totally the sensitive artist, nothing alpha about him in his looks or personality.

"Oh, I'm going to have to get details of this." Amelia went straight for the cupboard, pulling out wineglasses and one of the bottles Lincoln gave each employee as a thank you when profits were good.

"Oh yes, please." Skylar nodded in approval. "And I want to know about the Albuquerque men. Dev has been exceptionally tight lipped. What about you, Mel?"

Amelia grinned mischievously. "There's one I'm working on."

I knew it was coming; her feelings for him weren't secret to him or the bar staff. I still felt punched in the gut when she talked about him like that. After the exchange in Lincoln's office, he had backed completely off Mel. Even though her efforts had doubled, coming in the bar every chance she got and flirting almost painfully with him, he barely registered she was there.

One part of me hated something I said might prevent my sister's happiness, but most of me was relieved.

"He is so sexy and the things I want to do..." Amelia stopped, realizing her daughter was still in the room. "Mia, it's time for bed."

"Noooo! I want to stay with Aunty Sky."

"Sorry, kiddo." I steered her shoulders toward the hall. I knew it was about to get really X-rated in here soon.

Skylar dropped to Mia's level, grabbing her hands.

"How about *I* put you to bed?"

"And read me a story?" Mia jumped up and down.

"A short one, Bean." I brushed her hair back.

Mia went twirling and leaping down the hall, tugging Skylar with her.

"You asked for it." I laughed.

"I usually do." She hitched up her eyebrows in double meaning, then went skipping down the hall with my niece.

Skylar and I spent the next two days catching up, relishing every moment we had together. While I worked in the evening, she handled the business aspect of her trip.

She was a painter, but her main job was all the advertising and business for the small gallery she worked for. She enjoyed doing both, and it was the perfect fit for her complex personality. She was one of those people who flourished when challenged.

It was good to see her so happy with Christophe, herself, and work. It made me envious. If I weren't so damn tired all the time, I would strive to be fulfilled like that too. Happy.

I'd kept her up to date on Mom's condition through emails and texts, but she still wanted to hear it from me, letting me cry and vent, as she always did, being the shoulder I needed.

"So…Mel talked me into going to the bar with her tonight. She said for my last night, but really, we both know it's about her." Skylar rolled her eyes. "Who is this Lincoln she keeps talking about?"

"He's my boss." My eyes drifted out the window, my body shifting on the sofa.

Skylar tucked her legs underneath, her forehead furrowing. She slanted her head, reading me as only Skylar could. "Uh-oh. Do you like him too?"

"What? No." My head shook vehemently. "Not at all."

Skylar stayed quiet.

"What? He's way older…"

Skylar curved her eyebrow in an *Uh, hello. Look who I'm dating* expression.

"He's not at all my type. And a total jerk. Probably spends most of his days trying to see how he can fire me."

"Uh-huh."

"Skylar, stop looking at me like that. I don't like him," I exclaimed. "He and Amelia are much more suited. He's totally her type.

"And yet months later, nothing has happened." Sky propped her elbow on the back of the sofa, leaning against her hand. "You know the movie *He's Just Not That Into You*? Your sister should be taking notes.

Sounds to me this crush is completely one-sided."

"So?"

"Dev, you do this thing… You are a strong, capable, take-charge woman, but you become a doormat when you think you might hurt someone's feelings or be in the way. You don't just step back…you hide. I know your mother is a huge part of your life, but you've become comfortable with it being your *only* life." She touched my hand gently. "You can never say no, especially to Amelia. Choose yourself for once. If you want him, go after him. Who cares what Amelia is going to say? He doesn't like her, and she will get over it. I promise you. Also, it would be good for her, for once, to be the one to let you shine."

"I don't need to shine," I scoffed, feeling her words hit home. "I don't like my boss. And he certainly doesn't like me either."

"You might be right, but that's not the point. I'm ready to see you stand up for yourself for once, especially with Amelia."

Easier said than done. My sister felt like a force I didn't have enough energy to fight.

"No matter what, I'm coming in tonight and checking out this infamous Lincoln Kessler." She shot off the sofa, grabbing her empty glass. "And to really annoy the waitresses there." She winked, heading to the sink.

It wasn't the first time Skylar and I had a talk like this, but for some reason this time her speech sat heavy on my chest, ringing a bell until I picked it up and acknowledged the truth.

CHAPTER FOURTEEN

Nat waved me over the moment I walked in, her head poking around the corner down to the office.

"What's going on, Nat?"

"James is here again," she relayed and leaned farther into the passage. "I tried to eavesdrop, but shit, Lincoln must have soundproofed the room. I couldn't even hear mumbling." Irritation at the hindrance filled her voice.

"You little snoop." I prodded her playfully.

"In my world, information is survival. When you're useful, you live a lot longer."

Wow. Okay. Our worlds *were* perhaps more than slightly different.

"How long have they been in there?"

"James came in about ten minutes ago. He was…" She pushed her long-sleeved, black sweater up her arms. "I've seen that look too many times, when I was with Carlos. They all have the same expression…when someone is trying to pretend they aren't petrified out of their mind." She peered over at me. "Something has definitely happened. James has gotten himself in trouble."

"And he's trying to drag Lincoln into it," I added. She nodded at my words.

"James is weak. Whatever he's gotten himself into, he wants someone to get him out."

And who better than a sibling? I knew this routine. How many times had I helped Amelia when she had gotten into something sticky? I couldn't begin to count.

The front door opened and our regular, Rick, came in, sending Nat back to the bar. I stayed put, staring at the office as though my eyes could burn down the barricade.

Imagining what was going on behind the closed door, I jumped when it swung open. James's expression was pinched with anger, his face coated in sweat. Lincoln's impassive one right behind, stalking after him.

"Fuck you, brother." James hit the main room, flipping around. "Jesus, you've turned out exactly like him. He'd be so proud."

Every muscle strained along Lincoln's jaw, neck, and arms. "I am *nothing* like him." His voice was low, chilling my skin.

"Really?" James laughed maliciously. "Turning your back on family. Sounds like him."

"I have never turned my back on you, but there comes a time when you have to save yourself, *James*." He stressed his brother's name.

"Good time to give me a life lesson, *Lincoln*." James sauntered up to his brother until his chest touched Lincoln's. "Last time, I promise."

"You say that every time. I told you, I'm out for good."

"One call." James angled his head, almost in a taunting way. "That's all it will take. Poof. All gone."

It was subtle, but Lincoln's jaw shifted back and forth.

"That's what I thought." James patted his brother. "See you tonight."

James swiveled to us, blowing Nat and me kisses before he left, banging out the front entrance.

Lincoln took a beat before rounding to us.

"We have a group coming in tonight celebrating a twenty-first birthday. I want everyone's ID and their hand stamped," he stressed, his fists still locked at his sides. "It's just you two, so I'll be out here helping." With that, he turned back to his office, leaving me gaping after him.

James was a tornado every time he came here, spiraling through, causing chaos, and vanishing, leaving destruction in his wake.

He made my sister look like a gentle spring breeze in comparison.

The birthday party ended up being only ten people, who were actually low-key for twenty-one-year-olds. Still, between them and the regular Sunday crowd, Lincoln was out helping Nat to make drinks for my tables.

At nine thirty the door swung open and my sister sauntered in, her attention fixed on the man behind the bar. This time I really noticed the slight frown pulling his mouth when he saw her, as if he knew he couldn't escape to the back, especially when she tried to hug him.

"Wow. That was awkward." Skylar came up beside me, flinging her arm over my shoulder. "I was definitely right. Even from here, I can tell he is really not into her."

I tried to fight the smile wanting to curl on my mouth. It shouldn't make me happy.

"I need to get closer, but damn he looks sexy. Before Christophe, he would have *really* been my type." She tipped her head into mine. "So…who do I have to sleep with to get a drink around here?"

I snorted. "Well, since you've been sharing my room for the last three nights…" I nudged her with my hip. We so easily fell back into our adolescence, spending the night, gossiping all about the boys we liked, until one of the moms would yell at us to be quiet. "And you are being forced to spend an evening with Amelia. It's more than fair I get you a couple of them."

"*Only* fair."

I guided her to Nat's end of the bar.

"Nat? This is my best friend, Skylar. Anything she wants is on me. She's on babysitting duties tonight." I jiggled my head toward my sister.

"Oh, hell. Drinks are on the house." Nat winked, a knowing smile on her mouth. Nat liked my sister, but she could see right through her. Nat had even admitted she found it annoying how much Amelia came in to pursue Lincoln. "It's nice to meet you, Skylar. Any friend of Devon's, I know I will like." She waved to an empty seat at the bar. "Margarita with a side tequila shot for you?"

"Oh, I love you already." Skylar smiled back at her.

Nat went to work on her drink, while Skylar stepped toward the empty chair and came to a jarring stop, her regard on the other end of the bar.

"What's wrong?" I followed her gaze, confused at her reaction, which was locked on Lincoln. "Skylar?"

She jerked back to me, shaking her head. "Sorry, I just thought… I'm seeing things."

"What?"

"I'm not sure… He reminds me of someone, I guess." She tipped her chin at Lincoln, my stomach seizing with an odd sensation.

"Who?"

"I don't know, I can't place it, but there's something familiar about him." She rubbed her head and chuckled. "Clearly I need a drink." She laughed it off, plopping down on the stool. I made sure Skylar was good, then headed back to my tables, but every time I gazed back on my friend, she was staring at Lincoln as if he were a song she couldn't quite remember the lyrics to.

I knew the feeling. It was the same one I had every time I was around Lincoln Kessler. That Skylar also found him familiar twisted my guts in knots and again pushed up all those warnings I had shoved down earlier.

Now I couldn't stop feeling I had unwillingly stepped into quicksand.

Around eleven thirty, Lincoln disappeared.

"He's gone," Nat said when she noticed me craning down the hallway toward his office.

"Gone?"

"He left." She shrugged, giving me a pointed look. Unless Lincoln took the day off, which was rare, he never left before we did.

James said something about tonight. Did Lincoln leave to go meet his brother? Unease built in my bones at the growing mystery of Lincoln.

It wasn't long after that Amelia and Skylar went home. Amelia's reason for coming here had slipped out into the night. Skylar tried not to laugh as Amelia made excuses as to why Lincoln had left without saying anything to her.

"See you at home." Skylar hugged me, wobbling a little on her feet. "Leaving early tomorrow, so I'm going straight to sleep. Damn, Nat makes good drinks."

"You guys have a ride home?"

"Lyft is already waiting outside for us." She blew me a kiss and trailed after my sister into the chilly evening.

Nat and I closed the saloon soon after, then cleaned and shut down the bar.

"Dev, can you take these to the office, leave them on the desk for Lincoln?" She handed me the till reports before returning to stocking the empty fridge.

"Sure." I walked to Lincoln's office and clicked on the light. I placed the receipts on his desk, looking around. Nothing had changed. Same plain room, void of any personality. The bareness stirred anxiety I couldn't rid myself of. Skylar's reaction to him kept goading something in the back of my brain.

Peering back down the hall, I saw the kitchen staff and Nat were nowhere in sight. Quietly, I shut the door, closing me in his space alone. The room might be empty of decoration, but I could feel him everywhere, saturating the room.

I couldn't let go of the idea Lincoln hid something. Something I was not ready to voice aloud.

It's not him, Dev. That guy is in jail.

I crept to his desk, looking around once more before I opened the top drawer, my heart picking up speed.

Pens, paper, and other office stuff rolled around in a nearly empty drawer. Nothing important. I shifted to the side cabinet, finding a half-full whiskey bottle, painkillers, and an extra shirt.

I hummed in frustration. I didn't even know what I was looking for, but the lack of something personal or tangible made me more suspicious.

Being the daughter of a cop, figuring out mysteries or finding clues to what made people tick was in my blood. My dad also bought me all the *Nancy Drew* books from a garage sale, and I fell in love with putting hints together and discovering who did it before the story revealed itself to me.

Tiptoeing over to his filing cabinets, I only found bar reports, food and alcohol orders, and other business paperwork.

A voice boomed from outside the hall, freezing me in place, catching air in my throat.

Just one of the guys from the kitchen.

Shaking my head, I took another glance around the room. A few bartending books sat on a shelf, but nothing else revealed anything of interest.

Lincoln was smart. If he was trying to conceal something, he wouldn't leave evidence around. *Think, Dev. Where would someone hide something?*

I pulled the top drawer open again, feeling all the way to the rear for a false back.

Nope. It was solid.

Dropping down in his chair, I sighed. I was being stupid, trying to find something that wasn't there. My paranoia and need to fit everything in a box was getting the better of me.

I shoved myself up, needing to get out of the office soon, my hands gripping the lip of the desk. Like a snap of a magnet, the two-inch depth of the tabletop popped out, revealing a shallow drawer.

"Holy shit." Adrenaline filled my veins. I had never seen a desk do that. A secret compartment in the tabletop itself. Most would think it was solid wood, but really it was hollow, holding another drawer in its ordinary appearance.

Struggling to swallow, I listened for any noise in the hallway before pulling out the hidden compartment. My attention locked on the two objects held inside; a sealed puffy vanilla envelope about the size of a book and what looked like a driver's license.

Uneasily, I picked up the license, my eyes rolling over the picture, staring at Lincoln's face. He had black hair cut spiky and short and light scruff, but it was definitely him. I'd know his jaw and stern expression anywhere.

My stomach dropped.

Name: Jake Smith

Hair: Black

Eyes: Green

"What the hell?" I whispered, examining every detail to make sure I wasn't wrong.

No. It was Lincoln. It was the only thing I knew. But Jake Smith with green eyes and black hair stared back at me. Hair you can change, but eyes?

"You wear contacts?"

"Yeah. Nearsighted."

The moment we had in his office almost a month ago flashed back into my head. He had been curt and defensive. What if those contacts covered green eyes?

Who was Jake Smith, and what was Lincoln hiding?

"Devon?" Nat's voice sang from the passage. "Where are you?"

"Shit." I tossed the license back in the compartment and closed the drawer, the magnet clicking back in place, and I scuttled out of the office, like a thief in the night.

My gut had been right. Lincoln was hiding something, and I planned on finding out what.

Jake Smith or Lincoln Kessler, I would find out who they were.

CHAPTER FIFTEEN

After a tearful goodbye with Skylar, I was left alone in the house with nothing but my nagging thoughts. Mondays and Tuesdays were my days off. Opening the laptop my sister and I shared, I searched for Jake Smith and Lincoln Kessler on social media. The number of Jake Smiths was astronomical. It took all day and most of Tuesday morning to sleuth out the few contenders, and they all led to dead ends. Lincoln Kessler was no different.

Whoever they were, they stayed far from social media.

Unable to stop myself, I Googled Finn Montgomery. There were several, but none were the guy I encountered at Sue's Diner. I didn't see any reports about the guy in jail.

Frustrated, I sagged back in my chair, rubbing my forehead. The buzz of my cell jiggled on the table next to me. Picking it up, a name and number flashed across. My chest clenched, lashing fear into my lungs. I lifted the phone to my ear, dread burning down my neck.

"Hello?"

"Hi. Is this Devon Thorpe?"

"Yes." I swallowed.

"Nurse Bethany told me to call you."

Please. No.

"Your mother has taken a bad fall."

"But she's still alive?" My hand strangled my phone.

"Yes. She got a nasty cut on her head and a minor concussion. Bethany thought you should know. Maybe you could come see her. She thinks it will help calm your mom seeing a friendly face."

"Of course." I jumped from my chair. "I'm on my way."

Hanging up, I grabbed my jacket and tote bag and sprinted out the door to my car. Now that the weather was colder, the engine turned over and over.

"Come on! Not now!" I hit the steering wheel, but the car had no compassion for my emergency. "Damn it!" I slammed the door shut, stomping toward the bus stop.

Thankfully, the facility wasn't too far away, and I got there in less than twenty minutes.

"Hi." I ran to the check-in counter, out of breath. "Here to see Alyssa Thorpe."

"Devon!" Bethany came from the hallway, waving me over. "Follow me."

She led me down the passage to my mother's room.

Bony and fragile, the bed engulfed her frame. A large bandage was wrapped around her head and slightly bloody at the temple. Her lids were lowered, as if she were asleep.

"She got really scared and unsure where she was afterward." Bethany motioned me forward. "It might help even to hear your voice. She seems to have the strongest connection to you."

My shoes slid over the smooth floor, inching quietly to her.

"Mom?" I whispered, wrapping my fingers around the bars on her bed which kept her from rolling out. "Mom, are you awake?"

Her lashes fluttered, tilting her head to peer up at me. Blinking a few times, her dry, cracked lips parted. "Devy?" It was garbled and low, but I had heard it. My name. A relieved cry shot from my mouth, my heart constricting. She hadn't said my name in a long time.

"Yes, Mom. I'm here." I cupped her hand, holding it like a lifeline, a wobbly smile on my mouth.

Trembling, she drew my hand to her lips, murmuring almost inaudibly. "I love you."

The world fell away, her words filling a hole, an ache, I didn't realize was there until she verbalized it. "I love you too, Mom." Emotion clotted in my throat, tears stinging my eyes. She sighed, her lids closing. She tucked her head into the pillow as exhaustion took over. Clutching her hand firmer, I leaned over and kissed her head. "So much."

Sensing Bethany behind me, I rubbed away the stray tear, tucked the blanket higher around my mom's bony shoulders, and turned around.

"Sorry." I sniffled, wiping my nose.

"Oh, honey, you have nothing to apologize for. What you are going through… You have been so brave and strong." Bethany soothed me. "Honestly, you amaze me. Someone your age dealing with so much. Alyssa is so lucky to have you."

Laboring to swallow, my gaze went to my brown boots.

"I hate to add to your load. But we really need you to go over the papers."

"You don't need Amelia too?"

"No." Bethany rattled her head. "Your mom gave you the power of attorney over everything."

I'd known from the beginning she had made all the decisions. But it still felt it was up to me, the final decision to let her go or not.

Another loaded brick weighed down my bones.

Giving my mother one last kiss, I followed Bethany down the hall. My signature was about to solidify my mother's decisions. It really put things in perspective. My Nancy Drew quest earlier seemed painfully inconsequential. I no longer cared who Jake Smith or Lincoln Kessler were.

Nothing felt important except my family.

The bus to work was late, and I had left the apartment without my black work shirt or comfy shoes. Unseasonably early rain began to pour, so I had to run from the bus stop to the saloon, plastering my long hair to my face.

Reaching the front door, I swung it open, hoping I could slip in without too much notice, as I was thirty minutes late.

The sound of my boots squeaking over the wood as I jerked to a stop raised the few heads already at the bar.

Oh shit.

Nat and I always worked together, our schedules and days off in sync. Miguel worked weekends, Mondays and Tuesdays.

But it wasn't Nat or Miguel behind the bar.

"You're late." Lincoln placed his hands on the top, his gaze taking me in. "What happened to you?"

Approaching him like a wild animal, I peered around, hoping to see Nat coming from the kitchen or bathroom.

"Where's Nat?"

"She called in; her kid's sick."

"Oh."

His forehead lined, his eyes still roaming over me. "What's wrong? Did something happen?"

A tight laugh came from me. "Do I look that bad?" I nipped at my bottom lip, my heart still back in the office with Bethany. My signature set the truth in stone. It felt like my mother's life was in my hands and was too heavy to hold by myself.

"No, you're always gor—" He stopped, glancing away, clearing his throat. "Just curious why you're soaking wet and late."

"My car broke down, and it took longer on the bus to get here from the facility than I thought." I grumbled, unzipping my jacket, dripping water everywhere. "Oh, and I forgot my shirt."

"Facility? What are you talking about?"

"Nothing." I rolled up my jacket, my feet shuffling toward the lockers in the back. "Do you have an extra shirt and apron?"

"Devon. Stop." He stepped out from the bar, moving so close I had to look up at him. "What's going on?"

Irritation flashed over my expression, lowering my eyebrows. "Why? You don't care. I apologize I'm late. It won't ever happen again, boss."

"You don't think I care?" He frowned, tilting in even closer.

"Are you going to fire me?" I demanded. My temper always flared when I was barely holding on. It was the only way to keep from curling into a ball or falling apart.

"No." He eyed me, pressing his lips together, his rich, warm, manly smell curling in my nose.

Damn, even a total mess, my body still reacted to his. He was in his usual dark jeans and black T-shirt. He filled them out without being one of those who bought a size smaller to look bigger, like Miguel. He just was. Broad shoulders, huge arms and hands. His jeans could not hide his toned thighs. And I was tall, but he still towered over me.

Taking a step back from temptation, I rounded for my locker, needing to get far away from him.

"There're extra shirts and aprons in the bottom locker," he replied, his voice following me down the hall.

Out of sight, I banged my head into the lockers, sinking against them. The last thing I needed was to work with him all night. Being around him whipped my hormones into tiny bits, and it angered me. I was so good at being reasonable, logical, and organized. I had to be. But he had a way of slipping outside of my control.

Changing into the tank, I pulled my wet hair into a ponytail and walked back to the bar, shutting off all my emotions like a robot.

The room was a ghost town compared to normal Wednesdays. The rain kept everyone from venturing out into the cool, damp night.

I tried to keep busy, cleaning everything and staying away from Lincoln as much as I could. I faked a smile for my few tables but stayed quiet every time Lincoln tried to talk to me.

At nine thirty, the kitchen staff went home, and there were just two regulars at the far end of the bar, Rick and his buddy, Kyle, watching the game Lincoln turned on for them. We only had one TV and he kept it off most days, not wanting to become a sports bar, although he pulled it out for big games.

"Hey."

Refilling the already stocked napkins, lost in my own world, his deep voice made my heart leap into my throat. My gaze darted over to the wall of the small wait station.

He stood there with arms laid on the top, his chin on his hands, peering down at me.

"Did you want to go home? It's really quiet here."

"It's not even ten," I countered. Defensive. Now my stomach dropped at the idea of not being near him. "More people might come in." *Make up your mind.* I actively stayed away from him all night but now, given the opportunity, I didn't want to go.

He watched me for a few beats, the area around his eyes tightening as if he were trying to decide something.

"Fuck it." He wheeled around, rambling to the front door. "You guys good? Want to stay?" He pointed to Rick and Kyle.

They both nodded, drinking their beers, and going back to the game.

"What are you doing?" I padded after him, watching him slip the closed sign on the door and locking it.

"I'm shutting early." He left the keys dangling in the door, walking back to the bar. "Just let me know when you guys want to go, but you're welcome to stay until closing."

"Thanks, man." Rick lifted his beer in appreciation then went back to the TV.

"Why are you shutting early?" Did he want to get rid of me that badly?

"Because I'm the boss and I can do it." He smirked, traveling behind the bar. "What do you want?"

"What?" I gripped the backs of the barstools, stepping in between them, closer to the bar.

"To drink?" The side of his mouth edged up in a grin, flooding my skin with searing heat. "It seemed you had a really shitty day. Mine hasn't been great either. Thought we could watch the game and get drunk."

Nerves twirled and danced in my stomach. Getting drunk with Lincoln was the stupidest idea ever proposed, but once again, logic went out the door. I seemed to be in a really stupid frame of mind. A smile split my lips, and I scooted onto a barstool.

"Tequila."

"You don't fool around. Straight to it." His grin widened. "I like that."

Instead of grabbing for our house stock, he reached up to the top shelf, pulling down Gran Patron Platinum, one of our good tequilas. He cascaded a hefty pour over ice cubes, squeezing lime over it.

"This is the kind you can sip. It's smooth and smoky." He slid the drinks over the bar to me. Walking around, he took the chair closest to me, his knee brushing my thigh. My heart soared.

I grabbed the glass, taking a gulp. It didn't burn so much as warm my belly, and I didn't want to chase it with anything else. "That's nice." I coughed, my voice scratchy.

"Didn't I say to sip it?" He chuckled, rubbing my back, charging electric shocks up and down my spine.

Damn. Why do you have to touch me? I thought, sitting up. My willpower already hovered near the ground. One touch and I felt that girl, who was direct and went after what she wanted, open her eyes. The girl I had been in that bathroom so many years ago.

We finished our drinks, silently watching the game. He refilled both, my body becoming loose and toasty. The crushing weight I'd felt for so long eased and lifted, letting me breathe for a moment.

"No. Damn it," Lincoln shouted at the TV, taking another swig.

I glanced at him peripherally, trying to see if this time I could recognize anything which might confirm this gut feeling I had. But my memory was hazy, and I no longer knew if it were real or something I had made up over time. I had been tipsy then too.

My attention moved to Lincoln's lips as he licked the tequila from them. I almost didn't care who he was;

I wanted to feel *this* man's mouth on me. All over my body.

His head darted to me, almost as if he heard my thoughts, his intense regard pinning me in place.

"So?" His tongue slid over his lips again. "What happened today? Besides the piece-of-shit car finally breaking down. I know it's more than the car."

"Hey. My car has been faithful to me for a long time."

"Faithful?" He chuckled. "It sounds like your faithful companion just died on you."

My spine went straight, his words stabbing deeper than he thought.

"There." Humor dropped away, his voice going low. "This is what I'm talking about. You are so young, but there is such sadness in you."

His statement mixed up my head. He wasn't supposed to see my layers. He didn't know me well enough, and I was good at pretending things were fine.

"Now you are getting defensive." His hand circled my wrist, and he twisted to face me. "Don't worry, you hide it well."

"Then how do you see it?" All I could feel was the warmth of his fingers wrapped around my skin.

"You notice the same characteristics in someone else when you're also good at keeping up a wall."

"And what are you trying to keep out?" I whispered.

He let go of my hand, leaning in closer. "You."

"What?" My heart tipped over.

He swallowed, his brows furrowing. "I mean you go first."

"You're going to be sorry you asked." I twisted in my chair. His knee pressed into my hip, but neither of us moved. "Most people are."

"Try me." His breath seemed to glide straight down between my breasts.

I wasn't one to talk a lot about my private life. In my hometown, we never had to. The gossip spread for us. With him, though, I could feel his own pain sloshing around behind his armored walls.

"*Besides* my car breaking down..." I arched back, getting away from his nearness. "My mother was diagnosed with exceedingly rare early-onset Alzheimer's over five years ago. Early-onset is a really unusual form of Alzheimer's but more aggressive. It tends to run in families. She's in the final stages...and today I had to verify the paperwork that dictated I would let her die when she could no longer breathe on her own." *There. You asked for it.*

He blinked a few times. "Holy shit, I am so sorry. I had no idea."

Good to know Nat was a trustworthy confidante.

"Over five years ago?" He rubbed his beard. "How old were you when you found out?"

"Seventeen." I took a guzzle of my drink, chasing the feeling of weightlessness. "My birthday was right before the holiday."

"Seventeen? Wait, your birthday was a week ago?" He frowned and shook his head, then scoured his face with one hand. "Shit."

"Yeah, why?"

"Nothing." He chuckled sardonically, running his fingers over his cropped brown hair to his neck.

"You're so young to be dealing with something like this."

"Yeah, I am, but tragedy doesn't come with an age requirement."

Still smirking about a joke I didn't get, his gaze landed back to me. He shook his head, letting the strange reaction drop away, muttering, "Too late now."

"What is too late?"

"Everything," he answered evasively, clomping his boots on the ring of my chair. "You didn't tell me it was your birthday."

"I don't make a big deal of them." I shrugged. "I haven't made a big deal of them since my dad died. He was killed a few weeks before my sixteenth, and then the next year I was dealing with my mom." Birthdays became a reminder I was getting older, but my life couldn't move forward. Stuck. Because I would suffer guilt over feeling trapped, and knowing my mom didn't want this for me either, I began to ignore the birthdays, forcing my sister and Skylar to do the same.

"Well." He brought his glass up to mine, his head only inches from mine. "Happy belated birthday."

"Thank you." I clinked my drink against his, downing the rest. The room spun slightly, the heat of his physique alluring. I felt warm all over.

"You're blushing, Devon." He tipped closer, his eyes darting up and down, stopping on my mouth.

Mine mirrored his, trailing his full bottom lip, frozen by the urge to trace it with my tongue. The world around us blurred, the alcohol cocooning us in a heated bubble, filling it with desire and lust.

"Must be the tequila," I croaked, feeling myself leaning into him like a magnet.

"Too bad." His wide, wry grin was somehow carnal and suggestive.

"What?"

"I hoped it was me," he murmured, his focus entirely on my lips.

Holy shit. Did he just admit he was attracted to me? That he wanted this as well? Maybe I wasn't going insane thinking something was between us.

Lincoln inched closer, barely a sliver away from me, so close I could feel the heat of his mouth. Longed for it. I wanted nothing more than to feel his mouth on mine. Consuming me.

"Linc?" Rick's voice called over. Lincoln jerked back, his jaw twitching as his lips clenched together. Slowly, he glanced over his shoulder. "Hey, man, can we get more beers?" Rick pointed at the empty glasses, his attention still on the TV, clueless of what he interrupted.

"Fuckin' timing, asshole," Lincoln grumbled so low I didn't know if I heard him right. He shoved out of the chair, stalked behind the bar and poured two more beers for the guests.

He moved defensively. Like an animal always ready to fight off an attack. His shoulders rolled forward, dropping the beers in front of the men. He gripped the tabletop, keeping his back to me, sucking in a deep breath.

I could see the shift happening, but my eyes greedily soaked in his broad shoulders, tapering down his back, to his firm ass. Damn. That ass….

He rubbed his head again, then turned around; his demeanor had changed.

The wall had gone back up, cutting off the man who had almost kissed me. The man who smiled, laughed, and flirted, with the husky voice that had dampened the space between my thighs. Now he was empty, displaying his talent at hiding all emotions. Becoming stone.

"I'll call you a taxi." His clipped tone stabbed at my chest.

"No, it's okay. I'll take the bus." I slipped from the chair, rejection and sadness pulling the weights back on me like an overcoat.

"No, you won't." He tugged out his cell phone, his brown eyes drilling into me. This time no warmth came behind them. "Not at this time of night and in the pouring rain."

Not wasting the energy to fight him, I went back and collected my bag, pulling on my damp jacket. I turned, about to head back to the main room, and stopped.

Lincoln leaned against the wall in the dark corridor, his looming figure outlined from the light behind him.

My heart jackhammered against my ribs, my feet stepping up to him.

"Devon." His voice raked over my name, sending shivers through me, drifting my lashes up to his brown eyes. He stared down at me. He didn't move or speak, but his penetrating gaze burned into mine. All my words were locked behind my tongue, unable to find an escape. For a second, I thought I saw disappointment and frustration flick behind the façade, but I could never be sure.

His hand lifted, and I froze, watching him reach out. His fingers skimmed over my collarbone, feeling warm and sexual, robbing my lungs of air. Slowly he followed the trail of the bone, flipping out my tucked jacket collar, letting his hands slither over my jaw before he folded them back into his chest.

I wanted more. More of his hands on my body.

A buzz sounded in his pocket. "The taxi's here." His intensity still discharged from his eyes, his voice even. "You better go."

No was on the tip of my tongue.

"Please," he whispered, then yanked his body away from me, striding out like he had no care in the world.

Huffing out a shaky breath, I followed him. He unlatched the door, opening it to cool, damp air. A taxi waited out front, windshield wipers moving back and forth.

"Good night, Devon." Lincoln's voice wound close to my ear, tingling down the back of my neck.

"Good night." A hint of irritation braided through my farewell. I bolted forward, climbing into the taxi, but I couldn't help looking back at him as I shut the car door.

Our eyes locked. Something ricocheted between us, but I couldn't make out its meaning. It felt bottomless and unresolved.

Then he closed the door, shutting me out, again.

Rain trailed down the window, lights from the street glittering off the drops, fracturing me. I was a heap of jumbled feelings and thoughts, lost in what hadn't happened and what could have.

Buzzzz.

My cell joggled me out of my reprieve, a hopeful part of me wanting it to be him. Telling me to come back.

Staring at my sister's number lit up on my phone, I saw I had missed seven calls within a few minutes of each other, all from her. Four from an unknown number. My fingers trembled with dread as I hit the button.

When different people try to call you many times in a short time, it was never good news.

Mom. "Amelia?"

"Oh my god, Devon! I've been trying to call you. Why weren't you picking up?"

"I was at work." Actually, I was busy trying to make out with my boss, who has two identities, and who I should stay far away from. "What's wrong?" My tongue seemed to swell three sizes, struggling to let saliva and air in or out. "Is it mom?"

"No." Her voice rattled with grief, thick with tears. "Oh god, Devy…"

"Mia? What, Amelia? Tell me now!" My nails dug into the cell.

"It's Uncle Gavin… He's been shot."

The universe outside of the taxi shrank down to the size of a pea. Nothing existed except the scream ringing inside my chest.

No. No. Not again. No.

Every detail of my father's death flashed through my head. The phone call, my mom falling to the floor wailing, the surreal pain absorbing into me when I took the phone from her, hearing the news myself.

"Amelia…" My voice strangled.

"He's in critical condition. But still alive. It's all I know. His deputy called me, saying she couldn't get a hold of you," she bawled. "I don't know what to do, Devy. I can't…I can't go through this again. Mia won't go back to sleep or stop crying. She knows something's wrong." Amelia's voice barely climbed above a whisper. "We can't lose him."

No we can't. Uncle Gavin was all we had left. Life was playing a sick game of Russian roulette with us.

"I will be home in a few minutes."

"Okay." She sniffed, the tension in her voice easing because she knew I would handle it. Whatever was ahead, I would take the lead.

I usually did.

CHAPTER SIXTEEN

"When will you be back?" Amelia stood at the end of my bed watching me pack.

"I don't know." I was stuffing clothes into my bag, not caring what it was or if it matched anything else. I hadn't even slept, spending most of the night on the phone to the hospital or with his deputy, Lucy Vasquez.

She had stayed the night at the hospital but knew little more than I did. Lucy had gone through the academy with Gavin. They had even been partners at one time, but Gavin's ex-wife, Lisa, didn't want him working with a woman, probably jealous. He switched partners until becoming captain.

I had always liked Lucy. She was smart and compassionate and reminded me of my dad. She always looked at both sides of a situation and assessed it from multiple angles, whereas Gavin used the same regulations on everyone, no matter the circumstances.

"You know I would love to come with you…" She sat down on top of a pile of my T-shirts.

"I know."

It wasn't true. Amelia was relieved she didn't have to go. "I can't leave work or take Mia out of school." Like I could leave work. She wasn't wrong; it was because I knew even without those obligations she still would have found a reason. She didn't handle crisis well.

The one thing I made her promise was to visit Mom. I wanted to hold on to the moment of clarity where she'd remembered me, even though I knew it was like trying to hold water in my hands. Hopefully seeing Amelia's and Mia's faces would keep Mom tethered to this world until I got back.

"What about your job?" Amelia folded one of my shirts and placed it in the bag. It was still really early. The bus back home would take hours, and I wanted to get there as soon as I could.

Around three in the morning we finally got Mia to sleep, as exhaustion took over, but Amelia and I couldn't rest.

Lucy said they had been on a drug bust in the hills. A big meth area. The dealers weren't ready to give up their moneymaker without a fight. Uncle Gavin saw one of them sneaking around the corner, ready to shoot Lucy. He stepped in, pushing her away.

He was shot in the neck, right above his bulletproof vest, close to an artery. Lucy hadn't left the hospital since they rolled him in.

"I haven't called yet. It's too early." I was relieved I didn't have Lincoln's cell number, and I didn't want to wake Nat this early. I knew I was being a weenie. I just didn't want to call.

Anxiety at losing my job was high, and I didn't want any more bad news, but I had to be with Uncle Gavin. We were his only family. He had no one there either. Family came first. The rest I would figure out later.

"Lincoln wouldn't fire you, would he?"

"He's been wanting to since the beginning." I zipped my bag and started out the room.

"Do you want me to go talk to him?" She followed me. "It's the least I could do."

My hands rolled tighter around my bag. She acted as if she had sway over him, that she could bat her lashes and he would agree to anything. When in truth, it was a reason to go see him.

"So altruistic of you, Sis," I scoffed. "I'll call soon and explain what's happened," I said as I clomped to the hallway closet where I grabbed my jacket. A patch of it was still damp, reminding me of the night before. The feel of his lips so close to mine. My mind kept wanting to finish it, pretending we had not been interrupted. But it just made me more frustrated, grinding my teeth. I didn't want to imagine. I wanted to know.

Amelia stayed quiet for once.

"Tell Mia I love her and I'll be back soon." I buttoned my coat. "Please visit Mom. She needs to see you and Mia. It helps her."

"I promise." Mel bit down on her lip, sorrow filling her eyes. "Please call me when you know anything. I love you so much, Devy." She wrapped her arms around me, pulling me into a tight hug. I let go of all my negative emotions, hugging my sister back. She drove me crazy, but I loved her more than anything.

"I better go; the bus is leaving soon." I didn't trust my car to even start, let alone get me all the way back home. The bus was my only option.

To make myself feel better, I kicked my car on the way to the bus stop, where the local bus would take me to the main bus terminal.

It was going to be a long day.

卌 卌 |||| 卌 卌 |||| 卌 卌 ||||

Six hours later, I sat in the waiting room next to Lucy, anxious to hear anything from the doctors. The last we'd heard, the operation had gone smoothly, but we had to wait until he woke up.

Every time the doors opened, Lucy and I looked up hopefully, only to sag back in our seats when they walked by.

"Avoiding a call?" Lucy nodded to the cell sitting in my lap. For the last hour my work number had been waiting for me to push the call button.

"Yeah." I sighed. "I didn't tell work I was leaving. It's not going to be a fun call."

"Rip the Band-Aid." She smiled sympathetically. "Better to get it over with than have it looming over you."

I nodded, standing up. "I'll be right outside. Come get me if we learn anything."

"I will. I promise." With her elbows on her legs, still wearing her bloodied uniform, Lucy let her head fall forward in exhaustion, her loose braid falling over her shoulder. She reminded me a lot of the actress Michelle Rodriguez. Beautiful, strong, no nonsense, and could kick your ass in a second.

It was chillier than I anticipated as I stepped outside, so I burrowed farther into my jacket. On an exhale, I pushed the call button, putting the phone to my ear. About now, Nat would be there setting up. But what if her son was still sick? What if…

"Hello?" A deep voice answered.

Shit.

"Hey, Lincoln." I gulped. "It's me…" Were we on "me" terms? Would he know my voice? Was I being presumptuous? "Devon… It's Devon Thorpe."

"Yeah, I know who you are, Devon." His voice vibrated with slight humor, my cheeks flushing with embarrassment.

"Of course you do." I smacked my head. This was why I probably didn't have a boyfriend. "Listen, I—"

"Are you quitting on me?" He cut me off, irritation flaring up in his tone. "Because of last night?"

"No." I shook my head as though he could see me.

"Again, if I crossed any line," he was curt, bowling over my response, "it was a mistake. It won't happen again. You have my word."

Incense hurtled into my blood. Rejection. Hurt. I had wanted him to kiss me. Badly. And he was acting like our non-kiss was the worst crime he'd ever committed.

"You know what, Lincoln?" I snapped, my nose flaring. "Not everything is about you. I have bigger things going on in my life than getting all weirded-out over something that *didn't even happen.*"

My outburst silenced him, so I continued. "I called because my uncle was shot last night. He's in intensive care."

I heard a muffled swear come from him.

"I took the bus back home early this morning, and I was calling you to let you know I wouldn't be making it into work today...and probably the rest of the week," I seethed, fear for my uncle transforming into rage. And for once I didn't care if it was at my boss or if it would ruffle feathers. I was tired of being agreeable.

"Is it all right with you? If you're looking for an excuse to fire me, then here you go. You finally have it. But for your information, I was not calling to quit."

"Devon..." I could hear him scrubbing his forehead. "I-I'm sorry. Is he okay?"

As if his voice was a pin popping the rage in the balloon of my chest, my shoulders sagged down. "We don't know yet."

"Was he shot on duty?"

"Yes." My head tilted, my brows gathering. "Wait, how did you know he was a cop?" I had never talked to him about my family, except my mom. And that was just last night.

"Uh...something I must have heard from Nat."

Nat didn't talk, hadn't spilled one other thing about me, but she must have mentioned it. There was no way he'd know otherwise.

"Are you okay? Do you need anything?" His voice grew low. "You should have called me. I would have let you borrow my car."

"What?" His kindness made me reel. He was the first person who had asked about me. "You would have loaned me your car?"

"Your uncle's in the hospital, and you had to sit on the bus for what, four-plus hours? If it weren't breaking my word and crossing lines, I would have driven you myself."

Through my grief, a smile curled upon my mouth, butterflies crashing around in my stomach. "I would have been okay with that." The words fell off my tongue, my mind slow to filter my words.

"Damn," he whispered hoarsely. "You are so much trouble for me."

"Me?" I snorted. He was the definition of trouble. I had seen his other ID. I knew he was involved in something shady, but still I couldn't stop myself from jumping in the ring anyway.

"Yes. You." He growled, sending my butterflies into a frenzy. "You have no idea how much I need to stay away from you."

"Are you?"

"What?"

"Going to stay away from me?"

He didn't answer, but I could hear his deep breaths. Moments ticked by, my heart thumping in my throat.

"Lincoln?"

"How long do you need off?"

"Oh, um—" Jarred by the switch of topic, I tried to gulp back the sadness at his non-answer. "I don't know."

"We are going into the busy holiday season, and the bar already has parties packed through the holidays."

My lids squeezed together. "I understand if you need to hire someone else."

"We might. Julie can't handle it when it's too crazy. You know that."

I nodded, even though I knew he couldn't see me. "I understand."

"I have to go…" He went quiet again before I heard a weighted sigh. "Your job will be waiting for you when you come back."

The line went dead before I could respond. I gawked down at my cell, feeling once again I'd been through the Lincoln spin cycle.

"Devon?" a voice called out behind me. "The doctors are back."

I whirled around, forgetting my own drama, and jogged after Lucy to the waiting room.

The fate of Uncle Gavin demolished any worry outside of the here and now. Even Lincoln faded in the face of Uncle Gavin's life.

Or death.

Beeps from the monitor echoed in the room, mingling with the steady pumping of the machines. IVs and tubes draped over him, attached to his arms and nose. I was jolted back in time to another terribly similar situation. The similarity choked me, strangling me of oxygen.

I had been the last one to see my father. Mom was too distraught and my sister refused to.

Jason Thorpe had dangled in a coma for a few hours before death claimed him. It was long enough for me to see him hooked up to all the machines, unconscious. The shell of the man I'd looked up to. Ten minutes after I said goodbye, he passed away, like he had been waiting for me to leave.

Now his younger brother was lying in a similar bed, only a few doors down from where Dad died.

I stepped closer, my hand touching the blanket over his legs. Groggily, his lids fluttered and finally lifted enough to see me.

"Devy," he rasped, wincing over the word.

Relief at the sound of his voice filled my eyes with tears. My forehead fell on his chest as I sobbed, his weak hand running over my head. He let me cry, softly stroking my hair, my ear pressed to his beating heart. He was alive. It was all I could ask for right now.

"Don't ever scare us again like that." The tears had ebbed, and I lifted my head, staring into his dark eyes. "Please. You're all we have left." It was horrible not to be able to count my mother, but it was reality. Sadly, she would not be in our lives much longer.

His hand squeezed mine, understanding my meaning.

"Ms. Thorpe?" A man's voice spoke behind me, jerking me away from my uncle. I wiped my eyes, staring at an older, dark-haired man wearing a doctor's coat, his hands gripping a clipboard. "I'm Dr. Grant." I knew vaguely who he was already; he was the father of a kid I went to school with who was a few grades lower than me. He was so smart he took advanced classes way ahead of his class. Think he graduated early.

"How are you feeling, Mr. Thorpe?" Dr. Grant said, moving around to the side of the bed, his demeanor aloof and no-nonsense.

Gavin grunted, shifting in the bed.

"You are extremely lucky. The good news is the bullet missed your vocal cords. The bad news is the area is still quite damaged and inflamed. You will fully recover, but the healing process will not be easy. You will be our guest for a while. We want to monitor you closely."

Uncle Gavin's body wiggled when the doctor mentioned the slow mending process he had in front of him. He was not a patient person nor someone who liked having even a cold. If he could, he'd get up and walk out right now, forgoing the doctor's advice.

Dr. Grant checked his vitals, telling him to rest, but the moment he walked out the door, Gavin tugged at the blanket, wanting to get up.

"Oh. Hell. No." I slapped his hand away, re-tucking him in.

He glared at me.

"Sorry. Tough luck," I responded to his unspoken sentiment. "I am going to be here, make sure you heal properly."

He shook his head, his lids narrowing. "Mom. Work," he scraped out.

I shook my head. "Amelia is with Mom, and I got time off work."

His mouth pursed like he was going to speak again.

"Stop. Family is the most important. *You* are the most important. Don't even think about fighting me on this. You know how stubborn we Thorpe women can be."

He rolled his eyes to the side with a grunt, as if saying *you're telling me.*

"There's another woman who is stubborn as hell and won't leave." I tilted my shoulder to the door with a smile. "They won't let Lucy in because she's not family, but I want you to know she hasn't even gone home to change." I paused, winking. "I always liked her. How come you guys were never a thing?"

His eyes narrowed, lips pressing together before he let his eyes shut.

"Okay, pretend you need rest, but you're not getting out of this conversation," I teased.

He opened one eye, glaring at me, then shut it again.

I stood and kissed him on the forehead. "I'll be here when you wake up."

He nodded lightly, his body going slack, falling asleep.

Curling into the chair next to his bed, it wasn't long before I joined him, drifting off into a deep slumber.

CHAPTER SEVENTEEN

"I'm not kidding, Dev," Uncle Gavin growled with irritation as he sat on the edge of his hospital bed. The morning sun drifted over his scowling face. A small bag sat packed next to him.

"I can see you're not kidding." I shoved his slippers under his feet. "Ask me if I care."

"Devon, you've been here for almost three weeks. What about your job? Your mom?" He wiggled his feet into the soft shoes.

Mom was constantly on my mind. I called the facility twice a day at least. Bethany reassured me there had been no change in her. The moment anything happened, I would be home.

"I'm not leaving you." I stood, my hands on my hips. When they finally removed him from intensive care, he came to this room, where I had spent almost every moment. "You're just being released today. I don't want you to be home alone yet."

"Why? I'm a grown man—"

"Who got shot and almost died. Stop being stubborn."

"Me stubborn?" He huffed. "I thought Amelia took after your mom, but I was wrong. You by far out-stubborn your sister."

"Just when I'm right."

His head fell back and he stared at the ceiling, gritting his teeth. He took a breath and peered at me calmly.

"It's time, Devon. Don't get me wrong, every moment you've been here for me, I am grateful. I couldn't have gotten through this without you."

"Oh, I don't know. Think Lucy would have stepped in," I taunted.

"Stop evading."

"Who's evading?" I laughed. "She has been here every day. I've watched you two together… I haven't seen you smile like that. Ever!"

"She's my old partner. We have history. That's it."

I groaned, rolling my head around. "You are so blind."

"There are rules. It's not something I will even think about."

"Screw the rules." I tossed out my arms. "You almost died, Uncle Gav. You should throw all the bullshit out the window. Don't miss out on something wonderful because you're scared."

He watched me. "Why do I feel you need to be listening to your own advice?"

"What are you taking about?"

"You know I was lying in the bed for weeks hurt, not deaf. I overheard some of your conversations with Skylar."

Damn it. I had told her what happened between Lincoln and me, which she was thrilled about. But Lincoln's radio silence brought me to the profound realization…I was a fool. I threw myself into being Gavin's nurse, keeping my mind on what was truly important. It was what I was good at, forcing my thoughts not to drift to Lincoln Kessler.

Skylar, of course, thought I was wrong. Accusing me of taking the safe, easy way out. Shutting the door before it was even fully opened.

"I feel you are now using me as an excuse *not* to go home."

Folding my arms, I glanced away.

"Devon." He grabbed my hands, tugging them to him, forcing me to look at him. "I love you so much. If anything ever happened to you, I can't even imagine what I would do. I understand your fierce devotion to family. Believe me, I don't forget you girls are all I have in the world. But I don't want you to stop living because of me. I'm out of danger. I still need to heal, but believe it or not, I can feed myself and do my own laundry. Even put on my slippers."

I chuckled halfheartedly. He was right. At first, I stayed because he needed me, and then I didn't go because I needed him and this bubble of safety. It was nice to be around someone who was getting better, not continuing to deteriorate like my mother.

Here I could hide from the responsibility at home. From *him*.

I had talked to Nat a few times. They ended up hiring Miguel's younger brother, but Nat said he was awful and Lincoln had fired him after two weeks.

Amelia assured me Mom's condition had not changed, and she was visiting her three times a week. I accepted the lie, not wanting to fight with her about it. She seemed to forget Bethany and I spoke regularly. She had been there four times total in three weeks.

"Go home and be with Mia and your sister for the holidays." He let go of my hands. "All I'm going to be doing is sleeping and watching car shows."

"Ugh." I recoiled. "You really are trying to get rid of me."

"I'd have you stay forever, but this is not your home anymore. You are meant for more, and I don't want you to get trapped here because it's easy. It's not who you are."

"You are being awfully deep today."

"Blame it on almost dying." He grinned. "I want more for you."

"How about I get you settled and then—"

"Hey?" A knock on the door cut off the rest of my sentence. Lucy popped her head through the door. "Was going to go get you checked out." She thumbed toward the nurses' station.

"Thank you, Vasquez." My uncle addressed her formally, but a note of softness lined his voice.

"No problem. Bet you'll be happy to get home. I'll be back in a moment." She smiled and vanished.

"Now I know why you want to get rid of me."

"Shut up," he grumbled, but something flickered in his eyes.

"I'll make you a deal." I gathered my arms together, a smile on my mouth. "I'll go home *after* I settle you in…*if* you open your mind. Ignore rules and see the possibility of Lucy."

"Devon…"

"Scared, are we?" I challenged.

"Damn, you are so your mother's daughter."

"Is that a yes?"

He glared up at me.

It certainly wasn't a no.

The kitchen of our old house had been remodeled. Gavin's furniture filled the spaces, particularly the large TV screen, otherwise the house looked the same. But it felt different, another life, another person who lived here.

Even though the fire didn't destroy the house, in a way it burned any ties I felt to it. I used to hold on to it because it held memories of my father, of our life before. But now I felt nothing for it as I strolled in. My dad would always be with me, no matter where I was.

Lucy and I helped Uncle Gavin onto the sofa, and to his credit, he didn't even fight our help.

Habit directed me to the kitchen to make tea for everyone, but my focus halted on an open file on the table, a black-and-white Xeroxed picture on top.

My eyes widened, the pulse in my neck throbbing as adrenaline pounded through my veins.

From the counter, Finn Montgomery's face stared at me. A headline glared up at me.

Wanted: Escaped from prison.

The floor beneath my feet disappeared. Heat pricked at the back of my neck, sweat bursting down my back. *No. No way.* My feet slid to the table, my fingers reaching out, as if I had to touch it for it to be real.

It was the mug shot from the day he was arrested. The same mouth I kissed. The same shirt I had torn from his body.

Lucy sauntered in, her attention moving from me to the file, her muscles stiffening.

"He didn't want you to know about it." She moved in closer, dragging the file from me and shutting it in the file cabinet.

"Didn't want me to know what?" I breathed in and out through my nose, barely able to swallow.

She looked behind her, checking my uncle's sleeping form before turning back. "I argued you had the right to know, but he's your uncle and my captain."

"Tell me now, Lucy." The whole station knew I had been at the restaurant, but none had any clue how deep my ties to Finn went. My lies kept me safe from facing the stand. I helped condemn him with just a nod of my head.

"Finn Montgomery escaped from jail around nine months ago."

"What?" My mouth dropped open. "Nine months? And you're just telling me now?"

"He didn't want to worry you or add to your stress. And by now, if he had any resentment for those who put him away..." She left the rest unsaid, but my head filled in the rest. *"He would have already come for you."*

"You haven't found him?"

"No. I don't think there's anything to worry about. He doesn't seem the type to go after anyone. He's a nonviolent thief, nothing more. We've been on high alert and will continue to be so. Believe me, we will know if he sets a toe in this town," Lucy tried to reassure me. "It's really strange because he was only a year from going up for parole. The model inmate from what they told us. Doesn't make sense he would ruin that by escaping. Now when we capture him, he might be facing a life sentence."

She sounded so sure they would catch him, but I had this strange feeling Finn Montgomery was long gone.

"Again, you have nothing to worry about. From what your uncle told me, Montgomery probably didn't see you because you were in the bathroom."

"Yes. Right." I nodded, squeezing my fingers together as I tried to even out my breath, hiding the bristling warning driving over my subconscious like a semi.

The man I thought had been safely locked away was out.

Like you didn't know it already, a voice whispered into my head.

Finn Montgomery was a free man, and I had a good idea I knew *exactly* where he was.

CHAPTER EIGHTEEN

The apartment smelled of warm blueberry muffins when I stepped in, my belly grumbling. It was a tradition on Christmas morning from when Amelia and I were kids.

Our parents always tried to give us the best holiday, even without a lot of money. They instilled in us the best gifts were homemade or straight from the heart. We focused on family on Christmas. Mom didn't stay in the kitchen away from us, and we didn't spend it by ourselves playing with our toys. We would order Chinese food and filled the day sledding in the mountains or going to a movie or playing board games all day. I was pleased Amelia, for all her frustrating, selfish ways, had continued this tradition with Mia.

Stepping into the living room, I spotted what could only be called a Christmas bush, not a tree, but it was decorated with lights and homemade Mia ornaments: colorful paper rings, glued stick objects, and popcorn strings. Five stockings hung from the air conditioner:

mine, Amelia's, Mia's, Mom's, Dad's, and Uncle Gavin's

Emotion swirled in my chest at the sight of Mia and Amelia sitting on the floor, playing with a puzzle.

At the sound of the door, Mia's head jerked to me. "Auntie Dev!" She screamed, jumped up, and ran to me, leaping into my arms, strangling me with her skinny little arms. "I've missed you so much. Don't ever go away again. My heart hurt."

Oh jeez, why don't you stab me in mine, little Bean. I kissed her head, holding her to me, rocking us together. "I missed you too, Bean. I hated being away from you so long."

My sister got up then and wrapped her arms around us both, making a sandwich out of Mia. "We both missed you."

"Same." One arm reached for my sister, dragging her in to snuggle with us.

"Come help us with the puzzle Mommy got me." Mia wiggled out of my arms, tugging me to the coffee table.

"Let her put her stuff down." Amelia rubbed her head, glancing at me with a weary look and nodding toward Mia. "She's been up since six this morning. Is it too early to drink?"

"Hell no," I sniggered. "It's a holiday."

"Good thing." She wrapped her arm around my waist. "I really missed you, Dev. Three weeks without you felt like a century. I've haven't felt this exhausted since Mia was born."

Maybe you found out how much I do around here.

She hugged me again then proceeded to the kitchen, pulling down a bottle of wine. I had been up since six a.m. as well. The bus ride home took longer than usual, bringing me to the front door at eleven thirty…close enough to noon, right?

We enjoyed the early afternoon, Amelia making her obligatory phone call to her asshole ex so Mia could wish him a happy holiday. He couldn't care less, and Mia handed the cell back as soon as she said hello to her father and other grandmother. In the afternoon we visited Mom for an hour. She seemed the same as when I left, but no longer understood the concept of Christmas and couldn't hold a conversation, tiring quickly. Amelia and I took Mia to the park before we went home, ordered a bunch of Chinese food, and pigged out.

At nine, Amelia and Mia were both passed out on the sofa together. Times like this I could see the deep love between mother and daughter. Despite her aggravating ways, Amelia was a good mom.

Finishing the last of the wine, I called Nat to say hi.

"Devon!" Nat picked up on the second ring. "Chica, I've so missed you. When are you coming back?"

"Actually, I got home this morning."

"Really?" She crooned with excitement. "Yay! The bar has not been the same without you. Julie has threatened to quit every day, and Miguel's jackass little brother was more of a hindrance than a help. He was so bad he made Miguel's work ethic appear stellar."

"Wow," I snorted.

"Lincoln's also been a grump, not that he's usually in a good mood, but even more surly than usual."

Lincoln. He'd been all I could think of. My mind rolled around and around in circles. I needed to see him, needed to know.

"I figured the bar was closed today, so I was thinking of stopping in tomorrow, talking to Lincoln about coming back."

"Yes! I say you're rehired. No question," Nat burst out. "But the bar isn't closed tonight."

"What?"

"Yeah, it's just Lincoln, but he wanted to leave it open for those, like him, with nowhere to go."

Nowhere to go. The thought made me twitch.

Lincoln wasn't close with his brother, and he had no other family I knew of. What about friends? He also didn't appear to exist on social media or anywhere online for that matter. Someone as sexy as him with no girlfriend? No group of friends from school? You'd have thought he was trying to keep a low profile.

"Hey, Nat, I gotta go. Just wanted to wish you a happy holiday. Probably see you tomorrow."

"You too, girl. Glad you're back."

I hung up, already zipping my boots. Scribbling a note for Amelia, I pulled on my jacket and headed out into the cold, clear night, my determination overshadowing my nerves. The need to see him drew me to the bar like fish to bait. I could see the hook and line, but I still couldn't stop myself from chomping down on it.

Here's to more stupid decisions.

The warmth of the saloon burned my cold ears and nose as I soon as I stepped in, my pulse pounding in my ears.

The place was decorated with twinkly lights and glittery garland, giving the space an even cozier feel. A few people were nestled in the sofa area, and a handful sat at the bar, the TV playing *Die Hard.* Some people consider it a holiday movie. Rick and Kyle were in their usual seats, Kyle wearing a Hanukkah T-shirt, saying "Oy, to the World."

But they were all background as my gaze landed on the man behind the bar. My stomach tripped and stumbled like a drunk trying to stand on a merry-go-round.

"Holy shit," I muttered under my breath. In the last three weeks how did I forget how unbelievably attractive he was?

He stood with his profile to me, one large hand and powerful arm propped on the bar, his head glancing at the TV. He wore his usual black T-shirt and dark jeans, fitting every muscle just right, spreading need throughout my body.

I came here to see if I could find another face in his, of another guy I had once encountered. All I saw was Lincoln. All six-foot-four of him with muscles you could only get if you spent your days at a gym with nothing else to do. Yet I knew he spent most of his time here.

I was trying to put all the pieces together, but I really didn't give a shit.

"Devon! You're back!" Rick held up his beer to me. "*L'chaim!*"

Every particle of my body felt Lincoln react. His head snapped around and his gaze took me prisoner, robbing me of breath. I was so in trouble. Poker-faced, his regard pinned me to the floor, his jaw ticking back and forth. And all I could do was stare back, my chest heaving in and out.

He moved deliberately, coming out from behind the bar, prowling a few feet away from me before he stopped. He was so close I could smell him, feel his form over my personal space. Blood pounded in my ears, and my skin itched with the need to feel him against me.

Slowly, I lifted my lashes, staring straight into his eyes, meeting his intimidating stance with a raised chin.

He watched me, his eyes roaming over my body.

"Lincoln, I—"

He lunged forward, his hands cupping my face, and gripped the back of my head roughly. Pulling me to him, his mouth crashed down on mine, stealing the rest of my sentence, swallowing me whole.

The moment his lips touched mine, fire tore through my insides, detonating the desire I had been feeling. He pressed into me, warm and taut. I felt every inch of him and moaned softly.

His fingers dug deeper into my scalp, his lips parting my mouth with hunger, deepening the kiss. He growled when I nipped his bottom lip, his tongue sweeping into my mouth, devouring me in the flames.

The kiss consumed. Took. Gave. Incinerated.

And I knew without a doubt I had kissed him before.

He had ruined me already, and now I would stay that way.

"Whoo-wee!" Rick hollered, followed by a whistle. Lincoln's lips parted from mine, his hands still tangled in my hair, his mouth barely a sliver away.

"Damn. That's how you kiss a girl." Rick's exclamation made Lincoln and me snort.

"Like you would know," Kyle retorted.

"Maybe not with *girls*."

"Or me!"

"I did too."

"When? Name one time you kissed me like *that*."

Huh…I didn't realize Rick and Kyle were an item. They were so unassuming. I'd just thought they were best friends.

"Right, we aren't alone." Lincoln's mouth brushed against mine with a slow smile, his hands dropping away from my head, stepping back. I felt the loss of him instantly, wanting to yank him back in, claim his mouth again. "I think I completely broke my promise."

"That's…it's o-kay," I stuttered. He had completely *broken* my brain. I stared at him, feeling dizzy.

"Welcome back, Devon," he rumbled in his deep voice that made me crave him. Need him.

His voice was one of things which had stopped me from thinking Lincoln was Finn. It was not the timbre I remembered. Finn's had been deep, but not like this, where every word rolled through sand then jumped into a pool of whiskey. Rough, but it made your body melt.

"Thank you." I waggled my head, trying to get my feet on solid ground. "I had come to see if I could get my job back, but I think that was better."

"I told you your job would be waiting for you." He put his hands on his hips, peering down at me. We were close, but far enough away that his body taunted me. A smirk curved his mouth, and he took a step closer, as if he could read my thoughts. "You came down here, on a bus I'm guessing, late Christmas night, to see if you still had a job? Really?"

"It's what I told myself anyway."

The side of his mouth hitched higher, his eyes bright. Crap, he was totally distracting me from the reason I came here.

"Are you going to stay?" He lifted an eyebrow, the question traveling deeper than it seemed, asking me if I was going to stay until he closed. "I mean, you came all the way down here, so at least I can get you a drink."

"A drink sounds great." I grinned back. "It is Christmas after all."

He journeyed back to the bar, my gaze locked on his firm ass and broad back.

"Everything good back home?" He rounded into the bar.

I nodded, slipping off my jacket. "Yeah, he's doing well. He was ready for me leave and get off his ass."

A roguish grin cut across his face again. "Well, if you need another one to get on."

My cheeks burned, sizzling down my neck. He chuckled, my skin not hiding my reaction.

"What would you like, Dev?"

"Feeling I'd like the good tequila tonight." I put my jacket on the chair, thumbing over my shoulder. "I'm gonna run to the bathroom first."

He gave me a nod, reaching for the top-shelf liquor.

I scampered down the dim hallway, glancing over at my shoulder. Two guests had come back up to the bar to order, taking Lincoln's attention off me.

My heart reverberated in my head, sweat inching down my back. *Damn. I can't believe I'm doing this. But I wanted to know.* No. I *had* to know.

Another glance down the empty hall, and I slipped into the office. Turning on the light, I crept to the desk, even though I knew I was crossing a line. I hoped I could get back without getting caught, and it would give me the proof I needed.

Pushing on the magnet, the edge of the desk cracked open. Adrenaline pumped through me, my chest contracted and my breath came in short pants, making me feel I was about to pass out. Tugging out the slim drawer, my hand clutched the manila envelope, which I opened.

With a shaky breath and quick glance to the closed door, I returned to the packet, peering down. An old leather wallet sat at the bottom and I reached in, pulling it out. The leather creaked in my hands as I opened it.

It was mostly empty, but where you put your money lay a white plastic wristband, like ones you got at events or concerts. Or a hospital.

The name was worn so bad you couldn't make it out, leaving a barcode and a date of birth. Born April 12th, but the year confused me. It was two years older than Mia. Puzzled, I moved to the other item in the wallet. A picture. A man and a little blonde, blue-eyed girl.

I gasped. The man staring back at me…steel-blue eyes, blondish-brown hair, a cocky smile.

"Oh my god."

Finn Montgomery.

My fingers roamed over the picture; my mouth parted in shock. I was right. My gut had been trying to tell me, waiting for my brain to catch up.

Touching the writing on the back, I flipped over the picture. In cursive handwriting: Finn & Kessley.

Kessley?

Kessler.

I shook my head back and forth as my brain tried to absorb all the pieces. "What the hell?"

"I think that's my line." An icy voice came from the door.

With a cry, I jumped, my head snapping up to see Lincoln standing in the doorway, his arms folded, rage burning through his hard expression.

"Found my hiding spot, huh?" He stepped into the room, filling it with his large build. "You being a cop's daughter and cop's niece, I should have seen this coming." He shut the door behind him, trapping me in.

Terror dripped through me like an IV of ice water, taking in his aloof, detached demeanor. The guy who had kissed me was gone. This man, with his folded massive muscled arms and brutally set jaw, seemed ready to kill me without a thought.

"Y-you're supposed to be in jail."

"Am I?" He tilted his head, his tone condescending, as if he were batting me around like a toy, playing with me.

"I know who you are." I rolled my shoulders back, pretending I wasn't terrified.

"Since you recently had your tongue down my throat, that's good."

The bridge of my nose wrinkled, his words throwing me off. "You know what I mean."

"And why would you think I was supposed to be in jail?" He moved in closer, still blocking the exit.

"Because."

"Say it, Devon. I want to hear it." With another step, he came around the desk.

Unconsciously I stepped back, knocking into the desk chair, halting my retreat. I licked my lips, my breath catching in my lungs. Still, I held my ground, staring right into his fake brown eyes. "Because I may have helped put you there. You stayed at the diner partly because of me."

"There it is." With a derisive huff, he stepped closer, his boots knocking into mine. "I've been waiting awhile for that."

"You knew." It wasn't a question, ire cloaking my fear. "This whole time, you knew exactly who I was?"

"The girl I fucked in a diner bathroom five years ago?" His bluntness forced me to suck in, unwanted desire jolting my system. "Yeah. I knew who you were the moment I saw you." He tipped forward, his face close to mine. My brain said to run, but my body wouldn't move, wanting him to do whatever he wanted with it. "You think I could forget someone like you?"

My mouth opened to speak, but nothing came out.

"It's why I tried to fire you. Get you far away from me…" Fury mixed with humor in his throat. "But see, I'm a sick fuck. Any smart man would have forced you out. Made it certain you never stepped foot in here again." He moved in even closer, pushing me against the desk. "Tell me, Devon, what kind of fool, who might be recognized by the girl who helped put him in the slammer the first time, allows her to keep working here? Answer me that."

"I don't know," I whispered, my voice having deserted me.

"Fuck. Fate really wanted to screw with me. Of all places…you walk into mine."

Frustration vibrated through his shoulders as he placed his hands on either side of me.

"I want to hate you so much. You helped screw up my life." He sneered, the proximity of his mouth shifting the air between us. "The things in jail I fantasized about doing to you gave me focus. Drive."

Every muscle trembled, engulfed with lust and dread. "What are you going to do to me?" I whispered.

There was a beat, a moment, as his mouth arched into a wolfish grin, before his hands grabbed my hips and tossed me up onto the desk.

Neither of us hesitated, hungry and demanding. Our mouths collided together almost painfully, only turning me on more. My thighs clenched his waist, my nails skated through his short hair, wrenching him against me, opening my mouth deeper.

The kiss earlier had been passionate; this one was feral.

Desperate. Turbulent. Annihilating.

Lust burned away the hate, anger, and fear, using it as fuel.

His hands skimmed beneath my shirt, skating up my bare skin, lighting every nerve ending. Ripping it over my head, his mouth returned to mine with a deep growl. The sound melted my insides, pooling at my thighs.

I tugged at his shirt, pulling it over his head, my palms running down his muscular torso.

"Holy shit! You're gorgeous." I gaped, my eyes and hands greedily taking him in. My tongue wanted to lick every one of his ripped abs.

"Had a lot of time to work out." He bit my ear, and I dropped my head back. He nipped down my neck. "And a lot of time imagining you naked, screaming my name."

"You thought about me like that?" I gasped as his fingers moved beneath my bra.

"Far more often than the days I wanted to track you down and make you pay." He unhooked my bra, letting it drop to the floor.

"Are you going to force me pay now?" I grabbed the top button of his jeans.

"Most definitely." He winked, a wicked glimmer in his eyes. He bent forward, his warm tongue wrapping over one breast. With a loud groan, he tipped me back on the desk, his body following mine. I tore at the buttons of his pants, shoving them over his hips.

Not one part of me didn't want this or wasn't willing to second-guess it. He had been my fantasy for more than five years. I was tired of pretending. I wanted the real thing.

"I do have a bar full of people out there," he said, but his hands were working the buttons to my jeans. "And I don't have protection."

"I have an IUD and I'm clean."

"Me too. Prison doctors make sure." He unzipped my pants. "But I still left the bar unattended."

"Then I guess we skip the foreplay." I sat up, my hand pushing him back, peering at him. Wow. It wasn't just his build that seemed to get bigger. I yanked his boxer briefs down, desperate to touch him. "It's not as if we don't have experience with quickies in public places."

He groaned, riled up by my words as my thumb worked over the tip of his cock, moving down. "Fuck," he spit between his teeth.

Grabbing my hips, he turned me around, wrenching down my pants and underwear, bending me over the desk.

My breasts pressed against cool files, I gripped the lip of the desk, quaking as he dragged himself over me.

"Damn." He hissed, coiling my hair around his fist. "How many times I thought about fucking you just like this."

"Me too."

"Don't tell me that." He moaned.

"You think you were the only one fantasizing about that night? You've been *all* I've gotten off on for five years."

He swore again, parting my legs, dragging his fingers through me.

"Now. Lincoln. Please."

He pulled his fingers out, slapping my ass, drawing pain and pleasure from me. Then he thrust into me, filling me entirely, my mouth parting in a cry as he groaned loudly.

Oh god. I stopped breathing as he pulled out, then

pushed in deeper. My fingers clenched the desk as bliss gripped my body. I shoved back against him.

"Fuck!" He drove in, hitting my G-spot, his fingers digging into my hips, sending bursts of pleasure through my nerves.

"Oh god…harder!" I wanted more, to be closer. For him to destroy me.

He leaned over, nipping the back of my neck, his hips shoving forward. "Remember, *I* want to hear you scream, but do you want *them* to?"

"I don't care." I bent over farther. I didn't anymore. The bar down the street could hear us for all I cared, my embarrassment from before was long gone.

"Damn, you turn me on, Freckles."

His pet name for me only sent me more into a frenzy. I had heard it so many times in my head, wishing I wasn't alone in the bathtub.

Our rhythm grew desperate. Raw. The sound of us fucking volleyed off the walls, our moans and jilted breaths climbing higher.

I could feel the orgasm start as a swirl around my spine, compelling me to chase it with a ferocity. His hand reached around, finding my core. He seemed to be an expert at making my body explode. Ecstasy tore through me, clenching around him in pulses, taking him with me in a roar. I loved the intense sensation of him releasing deep inside me.

I knew I cried out. Loudly. But I felt no shame or embarrassment. Bliss sent me out into the atmosphere until slowly I fell back down, scattered in pieces.

Limply, my bones sagged onto the desk, my lungs trying to catch up. The feel of Lincoln still inside me sent tingles through my limbs. It was un-fucking-believable.

"Fuuuck." His chest pressed against my sweaty back, trying to hold himself up on his elbows, sucking in deep gulps of air.

I laughed. "You could say that."

"Next time," he kissed my shoulder, "I want to take my time with you."

"Next time?" I teased over my shoulder.

"Yeah." He grabbed my chin. "I'm gonna make you pay. For every day I was in jail, tenfold." He lifted off me, pulling me up with him, turning me around to face him, kissing me deeply. "Now this time, when I leave, I hope I won't find police waiting for me."

"It had nothing to do with me."

"You were frickin' seventeen, which could have put me in jail." He shook his head. "About had a heart attack the other night when I learned that."

"No one knew. And you weren't arrested because I was a few weeks from legal screwing age."

"No." He grabbed his briefs from his ankles, tugging them on. "But you were definitely the reason I got caught."

"What are you talking about?" I got redressed, pulling up my jeans, though all I wanted was to stay naked and go again.

"I would have been far away by the time they came, but instead…I ran into you."

"Are you blaming me?"

"Like I could have walked away from you." He stared down at me. "A breathtaking girl offering up hot sex in a bathroom. You were the perfect trap."

"Wait?" I jerked back folding my arms over my rumpled T-shirt, my mouth parting. "You really do blame me?"

"Didn't have a problem pointing me out in a lineup, did you?" Wrath skimmed the surface, his forehead contorting, emotions going from pleasure to anger.

"First of all, the entire restaurant was called in to identify you." I stabbed at his chest. "And I lied to the police, to *my uncle*...and *my best friend*." My anger drove him back a few steps. "I told them I was in the bathroom the whole time, and I didn't see or hear anything. They knew I saw you getting arrested, but that's it. I went in because we all had to. But I have *never* told a soul the truth of what happened. *Not one person*."

He blinked, his eyes narrowing as if he was trying to figure out my truthfulness.

"You were a thief and liar, but I still protected you... Don't ask me why now. Chalk it up to being young and naïve, but the boy I was with in the bathroom didn't feel like the guy they told me you were later."

"Devon..."

"No. Do you know how much guilt I carried because I lied to my uncle? Not something I do. My father was all about honesty and morality. It went against who I was, but I did it. For you. And why were you arrested? For stealing drugs and money from a hospital. From people who need it. Who does that?" I pushed him back. "Did you sell them on the black market? Are you still? Is it what you and your brother do? Brothers and *Thieves*. Very apropos."

His jaw gripped, his shoulders rising with fury. "You know *nothing* about me. Or my life."

"Does anyone? Who are you anyway? Finn, Jake, or Lincoln?"

"Jake never existed....and Finn is no longer anyone I know."

"He did in this life." My hand darted down to the picture lying on the desk, holding it up to him. "Is she yours? Kessley is awfully close to Kessler."

He plucked the image from my fingers.

"She's none of your business. And I'm done talking here." He stuffed the photo in his pocket and stalked toward the door.

"What?" I pursued him. "You decide when we're done talking?"

"*Yes*." He grabbed my arms, shoving me against the wall next to the door. Danger rose from his steely gaze as his body pressed into mine. "I have a bar to run, customers out there."

"No." Desire and anger wove a taut web inside me. "We're not done."

"Yes. We. Are." He growled, shoving off me, yanking the door open.

"So you get what you want from me, *your fill*, and you're done? I get it now."

"Get what I want?" He stopped, his stare searing me. He lifted his hand, grabbing the ends of my hair, his head slightly shaking, spitting out, "Far from it. And I certainly will never get my fill." He dropped his hand from me, clutching his fists, and stomped out of the room.

I slumped against the wall, gasping for air. I didn't realize I stopped inhaling. My head and heart were a tornado, spinning, wondering what the hell happened.

The sex—*holy shit*—I couldn't even put into words how unbelievable it was. My limbs were still quaking with the aftermath. It was better than I remembered or imagined, and my hormones were already asking for another helping. Demanding it.

But my logical side screamed at me to walk out of this bar for good and continue to pretend Finn Montgomery was a moment in my past and leave it at that. Except I couldn't seem to walk away from Lincoln Kessler, even when my gut had told me to run at the beginning.

He was dangerous. On the wrong side of the law. And definitely hiding a chasm full of secrets. Who was the little girl? Was he still thieving? And why did so much of his underlying anger and resentment seem pointed at me?

I'd grown up with a father who always told us to do the right thing, but over time even my father began to see the gray areas in every situation and treated each crime differently.

Uncle Gavin would have no such dilemma. Turning Lincoln in to the police would be the right thing here. The *only* option. He committed a crime and broke out of jail. He was guilty in the eyes of the law.

I was my father's daughter and before I did anything, I was going to figure out what Lincoln was hiding…and who the little girl was in the photo.

CHAPTER NINETEEN

"What the hell is going on with you?" Nat fixed her glittery party hat, frowning at me. "You have been in a mood all week. It's New Year's Eve. Time to put all the bad stuff behind you and start new."

I lifted an eyebrow at her.

"Yeah, I know, total bullshit." She swished her hand. "But seriously, you have been strange all week."

Strange. Yeah, you could call it that.

Being in the same vicinity as Lincoln was like being torn in half. He was a pull door, and I was pushing. In the week I'd been back, since…that night…we hardly spoke, and when we did there was so much underlying tension I was surprised the bar didn't turn into a boxing ring. The entire week had been painful.

I was pissed at him, but mostly infuriated with myself…or more specifically, my body's reaction to him. The more anger we spat at each other, the more I wanted to take him in the back office and really let my frustration go. Every time he brushed by me on accident, I had to bite back a whimper and stop myself from leaping on him.

"Is everything okay with your mom?" Nat asked while her hands deftly mixed cocktails. The crowds were already packing in, everyone happy and ready to celebrate the last night of the year.

I felt no such glee.

"No." I shook my head. "But it won't be. I saw her this morning, and she didn't recognize me at all."

"I'm sorry." She put two martinis on my tray. It was getting busy enough Lincoln would have to come out soon. Miguel was getting bogged down by customers at the bar.

I shrugged. I was starting to come to terms with the reality my mother would never get better or be all right.

"You aren't the only moody one around here." She rolled her eyes, grabbing a few beers. "Jesus, Lincoln has been insufferable. I thought you returning would put him into a better mood. He's worse now…and the tension between you two when you're in the same room… If I didn't know any better…" Nat tapered off, her eyes going wide, her mouth dropping open. "Oh. Holy. Shit!"

I peered around, my defense instincts kicking in.

"You did!" she exclaimed, her eyes glinting. "How did I not see this?"

"Nat…shhhh," I hissed.

"Oh my god, you and Lincoln?" Her voice lowered a notch.

"No. Nothing's going on."

"Don't lie to me. You screwed him, didn't you?"

"Nat…"

"You did! *¡Pinche, chica!* Tell me, was it in the office? Please tell me it was there because I've had so many fantasies about that room, and I'd like at least one of us to be living it out in real life."

"Is my order done?" I grabbed for my tray, wanting to get away from this conversation. Though, another side wanted to yell out, *Yes! And it was beyond mind blowing.*

"No wonder he was never interested in Amelia." She clicked her tongue, winking at me. "He wanted her little sister."

Of course this was the time Lincoln decided to step out, strolling behind the bar. Nat's expression blistered with elation, a knowing smile dancing on her face.

"Hey, Linc." She nudged him with her elbow.

He peered at her, perplexity scrunching his brows, wondering why she was grinning like a goof. "What?"

"Nothing. Just saying hi."

His lids narrowed farther; his gaze touched mine, sensing the odd tension going on before he jerked back to her.

"Get back to work. We're going to be extremely busy tonight."

"And here I thought you would be in a good mood now…satisfied and relaxed."

He went still, only the bob of his Adam's apple displayed the emotion he held back.

"It being the new year and all. Time to *release* old burdens." Nat patted his arm.

I was going to kill her.

“Get to work,” he ordered, moving down the bar to talk to Miguel.

“I. Hate. You,” I leaned over, whispering hoarsely.

“Please. You love me,” she replied, placing the last of my order on the tray. “I really should hate you. Damn, I’m jealous. So…what happened? Why are you both in such foul moods? If I were you, I’d be doing acrobatics from the ceiling or screwing him in the office on a never-ending loop.”

Picking up my tray, I turned, not answering her, but in my head, I thought, *the foul moods were because we weren’t in his office having endless sex.*

A one-time encounter. Well, technically two times I couldn’t stop thinking about or wishing to repeat.

The bar was packed with celebrators, keeping my mind busy. Julie was flustered as usual, making mistakes and freaking out when she got another table. She was overwhelmed by the mass of people, and I had to admit it was the worst version of a server’s nightmare. I couldn’t keep up with or get to some of my tables in reasonable time, but we tried our best and most people understood. Some people were drunk enough already and too much in the spirit of the holiday to complain.

I wasn’t surprised Lincoln kept Nat on making drinks, he clearly wanted to stay far from me. But this time on my way back, he was in Nat’s spot. She was in the middle of the bar taking multiple orders and trying to put a dent in the throng screaming at her.

Sidling up to the server section of the bar, I acted busy going over my orders, ignoring him.

"You told Nat?" His rough voice cut through the commotion around me.

Glaring, I met his eyes. "No. She figured it out."

"Really?" He scoffed.

"Yes," I snipped. "For some strange reason she picked up on the tension between us and came to her own conclusion."

He twisted away, grabbing a cocktail shaker, not responding. Anyone with half a brain could notice our hostility. Hostility drenched in sexual tension.

"I'm surprised you wanted to be this close…have to interact with me."

He huffed through his nose sardonically, grabbing for a liquor bottle, muttering to himself. The bar was so loud with music and chatter, I thought I heard him say, "I want to do more than interact with you." But I couldn't be sure.

"Nat kicked me out. I guess my attitude wasn't going well with the patrons."

"Whose fault is that?" I muttered to myself. We could both be in much better moods if he would let his guard down for a second.

"What?"

"Nothing." I smiled. Fake and condescending.

He clenched his jaw. His nostrils flared and a vein pulsed in his neck. My gaze wandered to the tattoo stretching down the side of his neck. This time I noticed a thick line underneath the dark ink. Like a scar. From far away it was hidden, but the way the bar light hit him, I really noticed it this time.

As I debated whether to engage in a conversation with him, I heard my name being called from behind.

Shit.

Peering over my shoulder, I watched my sister's hips swing up to the bar, a sexy smile lowering her lashes as she took in Lincoln.

"Hey, sis." She gave me a small hug but stared at the man behind the bar. "Thought I'd come down and bring in the new year with you guys."

It wasn't me she wanted to ring in the new year with.

"Hey, Linc," she purred.

"Hey." He lifted his chin at her, annoyance contracting his temples.

I steered far from the topic of Lincoln with my sister. In no way was I telling her something had happened between us, especially because it hadn't ended well. But I still felt irritated with her for flirting with him. It wasn't her fault; she had no clue, but my feelings didn't seem to care. Her appearance made me suddenly upset with both of them, as if it were his fault she was still sniffing around him.

"Perfect." I exhaled, tapping my fingers impatiently, wanting to be far from both. "Is my order ready yet?"

Lincoln shot me a surly look as he poured the cocktail into a highball glass.

"When you get a moment, can I get a shot? And I want to buy you one too," Amelia flirted. "It's New Year's Eve, and you guys should have some fun too. Maybe get a little wild."

I snorted, my lips pinching together so as to not say what I really thought. Getting Lincoln drunk and hoping he'd finally sleep with her was all my sister was thinking about.

Lincoln grabbed three shot glasses, pouring us some of the Kamikaze he was making, pushing it toward us.

"To a great new year. And amazing night." Amelia grinned at him, downing the shot. I could feel his gaze on me, but I slammed back the shot, trying to ignore him. Most of my life I had acted like an adult. Been responsible. Reasonable. Tonight my bitchy teenager was in full bloom. The combination of Amelia and Lincoln drummed on my patience like a marching band.

"You crazy kids have fun *getting wild*." I picked up my full tray, spinning around, ready to put distance between us.

A step was as far as I got before a hand grasped my wrist. As he spun me back around, he took the tray out of my hands, setting it back on the bar, his hold compressing on my arm.

"Julie," he yelled behind me, his raspy voice punching with annoyance. "Deliver these to Devon's table. I need a moment with her."

Amelia's gaping stare snagged on mine, her eyes wide, as if I had been caught by a teacher and was about to be reprimanded.

Before I could respond, he dragged me with him, his shoulders shoving through the throng of people like a linebacker. He marched us into his office and slammed the door behind us.

"I've had enough." He swung me around to face him.

Anger discharged my defenses. "Had enough of what?"

"This attitude."

"Mine?" I laughed. "Hello, pot, meet kettle."

“You are driving me crazy.” His hands went into his dark hair, scrubbing fiercely.

“Same.” I folded my arms.

His palm drifted to his face, rubbing his forehead before he dropped his arm with a sigh. “What are we going to do here? Do you want me to fire you? Do you want to quit?”

“No,” I said quietly.

He sat back on the edge of his desk, muttering to the ceiling. “I am so fucked.”

“Why?” I stepped between him and the chair, his knees grazing me.

“Because you’re good; you do the right thing. I’m a criminal. Jesus, you’re related to the person who put me away.” He tossed up his arms. “You could make one phone call, and my life is over. As much as I try to straighten out my life, something always drags me back. And most of all… because I want nothing more than to bend you over this desk again until neither of us can move.”

Yearning ballooned in my lungs, flushing my skin. I stepped between his legs.

“I suggest you stay away from my hometown and my uncle.” I cupped his face lightly, loving the way his scruff felt under my palms. “But I won’t turn you in.”

“You don’t know that,” he practically whispered, covering my hands with his. “There is so much you don’t know about me.”

“Then tell me.”

He turned his face, not looking at me. He wasn’t going to talk. Not yet. I wasn’t to be fully trusted yet.

“Okay.” My fingers slipped down his jaw to his

neck, skimming the raised scar under his tattoo. "Tell me how you got this."

He raised his lashes up, swallowing at my touch. "The first night in prison a group jumped me. Slit my throat."

"What?" Panic bolted my spine straight.

"I fought them off. Almost bled to death." His voice vibrated under my fingers. "No moment of doubt or weakness. You have to prove yourself. Fast. Or you become their bitch. They saw me as the new boy candy who they could dominate and control."

"Oh my god."

"I was in the infirmary for two weeks. Ruined the shit out of my vocal cords, but I was lucky to live."

That was why his voice was different, and why I didn't recognize it as the guy who growled in my ear five years ago.

"They tried again once I got out of the clinic. That's when I started to work out every moment I had. I wasn't going to be anyone's bitch."

"Did they…?"

"Rape me?" He bluntly filled in. "No. I may be sexy as hell, but I can fight."

A sharp burst of laughter surged from me. "Someone's cocky."

He grabbed my hand, lifting his shirt, and placed my hand slightly above his hip. My breath quickened.

"Feel that?" He rubbed my fingers over a deep scar wrapping around almost to his back.

"Yeah," I rasped. How did I miss this the other night?

"It was their second attack. Almost punctured my kidney. Not cocky. I had to fight like hell. Always on guard. Never show emotion. It's the only way to survive."

My gaze raised to his. How many nights had I thought about him? But not once did I ever think of what he must be going through or what was happening to him behind bars. I

pointed him out of a lineup and left, never to think of him as more than the one who captured my fantasies.

"I'm so sorry."

He rolled his lips together, shrugging. "Can't change the past."

"Would you? If you could?"

"What do you mean? Not get thrown into prison? Hell yeah."

"No…I meant." Chagrin shifted my weight to the other leg. "I mean you were caught because you *lingered* at the diner."

"You mean, would I take back *you*?"

"Yeah."

No response came, constricting my throat.

"Freckles…" He swallowed.

"No, I get it." I backed away. "I ruined your life."

"Look, I made my own choices." He stood up, following my retreat. "I only have myself to blame. But…being with you that day? What happened because of it?" He drew his hands up to his hips, staring at the floor. "I can't answer your question."

My teeth sawed together, my head bobbing. "I understand."

"No, you don't."

Silence stretched between us, both of us realizing there could be no win, no happy ending here.

"Listen, it'll be better if we go back to employee and employer. I think it's best for both of us if we pretend the other night didn't happen."

"Impossible." His low, rough voice sent a craving down my legs.

My lids shut, squeezing out the sorrow I felt building up behind my ribs, knowing my next words.

"I'll look for a new job next week." I couldn't stay around him. He was too much temptation and torture to be around.

"Devon—"

I held up my hand, cutting him off. "My relatives make it dangerous for me to stay around. The connection is too risky for you. We both know this is for the best."

He opened his mouth again, but I jumped in. "I'm putting in my two weeks' notice. That's the last of this discussion." I couldn't look at him, stepping back to the door. "I better get back out there, or you'll be down two servers instead of one."

When I left his office, all my anger with him earlier was gone, replaced with deep sorrow.

I stopped at the end of the hall, sucked in my willpower, and forced a smile onto my lips before I stepped back into the merriment. I felt none of the jubilant mood which sang and danced around me.

Only heartache.

CHAPTER TWENTY

Life had a funny way of continuing to run your ass over without stopping, even though you wanted no part of it. Besides being required to work next to Lincoln for the next two weeks, my sister couldn't stop talking about him. "I can't decide if he's gay, or if I'm not being obvious enough."

"Oh, I think he got it, Amelia." I unloaded our laundry from the washer. "The whole bar knows you want him."

It was Wednesday, my first night back after New Year's Eve, and I had spent the morning at the laundromat, doing Ikea bags full of our built-up pile. I don't think Amelia went once while I was gone, and the mound took me two trips.

Amelia sipped her iced tea, the remnants of her takeout lunch beside her on the dryer where she sat. The salon where she worked was only a few blocks down, so she came to join me on her break. Of course, she didn't help with any of the actual laundry.

"Did he say something to you?"

Oh, he's been saying a whole lot of things to me, but I doubted Amelia would want to hear it. "No. But you are not sly, Mel. And you've been stalking him for months now."

"I'm not stalking." She jolted with hurt pride. "And you need to spell it out for men. They're not as in tune as women are. You can't be subtle."

"Nothing about you is being subtle."

"What is his problem? I don't understand. He's the only guy who has been this obtuse. Hello!" She threw up her arms. "I'm a hot, sexy woman who wants to screw him. So what the hell is wrong? This should be a no-brainer."

I shoved the clothes in the dryer, slamming the lid shut.

"Can you talk to him? See if he's dating someone else? Oh god, the thought of another girl getting to fuck him… No. *He's mine*."

"He's *not yours*, Amelia!" I shrieked, something snapping in my brain. "He's not into you! Get it through your thick head. He doesn't want to sleep with you."

Amelia jerked back; her shocked expression transformed from hurt to anger. She thrust out her chest and shook her head in disbelief.

"Amelia…"

She pushed off the dryer, seizing her bag, and stomped out of the laundromat, fury riding on her shoulders, her heels slamming violently against the pavement.

"Shit." I slumped onto the dryer, palming my face. I didn't mean to be so harsh, but my patience for my sister was shrinking, especially when it came to Lincoln. Ever since Skylar visited, I had been feeling less willing to be Amelia's bitch. Or anyone's. It was time to start saying no.

She needed to hear it from me. I should have told her a long time ago, but I could have been kinder about it. I always stayed quiet, letting things build up, then I exploded. It took people back because they had no idea I was so upset.

"Don't ever be sorry for standing up for yourself. Sometimes you will be the only person who will." Lincoln's words came into my head. He was right. I needed to stop being a doormat.

I blew out my breath, returning to the loads of wash. I would let Amelia cool down, and tonight when I got home I would apologize, not for my words, but my delivery.

The weight of visiting Mom before work also sat heavy in my stomach. I dreaded the thought of going there today. Seeing the skeleton of the woman I knew, void of personality which used to light her eyes.

For once, do what you want, Devon. It doesn't make you a bad person. I could visit her tomorrow. Sadly, she wouldn't know. She didn't understand time anymore. Minutes felt like days to her and days felt like minutes. She didn't know me anymore either.

Unfortunately, doing what I wanted didn't include avoiding work. I would have to face Lincoln. Money would always override the desire to toss responsibility to the side, get on a plane, and never look back.

January was notoriously known as a dead month in the restaurant business, and this evening lived up to its reputation.

Nat chatted with a couple at the bar when I stepped onto the floor. I waved at Kyle and Rick, who filled their normal stools at the other end. Rick gave me a secretive wink. He had made a few jokes to suggest they had heard us or at least knew what had happened in Lincoln's office Christmas night. It didn't embarrass me more than make me sad because it would never happen again.

A couple of women who just got off work filled the sofa, already complaining about being back at work, cheering their wineglasses with each other. Besides them, I puttered around cleaning, my stomach in knots as I sensed Lincoln close by.

A buzz vibrated inside my apron, and I dug out my cell, glancing at the screen. Between Mom and Uncle Gavin's injury, I kept it on me at all times now. The facility's number scrolled over the screen, glowing against my face.

Probably Bethany, wondering why I didn't show up today.

Glancing around and not spotting anyone who needed me, I turned my back to the bar and put the phone to my ear, an apology already crawling over my tongue.

"I'm sorry, I know I was supposed to come today," I spewed out in a hoarse whisper. "Tell her I'll be in tomorrow.

"Devon."

"I got so busy today. I feel awful. Was she aware I wasn't there?"

"Devon!"

The force with which she said my name made me shut my mouth.

"Devon..." Bethany repeated my name. Heavy sorrow sank into my eardrum, trickling down to my soul. "I'm so sorry."

No. No. This wasn't happening.

"Your mother stopped breathing and because of the DNR...we let her go in peace. She passed away about fifteen minutes ago."

Time stopped.

My world stopped.

Everything went hazy around me, numbing me of anything except the anguish filling my stomach with bile.

"No." I pressed a hand to my stomach, shaking my head, not wanting to accept her declaration.

"I am so, so sorry, Devon." Bethany continued to talk, but I heard nothing after that, the phone dropping from my hand, tumbling loudly onto the wood floor.

I was supposed to visit her today. Be there. But I selfishly chose not to...

There would be no tomorrow. No visit to make up.

"Devon?" I heard Nat shouting my name as I dropped to the floor. Nothing felt real. It was all far away as if I were at the end of a very long tunnel. I didn't even feel I was in my own body. Producing no connection to the choked wail, bleating like a lamb, deriving from my body.

"Devon!"

My name didn't even belong to me, simply some consonants and vowels put together. I saw a blurred figure bound around me, trying to obtain my attention, but I continued to stare ahead, my mind and body floating off into another realm. "Lincoln! Lincoln, get out here now!"

Vague awareness of drumming vibrated the ground under me, legs and feet moving into my vision, a large form dropping in front of me.

"Hey." Strong, warm hands cupped my face, forcing me to look up. "Devon, look at me."

I took in the man speaking. His face was so familiar I felt as if I'd known him most of my life. Safety. Happiness.

Anchor. My heart thrummed, my gaze locking onto his, feeling his thumbs rub over my cheeks in a soothing rhythm. As if I were a balloon floating away, he grabbed for me, bringing me back down to earth. But with it came reality, turning Bethany's words over and over in my head. My mom was gone.

"She's dead." My voice sounded like a little girl, the last bit of innocence and purity being ripped from her. "She's gone…" Pain forced loud damp gasps from my chest. My mind fought back the crippling grief, switching into the girl who needed to handle things. Be the adult. The role I was good at.

"I need to call Amelia…and Uncle Gavin. Skylar. I have to get down to the facility. They probably need me."

"Devon." Lincoln gripped my face firmer, tipping my head to look at him. "It will all be taken care of. I am here. Whatever you need. I'll drive you down there."

"No…it's okay…taxi… I need to go." I shook from his grip, standing up, my attention fluttering superficially over everything but what was next. "Is it okay if I leave early?"

"Is it *okay*?" Lincoln bolted up, grasping my arms, pinning me in place. He shuffled his feet out, getting more in my eyeline, running his hands down my hair, trailing to my chin. "Stop! *I am* driving you down there. It's okay to ask for help, to let someone be there for you." His brown eyes lasered on mine. All I wanted was to see his real blue eyes. To peer into his soul without the barrier.

He didn't give me a chance to respond, whirling around to Nat. "You got this?"

"Yeah, go." She nodded, her expression pinched with heartache.

Lincoln pressed a hand to my lower back, moving me numbly toward the back door. Nat hugged me briefly, whispering to Linc to call her later. He nodded, ignoring the gaping silence coming from the customers while we crossed the space. I could feel their stares, but I wouldn't look at anyone, knowing I'd see pity and sadness in their expressions. Seeing myself in their eyes would break me.

The ride over was silent. I stared out the window. I had tried to call my sister, but she didn't answer. It was her night out with the girls at the salon, and the cell probably lay at the bottom of her bag as she giggled and drank with her friends. I didn't leave a message…just texted her *call me now*.

"Give me your phone." Lincoln held out his hand as we walked up to the facility, staying close to me, his hand comforting. "I will keep trying your sister."

I handed it over without argument. Normally I fought outside help, always saying "I got it," but right now I had no energy to get anything done. I let him take the lead when I wanted to crumble under the weight.

"Devon." Bethany greeted me the instant I stepped in, jogging over, wrapping me in her arms, whispering how sorry she was. She stepped back, taking in Lincoln. "Hello, I'm Bethany."

"Lincoln." He shook her hand.

"Thank you for coming." She patted the top of his hand, darting a look at me. "I'm so glad someone is here with her. As strong as she is…no one should be alone at this time." She tilted her head. "Devon is a remarkable girl."

"Yes, she is." His palm pressed into my back.

"Amelia?"

"Still trying to get a hold of her," he answered for me.

Bethany nodded, lips pressed together in understanding. "Would you like to see her?" Bethany reached out for my hand. "Say goodbye?"

You mean the goodbye I didn't say earlier when I ditched her for a day to myself? My guilty mind thought. I nodded, my throat constricting.

"Okay. This way." Bethany motioned for me to follow. I took one step when Lincoln grabbed my hand.

"Do you want me to go with you?" His willingness to be at my side during this brought another surge of emotion to my throat.

"No. It's okay." I squeezed his fingers then I turned to follow Bethany.

Bethany went down the hall, stopping at the closed door. "I'm sorry you have to do this."

My lips bowed in an agonizing smile. "It's not the first parent I've had to lay to rest."

"Oh, my girl." Bethany pressed a hand to her heart. "What you have gone through for one so young."

Youth had been wasted on me. How long had it been since I was young and carefree?

"This might not help now, but know your mother is finally at peace." Bethany opened the door and stepped to the side. "I'll be down the hall."

I stepped past her and crossed the threshold which held the last of my innocence.

CHAPTER TWENTY-ONE

There were no tubes attached like when I saw my father for the last time nor beeping machines as with Uncle Gavin. My mother lay on the bed, her eyes shut as if she were sleeping, her expression serene. I couldn't help hoping she'd wake up, look over, and smile.

My shoes squeaked loudly over the linoleum floor, making me painfully aware of the utter silence in the room. As if I could still wake her, I tiptoed to the side of her bed, staring down at her face.

My mom. My friend. My world.

Gone.

"I am so sorry, Mom." My breath hitched, the truth sinking in, burning tears filled the back of my lids and throat. "I should have been here earlier…"

She looked at peace and younger than she had for a while. With trembling fingers, I gently reached out, brushing my fingers over her cheek. Her skin was cool to the touch. It was then it really hit me—I would never talk or be with my mother again. A hiccupped sob gushed from the hole in my heart.

"Did you do it on purpose? Is this punishment because I was selfish?" A string of anger belted out as if a monster was taking over. "I didn't come to see you this one time since coming back from Uncle Gavin's and that's when you decided to die? Leave me like it's a big 'damn you, Devon.' Penance for the rest of my life?" I wailed, gripping the bars, tears gushing down my face. "You got me, Mom. The guilt I feel will be with me forever. Hanging over my head and calling me selfish and cruel. I wasn't there for you. I left you alone and scared here. How could I do that to you? How could you do this to me?"

Crushing grief bowed my legs, my body sagging down the side of her bed to the floor, wretched sobs howling through the room. Anger, fear, and sorrow heaved from my chest, pouring out over the floor, emptying my own soul. Time and the world didn't matter, my heart breaking into pieces.

I didn't hear him come in, but suddenly arms wrapped around me, drawing me into his warmth. Safety. Lincoln pulled me between his legs on the ground and held me tightly against him, as I fell apart, howls of agony shattering from my chest.

Time had no meaning. We could have been there minutes or hours. I curled into him, rocking gently. The world around me vanished and gradually the tears did too. I still couldn't leave his embrace; for once I felt completely safe. That someone had my back.

"I-I was supposed to visit her today. Should have been with her."

Lincoln didn't say a word. His lips brushed my temple, and he sighed heavily, relating to my pain.

"How do I live with this?" I pressed my cheek deeper into the soft cotton of his shirt, most of it soaked with my tears.

"I can give you all the advice in the world, but you know your mother loved you. She didn't die to hurt you or cause you more guilt. If anything, she picked this time to let go when you weren't here, so you wouldn't have to see her pass. It was her time to let go, Dev..." His hand stroked the back of my head. "But I know what it's like to fight guilt and grief. It's a hard devil to get off your conscience, which is accusing you of the worst things you've ever thought of yourself or what you could have done differently. The road of what-ifs and wishes. You step down that road, and you may never get off it. Your mother would not have wanted that for you."

I twisted my head to look up at him, my gaze fixed on his. I felt this went a lot deeper than he let on, a penetrating sorrow underneath the walls as though he knew the road well. My hand went to his face, feeling the tickle of his beard.

"Step off with me," I whispered.

"Too late." Despondency dropped his voice low.

In that moment I could feel the deep pain he carried, see through the barricades, comforting me in the fact I wasn't alone. We both knew grief and carried it every day.

I moved closer to him, my gaze on his mouth, my heartache wanting to relieve his, even for a moment.

"Your sister is on her way," he said, not moving a hair. He would not take advantage of me in grief.

It only made me want him more.

"Thank you," I muttered, brushing my lips over his. He stayed still, but a sharp breath hitched in his throat. My teeth tugged gently at his bottom lip before my mouth covered his. He inhaled through his nose, his hand sliding behind my head, responding to my kiss with his own.

Raw. Pain. Heartache. Grief.

Our mouths begged each other to take it all away. I straddled his lap, deepening the kiss, needing to be ever closer. I ground into him, yearning for release of the heartache or a tiny speck of pleasure in my sea of pain. My hands went up his shirt, strumming down his abs until I reached his pants. I needed him. Now.

"Devon." He tried to break away, but my desperation to keep feeling the tiny bit of relief he gave me drove me forward, my mouth hungry and urgent. "Devon. Stop." He clutched my head, pulling me back.

Annoyance flared like a punch inside me, hurt and despair on the fringes. I needed this. I wouldn't survive the moment otherwise.

"Hey." He shook me slightly. "Believe me, there is nothing I want more than to keep kissing you. To be inside you. But not now, Freckles…not here."

Right. My dead mother was lying in the bed near me. Ashamed, I bent my head to the side, wiping away my tears. Who does this? Who makes out with a guy right next to their mother's body?

"It's a natural reaction." Lincoln stood, pulling me up with him. He brushed his thumbs over my jaw, drying off the rest of my tears. “Seeking comfort and relief when you’re in pain is a human response when you are going through a tragedy.”

I peered down at my mom. I knew this was the last time I would ever see her, and I took time to greedily take in her features. Her face was no longer pinched with fear, anger, or pain. Now she would no longer stare vacantly out the windows, her mind deserting her.

She was no longer trapped in a body that killed her spirit. Traditional Navajos believed your body becomes part of new life, plants, and animals. Because my mom was never religious, she always liked the idea our souls were set free to be parts of other things. I hoped now she could soar free. Become part of an eagle along with my father’s soul.

“We’ll be okay. Go to Dad,” I finally said, and leaning over, I kissed her head. “I love you, Mom. Bye.”

Holding me against him, Lincoln escorted me out of the room and down the hall. We reached the nurses’ desk and came to a stop.

Amelia stood at the doors, her arms at her sides in fists, anguish trailing down her face in a steady stream. The moment she saw me, sobs hurtled out of her throat and she ran for me.

As Lincoln had done for me, I wrapped my arms around my sister and gave her a warm, safe place to grieve.

卌 卌 |||| 卌 卌 |||| 卌 卌 ||||

The next few days passed in a blur of planning and dealing with my mother’s funeral and memorial. Until you’ve been through it, you don’t realize how much needs to be done, like picking out a coffin, what she will be dressed in, or all the paperwork involved.

My father's death and burial had been taken care of by Dad's tribe, but then I still had Mom to help as well. With Mom's, one whole afternoon had been spent questioning the leader of my father's tribe. All tribes were different, but this one was exceptionally strict as to who could be buried on their sacred lands. Even though my mother was married to Jason, she wasn't Native, and so could not be buried with him. It still hurt my heart to think my parents couldn't be next to each other.

"They have already found their way back to each other. Space, time, and flesh mean nothing to souls," Chief Lee told me before we hung up.

I wanted to believe he was right.

Amelia was set on keeping Mom near us. Mom had never been fond of our hometown. She'd stayed because of family obligations. But besides Uncle Gavin, we had no reason to ever go back. Here, we could keep her close. Mia could visit her grandma's grave.

Everyone was being so generous and helpful: Uncle Gavin, Skylar, even the nurses at the home. Bethany helped me rent a small event space near the cemetery who would cater the memorial. Nat asked why I didn't ask Lincoln to use the saloon. It was the first thing to make me smile. Holding a memorial at Lincoln's bar, where my uncle and other sheriffs would be attending? Yeah, it sounded like a disaster in the making.

Just the mention of his name made my heart ache. I longed to hear from him, but I hadn't seen or heard from Lincoln since he disappeared after Amelia showed up a full week ago at the nursing home. I knew he thought my sister and I needed alone time together, to deal with our loss, but I missed him. Wanted him next to me. He had been so kind to me that day. We weren't a couple, so I couldn't ask for more, but I still craved him. Wished for him to step through the door and hold me.

Even when I heard the knock on the door, knew who was on the other side, I couldn't stop the moment of hope it would be him.

I swung the door open to my best friend, her arms already outstretched. She hugged me without a word. Amelia had been a basket case all week, unable to work, barely able to take care of Mia. Skylar had helped me plan things, calling and emailing people for me.

She was the one to contact my mother's old friends from town.

"There's nothing I can say but I love you." She squeezed me, laying her chin on my shoulder. "And I brought a case of wine."

A genuine laugh hiccupped up my esophagus. "I frickin' love you."

"I figured you would need it by now. This week had to be almost unbearable to get through." She stepped into apartment, placing her bag next to the sofa. "Where's Amelia?"

"Work." Mel had gone back to the salon this morning saying she needed distraction, and truthfully, I was relieved. Her understandable grief had become a little overwhelming.

"I'm more afraid of next week." I took the bottle of wine she handed me, answering her first question. "When the planning and the things keeping me busy are no longer there."

I remembered the time after my father's death when all the commotion died away, and nothing was left to take your mind off the loss. Even worse were the months down the road when others moved on, and yet those moments of debilitating sadness would still rip you apart.

Popping open a bottle, I poured wine for Skylar and me, then walked back to the sofa. "I'm so glad you are here."

"She was my other mom. And you're like a sister to me. There's nowhere else in the world I should be."

Emotion burned in my eyes, and I quickly blinked tears away.

"But tonight, no talk of the funeral or anything related." Skylar flicked off her shoes, sitting on the sofa, motioning me next to her. "We've talked all week about it. Sobbed. Grieved. There is nothing left to plan or decide. Tonight, I want to talk about nothing, laugh, get drunk, and watch stupid movies." We sat facing each other, and she reached over clasping my arm on the back of the sofa. "Or you will drown in misery."

Bending forward, I pressed my forehead to her hand in silent gratitude. Skylar knew me so well, knew exactly what I needed. She could sense me sinking under the weight of both mine and Amelia's sorrow.

"Now drink, because I'm going to start telling you juicy details of my sex life…unless you have anything to add," she teased.

"Well…actually."

Skylar's eyes went wide, not really expecting me to have something to contribute. I usually didn't.

"Oh my god." Her hand went to her mouth. "*Please, please* tell me it's the sexy man you work for, and it was earth shattering… and Amelia knows."

"You got one part of it wrong."

"Which one?"

"Amelia doesn't know."

"I knew it!" A squeal bubbled from Skylar. "Wait." She held up her hand, downed the rest of her glass, and set it on the table. "Okay, now tell me everything."

CHAPTER TWENTY-TWO

The sun shone down on the mild January day, the rays soaking into my black dress and chunky cardigan, but I felt neither cold nor warm. Just vacant. Numb.

Skylar's hand clutched mine, a pillar preventing me from crumbling to ground. Amelia's hand was locked in my other, wringing the blood from the tips of my fingers. Uncle Gavin stood on the other side of Amelia, Lucy next to him, as Mia sat at our feet, playing with the flowers lining around the grave, not totally comprehending what was going on.

Skylar's mom, Vivian, spoke lovely words, but I didn't really absorb them beyond a superficial level; everything bounced off me like I was made of rubber.

Amelia sobbed quietly and shielded her eyes under large sunglasses, Uncle Gavin pulling her closer to him. In a brief glance, I saw Lucy had laced her fingers through his, and I hoped it was more than a friendly gesture. He deserved happiness. Lisa had been so awful to him at the end, maliciously going after his mediocre sheriff salary, the house, and most important, the dog. I think the dog was what hurt him the most.

Amelia, Mia, and I moved to the lowered casket, tossing in flowers.

"Bye, *Enisi*." Mia kissed the little stuffed animal rabbit she'd been holding for security. Mom had given her when she was first born; it was her favorite. Mia leaned over and tossed it in.

"Mia…" Amelia gaped, staring down at the toy on the coffin below. "We can't retrieve it."

"I want *Enisi* to have it. I don't want her to be scared and alone."

My heart surged with love and grief at her pure child innocence.

"*Enisi* will love it. Thank you, Mia." Amelia picked up her daughter, hugging her tight.

My teeth carved into my bottom lip. I would not cry…because if I did, I wouldn't be able to stop. And I needed to keep it together for everyone and for myself.

People mingled, giving their condolences before heading to the venue. My eyes landed on a coworker of mine.

"Nat." I hugged my friend. "Thank you for coming."

"I wish I could go to the memorial." She rubbed my back before stepping out of my embrace. "Lincoln has left me in charge today, so I need to get over to the bar soon."

"Lincoln's actually taking a day off?" Lincoln. Just his name evoked butterflies in my stomach.

"He called me an hour ago, so not sure it was planned." She frowned. "Probably James. He's been in a lot the past few days." She brushed her curled hair over her shoulder. “Thank goodness I was able to get a babysitter.”

“Thank you for coming.” I gripped her hand.

“We miss you at work.” She grasped mine back. “Hope you come back soon.”

“Probably later this week. When everything is over, I’ll need something to distract me.”

“Devon, we’re heading out.” Skylar called to me, Mia high on her hip, one hand shading her eyes. Lucy, Amelia, and Gavin advanced toward the car.

“Okay, *chica*. I love you.” Nat gave me one last hug. I turned to head for the car, my eye catching an outline of a form in the distance, shrouded by the trees.

“You okay?” Skylar came beside me, pulling my attention away. When I looked back the figure was gone.

“Yeah.” I smiled meekly, taking Mia’s fingers. I kissed her hand as the three of us strolled to Lucy’s waiting sedan.

Food lined the tables at the venue, which had a view of the river out the large windows. Soft music played in the background. A couple dozen people were there. Most of the guests were nurses and police from back home. All too recently these same people had been at my father’s funeral, although the entire town showed up for his.

My mom had only a handful of friends, never feeling truly happy there. Vivian was her closest friend. Dr. Matheson was here with Jody and a couple of other nurses, talking with Bethany and a few of the doctors and nurses from Mom’s latest facility. The few from the sheriff's office gathered together, near the window, nibbling on canapés.

I moved throughout each group, robotically thanking them for coming and acknowledging their well wishes. No more than a zombie, I nodded, shook hands, and hugged people, their faces blurring together.

Amelia stayed with the women from the salon who could come, drinking a huge glass of red wine.

I cut to the refreshment table where soda, wine, and water were up for offer. I needed something stronger but opted for my own large glass of wine.

"Where's your mom?" A deep voice at the entrance coasted up my spine, and heat instantly flushed through my body. My heart lunged into my throat.

Swinging around, I spotted Lincoln holding Mia in his arms, her finger pointed toward me. I knew Amelia was by the window behind me, but it looked like Mia was pointing right at me.

His mouth pinched as he walked up to me, his gaze slicing into me. I couldn't help but notice he wore dark dress slacks and a white button-down shirt. He looked incredible.

"You have an excellent door greeter." He stopped in front of me.

Mia had a fascination with tall, bearded men. Where other little girls were shy, she'd march right up to them and tell them her name. The gruffer they were, the more intrigued she was, wrapping the huge guys around her finger. Like mother like daughter. Okay…like auntie like niece. The girl had no hope.

"You're her mother?" Alarm twitched his cheek, his voice going hoarse. "You never mentioned a kid…

How old is she?"

"I'm five." She fanned out her fingers proudly.

"Five, huh?" Each word stressed, his Adam's apple bobbing. "Really?"

If we weren't surrounded by cops and people who could recognize him, I would have laughed. I could see where his mind was going. She was at the perfect age.

Taking Mia from his arms, I set her down. "Go find your mom, Mia." I stroked her silky braided hair, watching her run toward my sister. "My *niece*."

"Oh god." He grabbed his chest. "I think I almost had a mild heart attack there. When she ran up to me, all I could see was a mini version of you. Amelia somehow left out the fact she had a kid."

"What are you doing here?" I hissed, jumping past the small talk, my gaze darting over the room, seeing all the off-duty cops, who *never* stopped working. "You shouldn't be here."

Lincoln rubbed his chin, not looking at me. "I don't know. I felt the need to be here for you."

"You should go. It's not safe for you." As if my uncle sensed the one person not supposed to be here, his focus went to Lincoln. He stopped mid-sentence, the bridge of nose creasing, as if he were trying to identify the six-foot-four man.

"Shit." I grabbed his arm, yanking him down the hall, right when I heard Amelia call out his name.

Damn it.

Hustling for the first door I spotted in the hallway, I shoved him into the one-stall bathroom, slamming and locking the door behind me.

"Are you crazy?" I flayed my arms.

"Possibly."

I narrowed my gaze at his cheeky answer. "Do you not get there are police out there? All who daily stare at your picture pinned on their wall?" I spat, wanting to pummel the grin growing on his lips. "Like I don't have enough to deal with? Keeping you from being arrested at my mother's memorial was not on the list."

His smile dropped, stepping closer to me. "I'm sorry. I know it was dumb. But of all days…" He trailed off. "I thought you might need someone to be here for *you*."

"Now? You've disappeared all week." Placing my hands on my hips, my high heels tapped at the tile.

"I'm sorry I haven't called." His voice fell over me, an awkward strain between us. He drew one hand over his head. "Things got kind of *complicated*… I've been dealing with some shit. And I thought it would be best if I stepped away."

No, my heart screamed. I didn't want him to step away; I wanted him close. But between my uncle and his past, he should *run* from me.

"Does it have anything to do with your brother?" Recalling what Nat told me earlier.

He snorted as if I hit the bull's-eye. "Like I said, it keeps pulling me back in."

"Can't you say no?"

"Can you say no to your sister?"

"Fair enough."

"It's more than that, but I don't want to talk about him right now." He shifted closer to me, his stare growing more forceful, our eyes really finding each other for the first time. "I came here for *you*."

"You can't. It's too dangerous out there."

"I don't need to be out there to be here for you. To make you feel better even for a moment."

A gulp stuck in throat, hearing the double meaning. He pushed me back against the counter, mischief glinting in his eyes. I didn't like the brown contacts. He could hide behind them and keep me at a distance. I wanted the real man before me, no games, no walls.

"Take them out," I demanded.

He tilted his head for a moment before doing as I requested. Tossing them in the trash, he peered down at me, making me gasp for air. Steel-blue eyes roamed over me with such intensity they seemed to shred me of my barriers, his regard as palpable as fingers brushed up my skin.

"There you are," I whispered. He was no longer the seemingly happy-go-lucky Finn Montgomery I had met so long ago. Prison had carved out this man I knew now. Lincoln Kessler. No matter what his birth certificate said, I wanted *this* man.

"Now let me *discover* you."

"What do you mean?" I whispered.

"Something I've wanted to do since the moment I met you." He grabbed my waist, shoving me up on the counter, stealing my breath. "Is it inappropriate to say you look fucking amazing?" His palm ran down my side to my bare thigh, curling around my calf.

Dresses and heels weren't my usual clothes, and I had one black dress. It was a sleeveless skater-style dress, far too short for a funeral, but Mom had encouraged me to get it. She would have approved. The black heels accentuated my long legs.

"You look amazing too." I felt my back arch, his hand running over my other thigh.

"I thought wearing torn jeans and a T-shirt might make me stand out." He nestled into my neck, nipping my ear.

"As if you don't already." I curved my neck for him, my body heating with every touch. "Doesn't matter what you wear."

His hand pushed my dress up to my hips, his mouth consuming mine in a ravenous kiss before he dropped down to his knees, his hands continuing to flame every nerve in my body.

"For five years I've been dreaming of this." Seeing his sparkling blue eyes peer up through his lashes, his expression hungry, spiked desire straight through me.

A soft moan parted my mouth as his tongue ran up my inner thigh. The heat of his mouth closed my hands into fists.

Working my other thigh, his fingers hooked over my underpants, snaking them down my legs. He pushed my legs apart, cool air rushing between them, exposing me to him.

"Damn," he muttered, grabbing my legs and yanking them over his shoulder.

A hissing inhale exploded from my mouth as he blew lightly over my folds, his tongue dividing them, discovering me.

"Oh god." My hands shot out on either side of the wall, trying to keep me upright. I had only done this a few times with guys passing through town. I had enjoyed it fine at the time. Now I felt none of them had a clue what they were doing. Not compared to Lincoln.

"Fuck, you taste better than I imagined," he growled against me.

Nipping, licking, and sucking, Lincoln's investigating changed. Gripping my ass, he tugged me farther toward him. Fingers joined his mouth. He was a man on a mission, incinerating every cell in my body with pleasure. A cry shuddered from me, and I grasped him by the head, moving my hips against him, ecstasy blooming inside me. Another loud moan bounced off the walls. I could hear chatter and activity bustling a few yards away, but I no longer cared. I gave in to unbelievable pleasure, chasing it like a kid after an ice cream truck.

A knock tapped at the door. Of course someone needed the bathroom now. "Occupied," I grunted, not caring who was out there. The risk of getting caught seemed to provoke Lincoln to strengthen the force of his objective.

"Fuck…*Lincoln*." My nails dug into his hair as he shifted, tongue in deeper, devouring me as his thumb rubbed my clit. I dropped my head back in a cry.

Sweat beaded at my back as my orgasm climbed every vertebra. Sensing my body starting to retract, my breath hitching in tiny gulps, he notched up the intensity, nipping down.

A choked moan was all I could get out as sheer bliss stole me from my body, taking me away from all the pain and heartache. All I felt was joy. Convulsing and jerking, I gradually came back into myself. Muscles let go of all their tension, and I crashed back against the mirror, trying to catch my breath.

I didn't move or speak for several moments, my mind and limbs mush.

Lincoln kissed me softly before rising up on his feet, a smug smile curving the side of his mouth.

"You don't know how many times I visualized doing this." He placed his palms on either side of my hips. "Far better than any of my fantasies. But again, this was half-assed. Next time I want to take my time, really make you lose your mind."

"Half-assed?" I sputtered. "Jesus, I don't think I could handle full-assed."

"Guess we'll have test it out." He leaned in, his mouth covering mine voraciously, his tongue and lips claiming mine, kissing me passionately. I went from sedated to turned on in a blaze, my knees gripping his hips as the kiss became frantic and desperate.

Abruptly, he pulled away, tipping his head into mine, our breaths ragged. "I better go."

My stomach dropped, my head spinning from the extremes this man could take me through.

"Yeah, you probably should. It won't be long before Amelia comes looking for you."

"I've told her I'm not interested. That there's someone else." He skimmed his lips over mine and then stepped back. "You haven't told her something's going on between us?"

"No." I brushed down my dress. "It never felt like a good time. She is so set on you… I didn't want to hurt her."

"Seriously?" He inched back farther, straightening his spine. "Keep me a dirty little secret to save Amelia's feelings. What about yours?"

"Mine? I have no idea what those are," I huffed, sliding off the counter, straightening my clothes, the façade I let down for a moment going back up. "I better get back out there, or they may start wondering where I am."

"Devon?" He caught my arm, exasperation written over him like his tattoos.

"I need to go. There are still a few guests I need to thank." I tugged out of his grip, sounding colder than I meant to. I didn't have the energy to get into it with him. Outside these walls was enough stress. "There's a side door down the hall."

"You do that." He nodded, tugging at the cuffs of his shirt, his voice impassive. "Get back out there, play the picture-perfect host and selfless sister."

"What the hell does that mean?" Irritation curled around my throat.

"Always the noble one. Righteous. I swear, I can hear your soul screaming from here to be let free. Be honest, Dev. You'd rather be anywhere but here."

It was as if he pried me open and scooped out my deepest thoughts. Few people ever looked beyond people's veneer, seeing into their soul. I hated Lincoln was one of the few who could really see me, see me suffocating.

"So?" I thrust my hands back to my hips, not bothering to deny it. "What does it have to do with anything? I have to be here… It's my mother's memorial. People are—"

"Counting on you." He finished for me, annoying me more. "Tell me, would your mom even like this memorial?"

No. My mom would hate it. She'd want a party or everyone sitting around a campfire getting drunk and telling funny stories. Before Dad died then she got sick, she was a bit of a free spirit.

"You know these memorials aren't for the person who died. It's to appease the living. Do what society tells you to do."

"Screw you." I bit down. "I am trying to get through without falling apart."

"Fall apart."

"What?"

"Fuckin' fall apart." He threw up his hands. "What will happen if you do? The world will end if you aren't in control? Of all the people who deserve to lose it, it's you. You don't think people would understand?"

My mouth opened then shut. It wasn't that I thought people wouldn't understand, I didn't want to…because somewhere along the road, I became a huge control freak.

"Who are you to talk?" I countered, my shoulders rolling forward. A moment ago his tongue was inside me, making me come, now I was contemplating punching him in the face. "You are so closed off I'm surprised you aren't constipated from your lies."

A gruff laugh hurled from him, but it dropped away as fast as it started. "My *life* depends on keeping private."

"Yeah, you're doing great at that." I waved my hand toward the main room. "But I know who you are. So why keep me out?"

"You don't want in. I promise you."

"Don't decide for me." My shoes knocked into his. Words spewed from me as if being around him made me lose all sense of control. "Or are you too scared I'll find you are a narcissistic, common, low-grade drug dealer? A thief stupid enough to get caught because he thought with his dick and not his brains."

His jaw locked down, his eyes narrowing into slits, his physique growing over me. I could feel the anger rising off him like steam.

"Is. That. What. You. Think?" He spoke slow and gritty.

"No. Uh. I don't know what to think," I challenged. "You won't tell me anything. You only slip in ambiguous hints here and there. You've never told me who the girl is in the photo. Do you have a kid? A wife?"

His head tipped to the side, anger contorting the lines of his face. "You really want to know?" He sneered, as if he were goading me, already knowing the outcome.

"Yes." I didn't back away. After all I'd dealt with, I could handle his story.

"Fine." He gripped my hand, swinging for the door. "Let's go."

"Where are we going?" I wiggled out of his tight hold.

"You said you wanted to know. Well, you're getting what you ask for. But you have to come with me to get the full story."

"I can't leave."

"Too bad." He shrugged, unlocking and opening the door. I knew in my gut this was the one chance he was giving me. If I didn't go, I wasn't sure he'd offer it again. Hesitating for a second, I watched him step from the room.

Go, Devon! Don't let him leave without you. A voice screamed inside my head, pushing me forward.

"Wait." I slipped out with him. He glanced down at me, seeing the choice set firmly on my face. I would send Skylar a text, asking her to apologize to everyone, that I needed a little time by myself. "Let's go out the back door." I pointed down the opposite way of the main venue.

Lacing his hand in mine, he rushed us down the hallway and pushed the door open to the back exit. With a final glance down the hall, I spotted Uncle Gavin, Skylar, and Amelia all talking in the room. Turning away, I ran from obligation and guilt, letting my control crumble away and leaving it behind with my discarded underwear.

CHAPTER TWENTY-THREE

"What?" I looked around in confusion. "Why are we back here?"

Lincoln climbed out of the Bronco, forcing me to follow. Heavy purple light shaded the cemetery.

"Lincoln?" I stepped around the Bronco, watching him stride toward a path opposite of where we just laid my mother to rest. "Lincoln!"

He didn't say a word, just kept walking. His legs were so long I had to jog after him, my feet aching as they struck the pavement. Why didn't I wear my Converse?

"Where are we going?" I caught up with him, but his walls were locked in place, not allowing a sliver of emotion out. "I thought you were showing me something."

"I am." The cords up his arms constricted, drawing my eyes up. His entire physique was rigid.

We curved down another path, the gate for the exit not too far away. But halfway to the gate he stopped, stepping carefully between a row of graves until he stopped in front of one. Heels sinking into the dirt, I came up beside him. My gaze shadowed his, looking down at the little headstone, reading the name.

Oh. God. No. I pressed a hand to my mouth.

The name carved into the stone: *Kessley Montgomery-Smith.*

"My daughter." His voice strained, his Adam's apple bobbing.

"Oh god…" My brain captured the dates. She had died around nine months ago. About the time Finn Montgomery escaped from prison.

He kept his head forward, his throat dancing with emotion. "I was so young when she was born." He blew out of his mouth, his body still tight, but he let the story come out. "When I met Kim, I was barely twenty and shallow. I didn't care about her personality, just that she was hot, experienced, and wanted me. We were oil and water, but we kept hooking up over the summer. Combustible. Toxic in everything but the bedroom. I didn't think anything of it after we parted ways. Then one day she showed up my doorstep with a baby. Mine. We had been dumb so many times..." He trailed off, shaking his head. I remembered his brother mentioning the name Kim, calling her a bitch. The mother of his child.

"I had no money, barely able to pay my bills, and Kim demanded more and more from my wallet. I wanted to be a good dad, unlike mine, and do the right thing. But I was drowning. My brother and I had always been on the gray side of the law. Pinching things from rich houses since we were kids to get by. It was more a hobby than anything." Lincoln scoured his head, wrinkling his forehead.

"It was *my* idea to do it more full-time. We were good at it, and it was the fastest and easiest way to get what we needed. We never used weapons, just robbed places when people weren't home. I did it because I felt I had to, but my brother took to it like a fiend. With his addictive personality, it was a high, a drug to him. He loved it. And similar to most drugs, you have to keep taking more to get the same high. He started talking about doing bigger jobs, like banks and businesses, bringing in guns, which was never my plan. I now had a precious blonde-haired, blue-eyed reason to stay out of jail. I was planning to get out, open a bar, have a proper job and be a good dad to Kessley. But of course, life always has to come along and fuck you…"

I didn't move or blink, lapping up his story like a sponge. He was letting me into his world, seeing his truth and his demons.

"She was only two when the doctors discovered she had a rare form of leukemia. Over the next four years it was one treatment after another and expensive hospital stays." He swallowed, pointing his face at the sky, squeezing his eyes tightly, holding back the pain. "With no family support on either side, it got harder and harder for us to afford health insurance. My brother and I came up with a plan. Steal enough to pay for her treatments. As you know, things didn't go as planned."

Oh. Holy. Crap.

He hadn't been some drug dealer selling medicine on the black market for himself. He had done it to get money. To save his daughter's life.

"It was supposed to be a quick in and out. A friend of Kim's stole us a nurse's badge and uniform, but a guard quickly realized I didn't match the name on the tag… I think I could have gotten out clean, but my brother's greed consumed him. Unknown to me, he was carrying a gun. He held up the gift shop on the way out, wanting cash, slowing us down and adding a huge weight to our crime. I took the gun. Told him I'd get rid of it."

"That's what you were going to hide in the bathroom." My brain trying to put all the pieces together.

"Stupid, I know, but I panicked. I figured someone would throw out the trash in the dumpster, the gun concealed inside, then head to the dump, where it would stay. I'd be back on the road, no one knowing I had ever stopped there. No gun for the cops to link to the crime." He twisted his head to look at me, a slight knowing grin on his mouth. "But that plan got botched too…"

"Me." I pinched my lips together.

"Jesus, Freckles, you were my fantasy come to life." He faced me. "Timing was awful, but even then, I couldn't seem to stay away from you. And you had this fierceness in your eyes, a sadness, that sealed my fate."

"A few hours earlier my mother had been diagnosed with Alzheimer's," I said. "And right before you walked in, my boyfriend sent a 'sext' to my best friend. I got it by mistake. They had been secretly having an affair. On our anniversary he was screwing her brains out."

"Wow. I'm sorry." He gripped my arms, running his palms up and down. "What a stupid asshole…but can I say I'm kind of thankful he was such a douche. I did not mind being your revenge fuck"

A snort rose up my throat.

His hands moved to my face, sliding under my jaw.

"Sex with you…it got me through most days in prison. For some reason I couldn't stop thinking or fantasizing about you…" He let his declaration taper away, his expression flattening out.

"But..." I filled in, biting my lip.

He let his hands go, stepping back from me, sorrow straining his features, tears permeating his eyes.

"Kim and I tested to be bone marrow matches. I was locked away when they found I was a match. Kim wasn't. The doctors were trying to prepare Kessley for a transplant.

"But I rotted in there while my little girl grew sicker… Kim told me she was no longer responding to any treatment and was failing fast." He sniffed and turned away from me, rage and grief twitching his neck. "I promised I'd never leave her side; I'd read her stories and play with her at the park. I told her everything would be okay." His voice strained. "Having my throat slashed was nothing to the pain I caused my little girl. Kim hated my guts, so she especially loved to rub it in when she did come to visit me in prison telling me Kessley cried every night, asking where I was. I had promised her I'd be there. I had broken my daughter's heart."

He kicked at the grass, resentment shredding his voice. "I was a model inmate. Kept to myself and did everything I was told. Knowing it was too late for the transplant, I wanted nothing to keep me from parole. But life once again, gave me a big fat fuck you…" He wheeled around, his eyes bright and wild, his teeth bared. "I still had over a year left, but my girl was done fighting. And guess what my daughter's last wish was?" He bellowed, a single tear falling through his lashes. "To see her daddy."

He heaved in oxygen, putting his hands on his hips, his head down.

"She was the sole reason I was being so good anyway, in the hopes I could see her, be with her. I decided fuck it. Seeing her for the last time was worth being recaptured and spending the rest of my life in jail. I broke out…" He choked over a whisper, a sob ripping his throat. "And I was still too late." He glanced back up at me, red streaking his eyes. "My little girl died before I got there, always believing her father failed her. That I didn't love her enough to show up. So, yes, Devon, *I know* the *devil*…the road of what-ifs and wishes," he seethed.

Tears tumbled down my face, feeling the anguish and guilt he held so deeply, caging him in a prison of his own making.

"Lincoln." I took a step to him, my heart empathizing with his grief.

"Don't." He took a step back, rage and heartache fighting under his skin. Ignoring his rebuff, I continued to him, wrapping my arms around his torso.

"Devon…" He stiffened, which made me hold him tighter. At last, he broke, his shoulders slumping forward, his arms engulfing me. His body started to shake, and he heaved with the sobs he was trying so hard to keep back.

In our mutual grief, we clung to each other, both of us broken and strong at the same time. We didn't talk. I didn't want to hear cliché sentiments, and I doubted he did either. This is where we could truly grieve, touch the darkness and heartache. Our connection tying us together even closer, buoying us above the sinking pit of crippling pain.

He held me close as our heartbeats slowed down, our anguish quieting. Slowly, he pulled back, gripping my face, dapping my drying tears with his thumbs.

"When you asked me if I regretted you…" he said softy.

"I understand. I would hate me too."

"No, you still don't get it." He expression severe. "I should. I should despise myself for deciding to stay…my mind will always wonder if I left, would I have been there to read her one last story? Would I have been there when she died?" He leaned into me. "But no matter how much I want to hate you, I can't. Nothing about you feels like a regret. And when you walked into my bar…yes, I wanted to blame you. Hate you. I thought fate really was trying to punish me. But strangely, you began to seem like the opposite."

"Opposite?"

"Yeah. When you walked back into my life, I felt as if I could breathe again, as if I had been holding my breath since the day I walked out of that bathroom. Every time I told myself I'd fire you…I couldn't do it. The idea of you not being near me…felt like a prison."

The meaning of his words cascaded over me. How many times had I said to myself he was a mistake? But not once did I ever feel it. He stayed with me, always haunting me; I didn't want to let him go.

I didn't think, I rose on my tiptoes. My mouth touched his, softly, discovering the taste and feel of him, tugging at his bottom lip.

A low growl ebbed up his chest, his hand sinking onto the back of my head, tangling in my hair as he pulled me in. His tongue parted my lips, desire escalating our need in a spike of adrenaline, our hands moving over each other. My fingers gripped his dress shirt and tugged it out of his pants.

"Wait." He gripped my arms, pinning them to my sides. "Not here."

My gaze wandered around. Shame quickly smothered my desperation.

"Oh my god, I am so sorry. I did it again." I palmed my face. We were standing at his daughter's grave. What kind of person was I? With him I seemed to have no civility; my yearning for him completely took over.

"Don't ever apologize. *Believe me*, knowing you're bare under that short skirt…I want nothing more than to strip the rest of you naked and lick every inch of you right now." My throat hitched, my blood sizzling in response to his words. "*But* this is not the right place or time. You probably need to get back."

I nodded, wanting nothing more than to stay with him and not return to smile and respond for the next hour with a variation of, "Thank you for coming. It *was* a lovely service. Yes, my mother will be greatly missed." I wanted to roll into a ball in the corner. Or get excessively drunk. The woman my mom had been before she got sick would have been all for that option. She did enjoy her wine.

"Yeah, I better get back to being the *perfect* host."

He smiled briefly, placing a hand on my lower back, leading me to his Bronco.

"Thank you for earlier, for bringing me here, for telling me your story." I stopped at the passenger door, staring up into blue eyes.

"What part of earlier are you thanking me for?" He smirked.

"All of it. But the bathroom? That was…*in-credible*." I shook my head, looking down at the ground, heat returning to my cheeks. "We do have a thing for public places."

He scoffed, rubbing his mouth with his hand, as if reliving the scene himself.

"But really, thank you for being there for me." I exhaled. "And for telling me about Kessley. I know it must have been horrible, and I can't imagine what you went through and still do."

He reached up and tucked a slip of my hair behind my ear. "I think you might understand."

"No, nothing like you. Being locked in prison while your daughter is dying… I can't fathom it. But you know she wouldn't want you to punish and hate yourself; she sounded too innocent and sweet for something like that. She'd want you happy."

"And how do you know?"

"Because I watched a little girl today, not much younger than Kessley, toss her I-can't-breathe-or-function-without stuffed animal into a grave because she didn't want her grandmother to be alone or scared, who she's really only known to be vacant or unstable." I touched his face. "And I doubt your daughter would've been any less pure of heart. She loved and believed in you. You may hate yourself, but I bet she never did. Someday she'd want you to forgive yourself."

"I can't." He bowed his head, his hand covering mine.

"I didn't say it would be easy. I'm working on a similar problem. Maybe we can try to step off the road of self-punishment together."

He stepped in, crushing his mouth to mine passionately, ending it almost as fast as it began.

"Get in the car, Freckles, or there is a good possibility you won't be making it back at all."

"I'm okay with that." But the moment I said it, I knew I better get back to the memorial. Being gone for a short time was one thing, disappearing the rest of the evening would not be okay. Skylar, Uncle Gavin, Amelia, and Mia needed me. With a heavy sigh I climbed into his Bronco, turning back into the steadfast sister and host.

When Lincoln returned me to the venue, the parking lot was almost empty and the cleaning crew was at work. Neither one of us realized how long we had been gone.

Remorse blistered up my throat, bile swishing around in my stomach. I felt awful, selfish, and ashamed as we drove home.

When I walked up to the apartment, I could still feel the sensation of Lincoln's mouth on mine from when he kissed me goodbye. An apology resembling groveling sat on my tongue as I stepped into our place, thinking I heard the voices of my family. Nothing.

"Hello?" I shut the door, spotting the jacket and bag I left at the place hanging on the coatrack, confirming they had returned. "Is anyone home?"

Silence.

Traveling to the living room, my eyes scurried around the empty room. Rotating toward my bedroom, I let out a yelp, spotting a motionless figure standing at the window.

"Shit, Amelia." I clamped down on my breastbone. "You scared me."

"Distracted?" She glanced over her shoulder. Her position had a perfect view of the front, exactly where Lincoln dropped me off. A sprout of nervousness wrapped around my vertebrae.

"When did you get home? I went back, and no one was there." I swallowed over the dry spot in my throat. "I'm so sorry. I sent a text to Skylar. I didn't realize how late it was."

"I wonder why that is." Her tone was punchy, disdainful. "Why you left *Mom's* memorial early…dumped everything on me. How could you be so selfish and cruel at your own mother's funeral?" Resentment layered every syllable.

My lids fluttered in annoyance, my earlier guilt was gobbled up by her hypocrisy. The two words, selfish and cruel, hit every nerve like a pinball machine. Lincoln and Skylar were both in my head, forcing me to see how much I catered to Amelia. I was sick of her always playing the victim card.

Tonight I had no energy for an Amelia tantrum.

"Where is everyone?" I shifted topics, ignoring her assessment of my character.

"They took Mia out for pizza and ice cream."

"And you didn't go?" I kicked off my heels, moaning with relief.

"No." She whirled around, her arms folded. "I wanted to talk to you."

"What is your problem, Mel?" I yearned to take a shower and crawl into bed. "I am sorry I left, and I wasn't there for the last bit. I feel awful, but for some reason I don't think that's what you are really mad about. Or are you annoyed because for once you had to take care of something?"

"Fuck you!" A storm heaved off her shoulders, her face pinching with rage. "I can't believe you! Always playing the sweet sister, when all along you were a backstabbing bitch."

"Whoa." Bewilderment stepped back, my hands going up. "What are you talking about?"

"You!" she spat out. "And Lincoln!"

Ah.

"I saw you just now. And I was the one knocking on the door…and I frickin' heard you screwing him. *In. The. Bathroom!* Found the panties you left on the floor," she screeched, charging for me. "How could you? You knew I really liked him. Was that the reason you went after him? To hurt me? To finally be the one picked over me?"

"What?" A sardonic laugh bolted up my throat. "Are you kidding me right now? Seriously?"

"Nailing you in the bathroom because you spread

your legs makes you easy, not wanted." This was the same thing she wanted to do with him, but *I* was the whore?

"Stop. Right. Now. Amelia," I seethed, getting right into her face.

"Why him? Of all guys. You knew how I felt about him. He was *mine*."

"He's not yours!" I exclaimed. "He never was. You are only set on him because he's the first guy who hasn't fallen at your feet. It became a challenge, but you don't actually like him."

"Yes, I do. I think I'm in love with him."

I laughed again, knowing my sister better than she knew herself. "Okay, what do you know about him? If you're so deeply in love, tell me something about him. His dreams? Ambitions? Start easy, where did he go to college?"

"It never came up."

"FYI, he didn't. Okay, does he have siblings?"

"I-I don't know. We didn't talk about that stuff."

"And you're in love with him?"

Her forehead wrinkled, fury riding her shoulders.

"You only want him because you can't have him." I pushed the balls of my feet into the floor. "There is something happening between him and me…there has been for a while. Yes, I should have told you a long time ago, but I didn't want to hurt you. I won't be staying quiet anymore."

"How long? Oh my god, did everyone at the bar know? You let me embarrass myself, throw myself at him, while everyone was probably laughing behind my back?"

"Yeah, 'cause once again it's about you, and therefore somehow my fault," I growled, getting back into her space, my anger cold and direct. "Shut your mouth before you say something even more stupid, which will really piss me off. Not a good time to push me. I mean, for crap sake, get over yourself. We *just buried* Mom today."

Amelia let out a crazed cry, her arms pinwheeling around. "You think I don't know that? I was there. The whole time!"

"Oh my god." I shook my head. "For one moment, an hour, I did something I wanted to do, which is you *all the time*, and I'm the bad guy?" Whatever Lincoln evoked in me, a new version of me rose from beneath, shoving the people pleaser back.

"You know what, Amelia? I am not always going to be here, taking care of you. For once in your life, you will have to start doing things on your own. Be a frickin' adult. You were old enough to get knocked up, so stop being the baby here. Just because you don't want to deal with something, like planning Mom's entire funeral, doesn't mean you get out of it. That's not how it works. I've let you slide for too long. Instead of fighting you, Mom and Dad let you get away with anything, always coming to me to pick up your part of the chores or responsibilities. But no more. I'm done with this…"

My arms flopped to my side, feeling the anger drain away to sadness. "I don't want this life. I want to travel, go to college, figure myself out. I love you… You and Mia are my heart, but it isn't my life's purpose to make yours easier. I want a sister, not to be the parent."

Her chest heaved, her eyes wide as she stared at me. I could see inklings of fear sprouting inside her at the thought of me no longer being there.

"Tell everyone I'll see them in the morning. I'm heading to bed." I veered for my bedroom.

"Devy?" Amelia's voice splintered over the floor.

I looked over my shoulder, but she said nothing, gaping at me with dejection.

"Good night, Mel," I said softly before shutting the door.

Amelia was my sister. I loved her more than anything, but our relationship needed to change. I hadn't realized how much I was suffocating under all this weight. It wasn't entirely her fault. I'd let her get away with it, but something had shifted in me, and I knew I would never be the same girl.

It was time for Devon Thorpe to get a life. Her own.

CHAPTER TWENTY-FOUR

It had only been two days since the funeral, but tension at home had grown thick as mud, sticking heavily to the air. Amelia and I hadn't really talked since our fight. We were cordial, but both of us were far too stubborn to bend first. And when Skylar left the day after the funeral, taking away our buffer, the strain only increased. It drove me out of the house on long runs where I could get lost in my thoughts.

Today, even after a run, I was restless, searching for something. I wanted to be around people, to feel life bustling by. I felt I had been in a cave for so long, solely focused on Mom and keeping my family afloat.

I was a mess. One moment, I felt shame for being relieved Mom was gone, that she was no longer suffering, and she was free. Then I'd flip to missing her so much and also feeling lost and scared, because I didn't know what to do without having the responsibility. Without her. And I knew myself. If I wasn't careful, I would turn my unease about my future toward Mia and Amelia, taking care of them so I wouldn't float away, never really asking myself what I wanted.

I was at a crossroads: either I allowed myself to fall into a safe life where I was needed, or I could let myself fly. Discover my own dreams. Waiting tables was fine for now, but it was not what I wanted to do with my life. All I seemed good at was taking care of people, though the idea of becoming a nurse or doctor made me want to cry. Taking care of my mom was one thing; I didn't want to do it professionally. My heart couldn't handle it. I'd toyed with the thought of opening my own café but didn't know how passionately I felt about it.

I guess that was what college was for. To figure it out. An education was necessary, especially if I decided to go into having my own business. But then the thoughts would enter my mind of what if I tried, took out hefty loans, and it wasn't successful? I hated the idea of not only failing, but of the loan money handcuffing me to years of endless serving jobs, the one thing I was qualified to do.

These contemplations looped around my brain until I thought I would snap. Requiring a reprieve, I went for a long walk to clear my head, my feet moving forward without much consideration, enjoying the late afternoon. As the evening descended, darkening the streets, I found myself stepping into the saloon, seeking a friendly face, my subconscious leading me here the whole time.

A wide grin from the other side of the bar warmed my heart, bringing me to the stools.

"Look who's back. We've missed your face." Rick and Kyle held up their drinks, welcoming me back. I waved, smiling at the bartender.

"Hey, *chica*!" Nat leaned over, hugging me. "How are you?"

"I'm okay. Good. Bad. Ugly."

"Don't I know it." She nodded. "I remember when I lost my nana. She had been sick so long, I felt both relieved and devastated, bouncing back and forth between them like a volleyball over a net."

"Oh. Yeah." I slipped into the chair, my gaze sliding quickly to the back.

"I don't think he's here anymore." I found a knowing smile on Nat's mouth. "He said he had to slip out for a bit." Noticing my pinched expression, she returned an affirmation. "Yep. James strikes again."

I now knew what happened to Lincoln, how he took responsibility for James, and I realized we weren't much different. It was easy to resent James and want to tell Lincoln to be strong and say no to him. But I would be a hypocrite, although Amelia wasn't dragging me into illegal activity, something that could put Lincoln away for good.

"You want a drink?" Nat reached for a glass. "Margarita?"

"Why not?" I shrugged. "I walked here. Also, I need to plug in my cell…ran out of battery earlier." I started to dig into my bag for the phone.

Nat grabbed the tequila, starting to mix the drink. "You know who else was here earlier?"

"Who?"

"Your uncle."

"My uncle?" My head snapped up. "Uncle Gavin?"

"Yeah." Her eyebrows crinkled. "He came in asking about Lincoln."

Ice. Fire. Both plunged down my airway, crashing into my gut.

"What?"

"He asked about you two and if I knew anything about him." She scooped ice into my cup, pouring the liquid over. "I know he's your uncle and probably seeing if he's a good enough guy for his niece, but my instinct around cops is to say as little as possible."

"What did you tell him?"

"The only things I really know. His name and he's been my boss for about seven or eight months. He was also curious who owned it before Lincoln and if I had seen him recently. What he looked like."

I could barely breathe or swallow. My uncle was smart, his intuition even sharper than my father's. He had raided so many drug houses, capturing criminals off a hunch and reasoning.

I had hoped Lincoln had skated past him, his attention on other things at the memorial. But no. By his expression I should have known he would compartmentalize, file it away until he had a moment.

Lucy had left town the same time as Skylar, needing to get back to work, but Uncle Gavin stayed. Told us he wanted to help with tying up loose ends for Mom. He had moved from the hotel to our sofa that morning.

"You didn't tell him, right?"

"He's your uncle and would know I was lying…so I said his name was James and a basic description of him. A million guys match the description I gave him."

Yeah, but only one had to fit if he knew who he was looking for. If my uncle put together who Lincoln's "partner" was… Shoving my chair back, I hopped off the seat.

"Where are you going?"

"I need to talk to Lincoln." Heading to the office, I needed to confirm he wasn't here before I started to truly panic. Stepping in the empty room, my shoulders twisted with tension. Shit.

Out the window behind his desk, through the partially closed blinds, I spotted Lincoln's Bronco. Headlights on, his shadowy outline reversing the car from the parking spot.

My legs bolted, leaping in long strides for the back door. With a burst, the back door cracked against the wall as I shoved through it.

"Lincoln!" I yelled, darting for the Bronco exiting the lot. "Stop!"

Oblivious to me, the car turned out, gunning down the street.

"Shit," I cried, racing back for the restaurant. Not only did I need to talk to Lincoln, I had to stop him. If my uncle was on to him, he needed to get as far from his brother and trouble as he could.

"Nat!" I bellowed, spurting down the hall. "I need to borrow your car."

"Why?"

The entire bar stared at me, every second ticking by, slipping him from my fingers.

"Please?" I ignored her question, bouncing on my toes in desperation.

Whatever she saw in my face, she went straight to

her purse and tossed her keys on the bar.

"Thank you." I swiped them up, pressing my hands together gratefully. "I will be back soon. I promise."

Without waiting, I ran, barreling through the back door, jumping into her tan Camry. The tires squealed as I veered out of the parking lot, turning the way I'd seen his Bronco go.

Two traffic signals up the road from me, I saw his Bronco turn, the black car glinting under the streetlights. I was usually a responsible driver, but I couldn't afford to lose him. Swerving around a group of cars, I slammed down on the gas, the sedan jerking with the effort. Speeding past the traffic, horns honked and people screamed at me, but I arched around the turn, barely slipping through the yellow-red light.

"Sorry," I pointlessly called back to the cars I'd cut off. Being around Lincoln seemed to bring out my reckless side, which I probably needed a little more of.

His vehicle slowed down, pulling onto a side street and stopping in a dimly lit empty lot. *What is he up to?* I was desperate to talk to him. *Is something happening tonight?*

Cruising past, I yanked the car into the first parking spot along the street. Then I rushed back to where I saw him, ready to quietly call his name, when my gaze darted over the sign on the store close to the lane.

Gold & Silver Exchange was etched in large letters over the banner. Dread filled my stomach like I had a gallon of water swishing around. *Please no.* Darting through the dark, my feet came to a grinding halt at the sound of voices near Lincoln's Bronco, my throat weaving into knots.

"What are you talking about? It's perfect. Smart." I recognized James's voice and crept closer behind a wobbly wooden fence. "Robbing banks always goes bad. They track the money by serial number or by dye, rendering it useless. This." James pointed at the store. "We sell it on the black market, triple the worth, clean money. It's ideal."

"I love your perception of ideal," Lincoln snarled. "And how do you think you're going to rob a store which has security guards and alarms all over? This isn't stealing from the houses of our father's clients. We can't sneak through a window."

"All covered, brother."

"What do you mean?"

"Bennie set me up."

"Bennie? Bennie who sells illegal guns?" I saw Lincoln's head waggle. "Hell no. I am out. I told you when I got of jail I wasn't getting into this shit again. I've already taken the heat for carrying a weapon at our last job. One that put me in prison because I didn't give you up."

"Jesus, Finn…you weren't always so fucking virtuous. Remember it was you who got us in this to begin with."

"Don't call me Finn," Lincoln growled. "And you can't keep throwing it in my face. This is all you now. You love this shit. I never did. I did it so we could survive. You do it for fun. Just another drug to you."

"Don't tell me this doesn't rev your engine…or is *someone* else doing that instead?"

Air strangled around them as Lincoln remained silent.

"After Kessley died, you were fine to dip your toes into the dark side. Now this girl has you all twisted up. Denying your nature. Is she making you all noble? An upstanding citizen?" James taunted. "Please. You're only fooling yourself."

"I'm not you." Lincoln's voice was so low I barely heard him. "And I'm not going back to jail. I'm out for good. And I'm done with you. Leave Albuquerque and don't come back." Metal squealed, the Bronco door opening.

"Is this how it's going to be? You turn your back on your brother? The only family you have? It has been just us since Dad kicked us out. Jesus. I was fourteen and had to take care of my baby brother on the streets. Remember, at sixteen, I jumped in front of a bullet for you? Saved your life. And who helped you break out of prison to see your daughter? Me!"

The only sounds in the long pause of Lincoln's silence were cars driving on the main road and my heart thumping in my ears.

"Last job. I promise. Then I'll disappear like you want. Pay off those guys and take the rest of my share and start a new life somewhere else so you can play house, pretend you're a good guy." I could feel the lasso James had tossed out, cinching in Lincoln. "Do this for me, brother."

Again, silence.

"I didn't want to do this…hoping you'd choose family first." James sighed. "You know how easy it would be for you to be found. Shit, you're walking the line now. One call. One tiny hint dropped, and you'll have cops swarming the bar."

"Fuck you." I heard anger, disgust, hate in Lincoln's gravelly response but worst of all a defeated sigh, as if his anger was all a front. He climbed back into the Bronco, slamming the door, his brother's laughter howling in the air as he tore out of the parking lot.

I stayed motionless behind the wooden fence, my heart pounding, hoping I stayed concealed in the dark as Lincoln's Bronco bounded right by me. It wasn't until I heard another car door slam and tires pulling out of the lot that I let the breath out of my lungs and tipped my head back against the fence.

This was bad.

Was my uncle curious enough to investigate Lincoln while his brother dragged him into a heist? With my luck and Lincoln's? The only way it would turn out was traffic.

The apartment was dark when I stepped in, a glow from the streetlight cascading into the room. Amelia was out with her salon gals, which had been happening more than usual lately. Mia was downstairs, undoubtedly happy to be out of this space, making cookies with Lucia, away from the sadness and strain.

Grumbling at my phone, I went to the kitchen to find a cord to charge my cell. My worry for Lincoln had doubled, but when I returned the car to Nat, his Bronco was nowhere in sight. I had given Amelia grief for not knowing much about him, when I barely knew the real man myself. I didn't even know where he lived.

I flicked on the kitchen light and let out a scream. Sitting at the dining table, my uncle silently stared out the window, a glass of scotch beside him.

"Shit," I gasped, patting at my chest. "I need to put bells on you and Amelia."

His response was to pick up his glass and take a sip. My uncle only drank on very special occasions or when he was deeply troubled by a case. When I was little and a case went cold, my father and uncle would sit and drink a glass of their favorite scotch and go over every single detail of the event, trying to find anything they missed. Neither brother liked a case or criminal getting the better of them. They would fret over it until they figured it out. That was exactly what he looked like now. As if my father was sitting across from him, both silent as their minds worked out the details.

"Uncle Gav?" The knots in my belly wound together, a pressure spreading across my shoulder blades. Hesitantly, I moved over to the table, sitting in the chair across from his. "Everything okay?" Although I had a pretty good idea what was churning in his mind, I feigned complete ignorance.

He took another sip then set the glass down with a deliberate tap. "Besides losing my parents, brother, and sister-in-law?" he replied impassively, watching the ice cubes swirl around his glass. "But I don't think that's what you mean."

I kept my mouth shut, sensing a turbulent undercurrent to his words. Sweat dampened the base of my neck. I watched his profile staring back out the window, my heart picking up speed. Silence smothered the room. How much did he know about Lincoln? Had he tied Lincoln to Finn?

"What do you do when you watch someone you care about making reckless decisions?" He kept his voice low and even.

Shit. Shit. Shit.

Anxiety wrapped around my lungs and throat. Growing up in a family of cops, you learned about both sides of the law. How to interrogate and how to tactically respond to an investigation. How to keep calm and divulge as little as possible. How to stay ambiguous and vague.

“It’s a tough one. Some people need to learn from their own mistakes.” Muscles squeezing around my neck, I responded. Composed and steady.

“Even if their life could be completely destroyed because of their *wrong* choices?”

“What’s wrong to you might not feel wrong to them.”

He knew. I knew. And we both knew the other was aware, but both of us stayed controlled, revealing nothing.

“If it’s illegal, the law cares nothing for personal feelings or motive.” He turned his head enough for his gaze to lock onto mine. I expelled a quick breath from my lungs but held his gaze. “Don’t you think a loved one has an obligation to step in?”

My heartbeat pulsed in my throat. I did not have any response to his question. I would force him to be direct. “Why did you stay?” I coerced the words through my teeth, clasping my hands painfully together. “Why didn’t you go with Lucy?”

“You mean you don’t want me here?” His eyebrow lifted.

“Of course I do.” I pretended to not hear the implication oozing off his tone. “I’m just surprised since she drove you down.”

"I wanted to spend more time with my nieces and Mia. Is that so wrong of me?" I shook my head at his question. "Plus, Lucy needed to get back to Max."

"Max?" Defensiveness on his behalf filled me. She was with someone else? The way she looked at Gavin, it was obvious she was completely in love with him. Had been since they were partners. "Who is Max?"

"My—*our*—German shepherd puppy."

My mouth dropped open, repeating. "*Our* puppy?"

A tiny smile twitched on his mouth, but tension still lay coiled beneath like a tiger preparing to pounce. "She thought he would cheer me up when I was recovering. Told me no true cop should be without a police dog. So now I have a dog."

This was huge. He had been adamant about not getting another dog after Lisa took Oscar, the shepherd they had together. He didn't want to open himself to love something again.

"You two have a dog? Together?"

"Dev…" Warning peaked in his voice.

"Stop fighting your feelings for her. Lucy is amazing. The best thing to ever happen to you. So don't let it slip away because you're scared of letting someone in."

"There are rules…"

"Stop. The rules are bullshit. Officers Camia and Danny have been together forever. No one seems to care."

"I'm captain. It's different. I must lead by example."

"You're using it as an excuse and you know it," I chided, leaning my elbows on the table. "You don't want to be hurt again or show vulnerability to someone.

But you forget, Lucy knows you. She's seen all sides of you, probably far more than Lisa ever did, and she loves you."

He rolled his shoulders back and took another gulp of his scotch. Lucy was breaking down his walls, infiltrating his world, and as much as he wanted to fight it, I think deep down he wanted her to. Their friendship and bond had been blatantly obvious from the start and no doubt why Lisa hated her so much.

"You really are your mother's daughter," he muttered into his drink. "Let me get used to the dog first."

"The one you *share*."

"Yes." He rolled his eyes. "The one we share."

This was a big step for him, and I knew when to back off.

"Okay, I'm going to head for bed." I stood up, wanting to escape before we could return to the earlier, more dangerous conversation. I reached the hallway before I heard my name. I turned to look over my shoulder. Uncle Gavin's grave expression watched me.

"You know how much I love you, right?" He didn't wait for me to respond. "There's *nothing* I won't do to keep you protected and safe." His gaze dug into my soul, churning the guilt around like an ice cream maker. "Good night, Devon."

"Night," I whispered, turning back down the hall.

It wasn't a loving sentiment. It was a warning.

CHAPTER TWENTY-FIVE

The sofa was empty when I got up in the morning, Uncle Gavin already gone. I stumbled for the coffee pot. This time I didn't wait for it to fill, holding my cup under the drip as Amelia did.

Sleep had escaped me most of the night, worry, guilt, and fear spinning me in my bed like a Ferris wheel as I thought over everything that had happened in the past few days. No doubt Gavin knew something. But how much? I guess it didn't matter; it was enough to put Lincoln in jeopardy. Lincoln needed to disappear. And soon, before his brother pulled him back in.

I grunted, blowing on my full cup of coffee. That thought was like a pitchfork stabbing me in the gut. I didn't want him to go, but his welfare came first, no matter how selfish I wanted to be.

He would leave, and it would be the best for all of us. Associating with me would only bring about his downfall. And mine. Uncle Gavin was right; I was reckless when it came to Lincoln. The way my heart swelled when he was around. The way I longed for him…had always longed for him. Since the day he walked into that restroom, it felt as if I were destined to love him. It was ill-fated and tragic. My feelings for him would result in catastrophe. I realized I would do anything for him, even if it meant going against the law. Against my family. When it came to Lincoln, all I saw was gray, not black and white.

Picking up my cell, I called him, scared the sheriff was already on his way to him. The bar didn't open until later, but I didn't put anything past my uncle. It was probably why he'd left early, to sniff out Lincoln. No answer. I sent a text telling him to call me ASAP. Ten minutes passed, and my phone stayed silent.

"Damn it." I set down my cup, marching for my bedroom to get dressed but collided with my sister.

"Owww, Dev!" Amelia rubbed her nose, her sleepy lids still half closed.

I opened my mouth to apologize but stopped myself. I was tired of saying sorry to Amelia. I was done with a lot of things. Moving around her, I started for my bedroom.

"Devy, wait," she called to me, stunting my progression to my room. "I want to talk with you."

"Amelia, I'm kind of in a hurry."

"Please," she asked softly, misery in her gaze. I hated I didn't know if she was being real or playing the suffering sister. She was good at adapting, playing people. When it came to my sister, I never knew for sure.

Pivoting to face her, I folded my arms over my stomach. At first neither of us talked.

She released a sigh. "I see you're not going to make this easy for me."

I blinked back at her.

"Okay. Fine." She huffed. "I'm sorry, Dev. I hate this. I hate not being able to talk to my sister."

I shifted on my feet. I really didn't like fighting either. As much as we could drive each other crazy, she was still family.

"I'm still hurt, and I hate how you lied to me about Lincoln." She rubbed at her nails.

"I mean, I *really* liked him. And to know the whole time I was making a fool of myself and everyone was laughing at me… That was really cruel."

This was her apology? I sighed.

"I'm sorry I didn't tell you earlier. I thought I was saving your feelings. But I am not sorry for any of the rest." I held my ground. "And not for wanting to be with him." *And possibly falling in love with him.*

A streak of anger flared in Amelia's eyes, but she bit down on her lip, jerking her head to the side.

I pressed on before I lost courage. "You may think I'm being unkind to you, but I'm tired of walking on eggshells around your feelings all the time when you have no consideration of mine. You are so wrapped up in yourself, you never see me. You never notice or acknowledge what I do. I love you. That will never stop, but I won't cater to you. I won't keep you pacified. You have to grow up, Amelia."

My words were direct, but my voice was calm.

"In the not-too-distant future, I'm going to apply to community college. I will probably move into some inexpensive housing near the college and experience what it's like to be my age."

"What?" Her head jerked to me. "When did you decide this?"

"I've wanted to go to college way before Mom got sick. You should know this about me. It's no secret."

"You'll move out? But what about Mia? Me? I can't afford this place by myself."

"Then I guess you'll have to move into a place you can." I shrugged one shoulder. "Mel, I want a life. My own. Mom's illness took it from me, and she hated it. She made me promise the moment I could, I would run. Spread my wings. She'd want this for me. And she'd want you to be able to stand on your own. Because of me, you've never even bothered to ask Shithead to pay a cent for Mia. He needs to step up too, or you need to figure out if you even want him in Mia's life at all."

A tear trickled down Mel's cheek, her chest quaking.

"You are so much stronger than you think." I took a step to her, touching her arm. "I know you. You are a force. When you set your mind to something, you don't let up until you get it. I don't doubt you will be more than okay."

She sniffed, a few more tears cascading down.

I wrapped my arms around her neck, tugging her in tight. It was a beat before her limbs circled my waist, her sniffles turning to blubbers. We stood like that for a long time, hugging while she cried. I knew she was scared. For someone who jumped from trend to trend in a blink, she didn't like change. Not when it was forcing her to step up.

"I love you too, Dev. So much." Her tears abated, and she stepped back, wiping her face. "And I'm sorry for what I said to you the other night. I'm truly happy for you."

I snorted, tipping my head to the side.

"Okay, I am still working on that one. But I promise I will try. And I will try to be a better sister. Stand on my own more."

I had heard it a thousand times. I knew in the moment she really believed it, but the promise never came to fruition.

Let's hope this time it stuck.

The saloon was dark and locked up, but I knew Nat and Lincoln would be behind the doors, setting up and handling the business part of the job.

At the back entrance, I spotted Lincoln's Bronco in its usual place. For some reason it ticked me off. I was freaking out, calling and texting him all day, and he was at work, acting like everything was okay. Ignoring me. Why the hell hadn't he called me back? What part of *"Call me now! This is URGENT!"* didn't he get?

I marched to Lincoln's office.

"What the hell, Lincoln? Is there a reason you're ignoring my texts?" I swung the door so hard it bounced back off the wall. Three heads jerked to me.

Ah. Crap.

Two men I recognized as liquor distributors sat in chairs in front of Lincoln, anger oozing off them, their eyes narrowed on me.

"May I help you, Devon?" Lincoln raised his eyebrows, a smirk on his mouth.

"Oh. Wow. I am so sorry." Chagrin flamed my cheeks. "Forget you saw me…or heard me." I took a step back, gripping the doorknob.

Lincoln shoved back his chair, standing up.

"It's okay. I think we're done here." Humor vanished from his face, a darkness creeping in as he looked at the two men. "I think our business is finished."

The men stood, glaring at Lincoln, their demeanor threatening

"Last chance, Lincoln. You might come to regret this."

"Maybe, but I doubt it." He walked to the door, moving me out of the way and motioning for the men to exit.

They stalked out of the room, still scowling at the bar owner. Something about them ran a chill down my spine. Lincoln watched the men carefully until he saw them exit through the door, letting out a breath.

"What was that about?" My gaze darted to the closed door back to Lincoln.

"Shady assholes my brother started business with when he was running things. He owed them money." Lincoln dragged his hands over his face as if he had gotten no sleep either. "I decided it was time to end the connection. Have a fresh start for the bar. They were used to getting a take off the top of the liquor profits. They did not like that I took it away from them or my threat to make them regret it if they touch my brother."

"Will they come after you?"

"I've met some truly scary and dangerous men in my time. Those two aren't even close. They're shadows of formidable men, enough to keep my brother in their hip pocket." Lincoln leaned back on his heels, his gaze roaming over me with hunger. "But not me, Freckles. My connections are scarier than theirs."

Damn… Was it sick I found this so sexy?

"Now, what did you come storming into my office about?" He shut the door, taking a large step to me. "All fluffed up and hot as fuck." His body hit mine, his hands curling around my face.

I stared up at his eyes, lost in their heat. Shit, what was I here for?

"You need something?" He leaned into me, his voice husky, his mouth brushing mine.

Yeah, I needed something. Him. On the desk in about ten seconds. But my stupid conscience nagged and nipped at me, forcing me to push him back.

"This is serious." I took another step away, the heat of his body close and far too tempting. "Why haven't you called me back?"

"I turned off my phone when those two showed up." He tugged out his phone. "What did you need?"

"My uncle knows." I got to the point. "If he doesn't know who you are yet, he's going to figure it out soon."

Lincoln watched me for a few moments, my anxiety tripling at his strange calmness.

"I know."

"Wait. What?" I sputtered. "You know?"

"I've been running from police and keeping under the radar most of my life. You become extremely aware of your surroundings. You notice when a cop comes into the bar and asks about you. Or stares at you like he's seen a ghost. I didn't miss him at the memorial. Or in the rented car parked out front right now." *Duh. Of course he would know Gavin came in. Nat would've told him.*

"Seriously? He's out there right now?" I exclaimed, panic waving my arms around, my voice rising a few octaves. "What are you doing here? Why aren't you running? You better go!"

"Devon." Lincoln recaptured the space I put between us, his hands clutching my flaying arms, rubbing them softly. "Calm down."

"How can I calm down when my uncle, a sheriff who's been hunting you since you escaped from jail, is on a stakeout in front of the bar?" I wiggled from his soothing hands. "Why aren't you freaking out? How can be so relaxed about this?"

He pressed against me. "If I freak out or do anything out of the ordinary, like run, I'm the man he thinks I am. I will give him exactly what he wants."

Right. Only someone guilty would flee.

"He thinks he knows. He has no proof. I have to keep going about my day." He tipped my chin up, his breath curling down my breasts. "Find something to do to keep me busy." He drew my mouth to his.

"He will find proof eventually," I whispered against his lips before his parted mine, kissing me deeply. His fingers pressed into the back of my head, walking me backward to the desk until my ass hit the edge. "Especially if you comply with your brother and rob a jewelry store."

He jerked back, hand still in my hair, but his lids narrowed on me. "How do you know about that?"

"I followed you last night." I didn't shy away from the revelation.

"You did what?" His arms dropped, his forehead creasing with incense. "You spied on me?"

"Yes. I won't apologize for it. I went after you to warn you about my uncle. I overheard everything." I shook my head. "Aware of your surroundings, huh? You're lucky it was me who followed you. It could have been a cop overhearing you both."

"Lucky? Is that what you call it?" He scoured his head. "Jesus…what is it about you? From day one you slipped under my skin and totally fucked up my head. All sense goes out the window."

"I could say the same about you."

"That's the problem." He started to pace. "We make each other stupid. Reckless. Forgoing any logic. We are living in this fantasy where things will work out for us. That we are not unlucky. That *we* will work."

I wrenched back, the sting and truth of his words burrowing in.

Putting his hands on his hips, he exhaled, his shoulders sagging. "But you know what is even more absurd?" He caught my eyes, his voice softening. "I don't care."

"What do you mean?"

"I mean, I know I should have left by now, should already be in Cabo, drinking a beer with a new name and appearance." He glowered as if it were my fault. "I sat up all night, keys in my hand, ready to drive away…but I couldn't make myself go."

My mouth wouldn't move, didn't dare ask.

"Want to know why?" His hands glided up to the back of my head. "The same reason I didn't leave that bathroom when I should have. A girl with the cutest freckles, gorgeous blue eyes, and sexiest mouth I've ever seen has utterly bewitched me." He kissed my lips. "You have completely fucked me, Freckles."

I felt the same. And I didn't care. My mouth moved over his, our passion devouring us, my hands fumbling for his jeans.

"Stop." He groaned as if he couldn't believe he uttered the command, pulling back. "You make this so hard."

"What's so *hard*?" I pulled on his shirt with a smirk, bringing him back into me, tugging the zipper of his pants. "I can help with that." My lips claimed his with urgency. He gave in, his tongue curling around mine, exploring, until I heard him grunt, shoving back.

"I'm still leaving."

"What?" His statement kicked my head back. "You just said…"

"I was being selfish. My feelings for you clouded my judgment. Seeing you, knowing your uncle is right outside, I realized I have put you in an impossible situation. You're a good person, Devon. You live life on the right side of the law. I never have. I am a criminal. Escaped convict. I will not force you to decide between your belief system, your *own* family, and me."

"But what if I want—" He put a finger to my mouth, stopping the rest of my declaration.

"You're also logical. You know this can never work. I will always be on the run, one step ahead of the police. You don't belong in my world."

"You mean the world of a man who owns a bar, who's done nothing but the right thing for others, now lives completely above the law?"

"He's pretend."

"No." I rammed my palm onto his firm chest. "He's not. I work with him every day. There is nothing pretend about that guy. He's kind, smart, will do anything for those he cares about." I grasped his waist. "I don't think the other guy is real. He was a kid who had to learn to survive, grew up with unfortunate circumstances, and got caught."

"Devon." He shut his lids briefly. "It doesn't matter. Why I did it is not relevant. I'm guilty; it's all they care about."

The law cares nothing for personal feelings or motive. My uncle's statement came back into my head.

"I don't want you to go."

A pained smile twisted his face. "After our last job tonight, I'm leaving with my brother. I put the deed in Nat's name this morning. It's why I got rid of those assholes. I wanted her to be totally clean and legit."

"You're still going to rob the store?" My gut dropped to the floor. "But-but I thought those guys were why he needed money. Why do you need to do this?"

"Because we will need something to live on in Mexico."

"No." I shook my head. "Lincoln, please, don't do it."

"I warned you I wasn't the good guy."

"Everything you've done so far has been for own survival or your daughter's." I fisted my hands. "This is completely different, and you know it. Not only is my uncle up your ass, but if you do this, you prove you are nothing but a common criminal."

"Too late, Freckles." He pulled his cool façade back into place. "Once a felon, always a felon." Roughly, he kissed my forehead. Grabbing his backpack, he sauntered to the door, and opened it. "I know it's a lot for me to ask, but I hope you won't tell your uncle until I've left town." He clasped the doorframe, pain straining the corners of his eyes. "I will never forget you, Freckles. You are embedded far too deep under my skin. No one will come close."

Stupefied by his claim, my body and voice locked up, watching him walk out of the exit door and out of my life.

"No." Panic melted my muscles, and I darted to the back door, stumbling out into the bright day. His Bronco was already backing out. "Lincoln! Please...don't..." *Don't do this. Don't go. Don't leave me. I'm in love with you.* The cries burst inside my chest, not making it to my mouth, devastation engulfing me as I watched his Bronco drive away.

The first time he walked out of my life, I could do nothing to prevent his fate. This time?

You think I give up so easily? Screw you, Lincoln, I will save you...even if it's from yourself.

CHAPTER TWENTY-SIX

Nibbling on my nails, I transferred the ache in one side of my ass to the other cheek. The sun had long since disappeared behind the distant mountains, streaking shades of purples, oranges, and blues across the skyline. Now the bright stars above twinkled happily, opposing the grave feeling in my gut. I had been sitting here for hours and losing my mind with boredom and worry. Nat's radio was broken and the only CD she had was a *Sesame Street* sing-a-long. Nothing said dangerous-and-thrilling stakeout as "Rubber Ducky" and a car seat in the back.

When I had run into the bar after seeing Lincoln take off, Nat didn't even ask. She just set her car keys on the bar and said, "I'll take the bus home. Go get our guy, Devon." She slid the set to me. "Whatever he's about to do…stop him."

"I plan on it." I clutched the keys to my chest. "Thank you."

I ran for the car, realizing as I pulled out I had no idea where he'd go or what I'd do if I found him. I needed to stop him. Whatever it took.

I drove around searching for his car or any sign of him. He was like a ghost, fading to whispers in the wind, tendrils of smoke I saw from the corner of my eye but were gone the moment I looked over.

The one place I knew for certain where he'd end up was the store they would try to rob tonight. I headed there. Double-checking the street, I didn't see my uncle's car or a rental car, which suggested he had trailed after Lincoln instead of me. What was Lincoln thinking? Surely he knew my uncle would follow him. Nothing about this sat right with me. My gut screamed disaster was about to befall. I could lose him again.

"*Rubber ducky, you're the one…*" I unconsciously hummed along before crying out in frustration, stabbing the off button. Stakeouts weren't as exciting as movies led you to believe. My dad had dreaded them, saying, "You get ten seconds of thrill for eight hours of mind-numbing boredom."

An hour ago, I had eaten the bag of cheerios Nat hid in the glove compartment. I was out of fun. Sighing, I glanced around. The store had been closed for a while, but they probably wanted to make sure the town was asleep as well. Along with my ass.

Curbing the boredom, I kept trying to come up with a plan. Something I was usually good at. Tonight seemed to be an exception. Lincoln was stubborn and had such a strong responsibility to his brother. All I knew is I couldn't sit at home and allow this to happen…to let him go.

I was stubborn too.

Glancing at the clock, I saw the night had ticked into the witching hour. Nothing good happened at this time. The streets throbbed with an eerie silence, pregnant with sinful deeds.

I started to tap my head against the wheel, tension and tedium straining every nerve, when headlights flashed across the windshield. My head bolted up, my heart sticking in my throat. I ducked down in the seat. I recognized the car from the other night.

James.

The exceptional plan I was supposed to come up with while I waited still alluded me, nerves raking over my gut. It was beginning and I still didn't know how to convince Lincoln not do this.

James tucked the car into an abandoned lot across from me, well-guarded from view of the main street, the dark car almost vanishing into the shadows. It was a perfect spot, as it was close to jump into and escape, but it would not be noticed with the tall fence and bushes hiding it from witnesses. Because I had followed Lincoln here, I knew where to look.

I watched James get out of the car and pop the trunk. A putrid yellow-green streetlight glowed behind him, framing him in a dark outline. The car was a black Dodge Challenger, a muscle car with a supercharged engine. Perfect for a getaway…to run for the border. He grabbed items from the trunk, shoving one into the back of his jeans, and the other one in the front.

Guns.

He slammed the trunk, leaned against it, and lit up what looked similar to a cigarette, but knowing James the little I did, it was probably a joint. “Shit, James,” I grumbled. “Getting high before a robbery. Brilliant.”

Another forty minutes passed as I watched James pace and smoke until a motorcycle turned into the lot. I instantly recognized the man on it. Lincoln. Somewhere during the night, he switched his car for something he could hide or run from police a lot easier.

Slipping out my door, I slunk over to the same fence I’d hidden behind last time.

“What the fuck took you so long?” James hissed, walking over to his brother. “I’ve been waiting here like a sitting duck.”

“Listen, I told you I had a tail. I had to get rid of him. Change vehicles.” Lincoln kicked out the stand, flinging his leg over to stand up. “It took longer than I thought to lose him. So fuckin’ relax.”

“Relax?” James snorted. “I’ve been trying to for the last forty minutes.”

“Jesus, are you smoking pot before we do a job? Are you an idiot?”

Yes, yes, he is. Another reason you should turn around now.

“The fact you haven’t been in jail and I have baffles the hell out of me,” Lincoln snarled, tossing his backpack into the back of the Challenger.

“Because I don’t get caught.” James rounded on his brother. “Don’t get me wrong, you know how much I love some pussy, but I’m smart enough not to let it distract me from a drop and I run.”

“Shut the fuck up.” Lincoln loomed over his brother.

“Jesus, brother. You’re still so defensive about that girl. Was her pussy *that* tight and magical?”

In a blink, Lincoln grabbed James by the throat, slamming him against the car. "I told you *never* to speak of her like that again. Ever."

"Shit." James tried to shove him off but couldn't even lift Lincoln's pinkie. "Okay, sorry."

Lincoln shoved him again but let go and stepped back.

"I don't get you." James tugged at his collar. "You had sex with her *once*, *six* years ago or something. Why was she so special? I'd have thought the new little piece at work would've eliminated the fantasy girl from your head."

I exhaled with relief. I preferred James not knowing I was the same girl.

"Let's get this over with and get out of this town," Lincoln grumbled, stalking to the passenger door. "You brought everything?"

"Yep. Gloves, black sweater, mask, bolt cutters, smokers, blackout paint for cameras, alarm scrambler, and bags," James said as Lincoln gathered the items from the front seat, pulling on the black jersey.

"Okay, let's do this." James tugged a ski mask onto his head and grabbed the bolt cutters from Lincoln. "Soon we'll be lying on a beach, drinking endless beers delivered to us by gorgeous *señoritas* in bikinis."

Lincoln huffed, pulling on gloves, both of them creeping toward the edge of the lot.

Come on, Dev. Now or never. "No!" I didn't even think, leaping out in front of the pair. "Lincoln. Stop."

"Shit!" James pulled the pistol stashed in the back of his jeans and held it on me. Lincoln moved in front of me, his eyes wide.

"Holy hell, Devon," he growled, his arms outstretched, blocking me from James. "What the hell were you thinking jumping out?" He didn't stop to hear my answer. "What are you even doing here? You need to go now."

"I almost shot you, girl." James tucked the gun back.

"I'm not leaving." I held my chin up, ignoring James, my attention locked on Lincoln. "Not unless you come with me. Don't do this, Lincoln. Please."

His gaze moved over my face, the light illuminating his back-to-blue eyes.

"I can't." His features wrinkled in regret. "We already went through this."

"I don't care if we have to go through it a hundred more times. I will not stop until you are walking away with *me*."

"I made up my mind." He took a step closer.

"Me too." I moved in even closer, my hands on my hips. Neither of us backed away. The heat of our bodies warred for dominance with our heavy breaths.

His nose flared and his pupils dilated as they dipped down to my mouth. My breasts tightened in response, igniting the fire in my stomach. "Go. Home. Devon."

"You first."

"No."

"Yes."

"Okay." James held up hands between us. "We're wasting time. Holy shit, did I call it with this one. I knew she was clearly your type, brother." James pointed at me, then shook his head. "Not the point. Devon, is it? You need to go. And if you know what's good for you, never speak of this night or seeing us."

"You mean not tell the cops you're heading to Mexico?"

James swore, stomping his foot. "She knows? Just fucking great."

"Relax." Lincoln tilted his head. "She won't tell."

"I won't?" I went back to my standoff with Lincoln, the feel of him gazing at my frame sending heat throughout my body.

"No." His mouth moved around the word, a smirk lying beneath, his gaze ardent, blistering my heart.

We may have started our relationship in lust, but our connection went much deeper. I had no idea when it happened, but I knew this disemboweled sensation pitting my soul. I was in love with him. Deeply. And I was going to lose him. Again.

Tears stabbed the back of my lids. "Please don't do this," I whispered, choking on each word. I took a deep breath, letting the confession tumble out. "I love you."

Agony strained his face; his hands glided up my jaw, his forehead falling against mine. A sound similar to a hurt animal vibrated in the back of his throat, crushing me against him. His mouth was hot and passionate, burning what was left of me as his lips took mine.

He pulled away almost as quickly as he began. "It will always be you, Freckles," he muttered against my mouth. His lips pressed against my head, then he shoved away and walked around me, gutting me as if I were about to be thrown on the barbeque.

"Lincoln…" I swiveled around, blinking back tears, staring at the backs of the brothers walking away from me.

A chill ran up my spine. I sensed something in the atmosphere changing. I had sharp instincts. My father always said I'd make a great cop because of my attention to detail, logic, and need to help people.

My intuition knew what it was before I even heard a gun clicking. My world tipped, both slowing down and speeding up around us. My mouth dropped open to yell as a silhouette stepped out from behind the fence.

"No!" I cried at the same time my uncle's voice boomed through the night air, a gun pointed directly at the brothers: "FREEZE!"

James jolted back, sucking in a yelp of air, his arms going up. Lincoln stopped but didn't even flinch, an eerie calmness radiating off him. Composed. Detached. Not a single emotion filtered across his face, and this was the man who had been in jail, who had to survive under constant threat and soul-destroying situations.

"Devon, what the hell are you doing here? Move away!" My uncle waved his gun for me to step next to him. I didn't budge. "I was going to wait until you guys did something stupid, lock you up for good. But…" Uncle Gavin shot a deadly glare at me. I had changed his plans.

"Thought you lost me, didn't you?" Gavin scooted in, flickering his gun from one brother to another.

"Hoped was more like it." Lincoln's voice remained even.

"I've been looking for you for a long time," my uncle seethed. "And here I find you up to your old tricks. Not really a surprise. Stealing from others is the only thing you know how to do. But you involve my niece in your shit? You now made this personal." Gavin inched even closer, motioning his gun at both guys. "Turn around and put your hands up. Now!" His thumb tapped at the trigger. Lincoln looked at me, his expression almost apologetic before he turned around doing what my uncle asked. James twisted around as if he had all the time in the world, a smug smile on his mouth. Uncle Gavin reached out to pat down Lincoln first. "I've done a lot of research on you two. Born Finn and William Montgomery, to a wealthy Texas tycoon, Finnick William Montgomery, III."

My head jerked to James. Of course James wasn't his real name.

"Your mother was killed in a car accident when you were kids. That's when it started. At first just little burglaries. Stealing from your father's clients. Was this your way of getting Daddy's attention? But it backfired, huh? You became an embarrassment he couldn't cover up, so he kicked you out on the street. Disowned you. Got remarried and started a new family."

Lincoln told me a little about them being on the streets but not why. Shit. They were only teenagers, and their own father kicked them out? Bastard. How could you turn your back on your own children, young boys, who recently lost their mother, and throw them out on the street with nothing?

"Wow, that was a fun trip down memory lane." James shifted on his feet, his arms lowering slightly. "Is there a point?"

"You guys were smart. Moved around. Only took what you needed from wealthy houses, never used a weapon. Until the last time. Something changed. Your target. Your MO. Why?"

Uncle Gavin didn't know about Kessley or about James's need to continually raise the stakes.

My uncle sidestepped toward James, ready to pat him down. While he busied himself with relieving James of the gun tucked into the back of his pants, I saw James reach down his front.

"No!" I screamed, leaping forward, bulldozing into Lincoln's brother. We went crashing to the ground, taking Uncle Gavin with us. The revolver in James's hand hit the ground, skating across the concrete into a pole. In a frenzy of yelling and hands clamoring for the second weapon, Lincoln bolted over and plucked it from the cluster of groping fingers.

"Lincoln!" I shouted as my uncle bounced up, pointing his own gun at Lincoln's chest.

"Put it down, Finn. You do not want to do this."

"Don't call me that. That was *his* name," he snarled, still clutching the weapon. Getting back to my feet, I took a step toward him, but the slight shake of his head ended my advance.

"I know he beat both of you. Your records are full of hospital visits with mysterious bruises and broken bones," my uncle's voice softened.

"When a top client is also a well-respected doctor, funny how much you can spin child abuse as boys being boys." Lincoln's face darkened, his fingers strangling the handle of the gun. At the slight movement, my uncle's arm twitched.

"Put. Down. The. Gun," Gavin ordered, an edge to it. "*Last time* I will ask."

I feared that ever since my father was shot by a man who wouldn't put down his gun, my uncle's trigger finger was a bit more fidgety. Panic hammered my heart. In a split second and things could shift so easily. On either side of those two guns were the two men I loved most in the world.

"Lincoln…" I cautiously moved toward him. "Please do what he says."

"Devon! What are you doing? Stop!" Uncle Gavin cried out to me, terror coating his words. "Devon?"

I ignored him and stared into the blue eyes I loved, my hand gently wrapping around the hand with the gun. He didn't move or try to stop me as I peeled his fingers away, taking the gun in mine.

"Like I could ever fight you." A sardonic huff tipped his mouth. "You demand. I obey."

"If it were true, we'd be home…in bed, not here," I replied, only a few inches away from him. I tossed the gun to the side, the metal scraping as it hit the pavement. "Instead, I will be visiting you in prison." Grief bowed my mouth.

Lincoln's hand ran down one side of my head, cupping my face. "As long as they're conjugal." He smirked before his mouth slanted over mine, quickly kissing me.

My uncle gave a small gasp. When I turned around, his face was contorted in disappointment and shock.

"Uncle Gav…"

"You knew he was Finn?" Gavin cut me off, his feet taking him back a few steps. "This whole time?"

I couldn't find words to speak, just stared dumbly at my uncle.

"Holy shit. How long have you known?" He shook his head but lowered his gun. "I thought you knew him as Lincoln, and he was snowing you, pulling you into his world without your understanding …but…" He trailed off, his eyebrows pinching together. "I mean, you saw him for a brief second…"

Pain flinched in my expression.

"No…no… Were you in on it the whole time?" Uncle Gavin looked as if I had kicked his dog. The image he had of me fractured into a million pieces. "Were you helping him all along? Lying to me? To the entire station from the start?"

"No," Lincoln said from behind me. "She had no idea who I was until a few weeks ago, and that's because she has good instincts. She sensed something was off. Started to put the pieces together. She's completely innocent."

Not completely. He left out a big chunk of our meeting to protect me.

"But still…Devon." Uncle Gavin's eyes pleaded with sorrow. "You knew what the right thing to do was, and you protected him instead. Aided a *criminal*."

"I did." I didn't try to deny it. "But you don't know the whole truth. You asked what made their last job different? Why it changed?"

"Devon," Lincoln growled from behind me.

I didn't respond, needing my uncle to understand.

"You only see it changed, but you didn't look deeper, as Dad did. He always looked into why a behavior shifted." I stepped closer to my uncle. "Lincoln stole from the hospital because he had a little girl dying of leukemia."

My uncle's body went stiff.

"He was her match. Bone marrow which could possibly save her life, and he was in jail. The reason he was a model inmate was to get out quickly. But she was dying, and he chose to be with her on her last day, to kiss her for the last time before she died…"

"Nine months ago." My uncle finished for me, putting the puzzle together. His Adam's apple bobbed, his gaze darting around to all of us. "It's incredibly sad, and I'm sorry. But it doesn't take away the fact you have robbed people, broken out of jail. Held up the hospital at gunpoint."

The police had the gun, but I knew there were no prints on it. Because he was caught with it, they had linked them wrongfully to Lincoln.

"Wrong brother." I nodded to James. "He's the one who held up the gift shop. Lincoln was protecting him."

My uncle snapped to James, raising the gun again. In a blink, everything transformed, blurring the lines of comprehension.

James bolted forward, grabbed me, and yanked me in front of him. Tugging a blade out of his boot, he whipped the blade to my neck, its edge piercing the tender skin of my throat. I barely dared to breathe, terror turning my limbs to liquid.

"William, no!" Lincoln yelled, the gun I tossed to the side back in his hands. My uncle snapped his weapon between the two brothers, a wild look flicking his finger on the trigger, not knowing who was the real threat, forcing Lincoln to respond in kind.

A slip of the finger or an adrenaline surge could lead to catastrophe.

"You're fucking talking, brother? Spilling our secrets? Was she worth breaking our number-one code for?" He jerked me farther back, digging the knife in deeper.

"Will. Stop." Lincoln's blue eyes looked like ice. Cold. Ruthless.

"Oh, we dropping pretenses now, *Finn*? What happened to brothers above all? Brothers and thieves. Always first, always together," James sneered, his voice frantic, angry. Unstable. On more than pot. "How dumb did she make you? Now I get it. The same girl from before. She's a cop's niece. Fuck… Is her pussy that miraculous?"

"Drop the weapon and let her go. You're just making this worse." My uncle shuffled forward.

"No. You are," James growled. I gasped, the blade puncturing my skin, a groan of pain escaping my tongue as I felt tendrils of blood slide down my neck. "Back off!"

Gavin halted, his chest rising with anger and panting heavily, eyes creased with concern and fear for me.

Lincoln's shoulders rolled back, his jaw cracked down, rage flaring in the set of his face. "You hurt her, *brother*, and I. Will. Kill. You."

"Ooooohhh… *Damn, girl*, you must be special." James's sardonic laugh crackled in my ear, his grip cranking down on my arms. "This guy hasn't committed to any girl in his life. Fucked a shitload, but not one did he give a rat's ass about, even his baby's momma. But you see, this is where it becomes a problem for me and for him."

James shuffled me back toward the car. "He should know better than to let anyone in. Nothing good ever comes of it. Accidents happen."

"Don't," Lincoln snarled, his finger sliding over the trigger, countering our steps.

"You take one more step. You shoot me and I will make sure the knife slices her neck. Even think about shooting at the tires, and *I will kill her*." He was jittery and slurring.

James poised the blade at the side of my neck, cutting in deeper, showing he had no problem slicing it. I tried not to cry out, but tears of pain leaked down my face.

Lincoln stopped where he was. For a moment Lincoln's steel eyes met mine, terror drenching them, before they went back to his brother, where they filled with wrath. I could see the man who had to fight every day for life, to protect or kill if he had to. Palpable anger shook off his magnificent body like a wild animal trying to free itself from a trap. He'd had his own neck slit in jail. Would it be some sick poetic justice for the same to happen to me?

My body trembled with fright, pain and blood loss spinning my head, but I tried to keep breathing, keep thinking. Assess the situation. What would my dad do?

"*Shoot me*," I mouthed to both my uncle and Lincoln. Best way to render a hostage useless was to get them out of the way. Shoot them in the leg. I remember one time my dad told me he had to implement that strategy. Of course, the bank teller sued the police station, but she was alive.

The area around Lincoln's eyes tightened, a nerve in his jaw twitched. But Uncle Gavin's head shook, telling me there was no way in hell. My father had made the call, but it was something my uncle never liked. It wasn't by the book; it bent the rules.

"Well, this night didn't go as planned." James dragged us back more, the pain in my throat now throbbing, making me cringe. Tears mixed with the stream of sticky blood soaking into my shirt. "I am *not* going to jail. Remember, you are forcing me to do this. She could have stayed out of it. It's your fault she's involved." James opened the driver's side door. "Devon is coming with me. If you follow, it's your responsibility if she dies."

My gut told me I was going to die anyway. He would let me bleed out.

"Do. It." I choked in a hiss, trying to swallow over the hunk of metal cutting deeper into my throat. Soon he would have me in the car, and it would be too late.

My uncle and Lincoln exchanged a look, desperation crimping Gavin's features.

It happened in an instant. One beat of my heart.

Uncle Gavin darted out to one side, while Lincoln went to the other.

Boom!

A single shot exploded into the calm sky, the bullet cutting through its victim.

A scream tore through the night.

"Fuck!" James bellowed as I fell against him, tumbling onto the pavement with agony, grabbing at my leg. Pain detonated through my calf and up every nerve.

Holy shit…it hurt.

James screamed again before another gunshot rang in the air. Out of my periphery, I saw James drop next to me, groaning and shrieking.

"Devon!" Lincoln's voice boomed as he scrambled down next to me, pressing his hands to my face and searching my neck for the wound. "I'm so sorry."

"Hell." I gulped. "You really shot me."

"It's a graze; it didn't go in." He ripped off his jacket, peeled off his shirt, wadded it into a ball, and pressed it to my throat wrapping his coat around my leg. "And you told me to."

"This time you listened?" I struggled with every word, trying to talk through all the pain.

"I told you, Freckles. You demand. I obey." He tried to smirk but worry streaked his features.

"Dev? Are you all right?" Uncle Gavin came down on my other side, his gun still pointed on the moaning James behind me.

"Feel awesome," I wheezed. "See, my neck is smiling."

Both Gavin and Lincoln groaned.

"Tough crowd," I mumbled softly. I felt light headed and dizzy, the world going hazy at the edges. I was losing too much blood.

From the distance I heard sirens, like warning bells tinkling in my eardrums. Gavin's head bolted to pinpoint the alarms heading our way. He turned back, licking his lips.

"Get her out of here." He met Lincoln's gaze. "They don't have to know. My gun only fired on him. I can say he was alone in this."

"What?" Lincoln's mouth parted. "You'll lie?"

"Don't make me rethink this," Gavin growled, rubbing at his head. "She has no reason to be involved."

Between the blood loss and my shock at Uncle Gavin, I felt I might pass out. Mr. Black and White, By-the-Rules Cop, was bending them to the breaking point.

Lincoln looked as if he were about to say something else before my uncle yelled, "Go! They're almost here."

Lincoln didn't hesitate, scooping me up in his arms, his warm chest cocooning me. I shut my eyes. He hustled across the lot, digging the keys out of my jacket pocket. The click of doors unlocking set his course to Nat's car. Flinging the back door open, he lay me in the backseat, forcing a cry out of me. Fire also raged down my leg, and I struggled to take full breaths.

"Keep your forehead propped on the car seat; keep your chin down to your chest. It will slow the blood from your neck." Panic in his voice tangled with the encroaching sirens. "Jesus, Nat's gonna love blood all over her backseat."

Doors slammed and I felt the motion of the car, but the hazy world turned into darkness, consciousness seeping from me with every breath.

"Don't you give up on me, Freckles. Stay awake. I *will not* lose you. Fight for me, Dev."

I tried, but his rough, sexy voice rumbled in my ear like a lullaby, compelling me to slip into the blackness.

CHAPTER TWENTY-SEVEN

Sunlight trickled through my lashes, and I pressed them together, rejecting the obscene light. The brightness flipped my peaceful oblivion into searing consciousness. A groan clogged my throat but didn't make it past my lips. Every muscle and bone in my body ached as if I had been through a wringer.

My lids flickered open, the impulse to vomit climbing up each rib. I struggled to swallow, my throat raw and sore, and grasped at a bandage wrapped tightly around my neck. With that, memories of last night rushed into my head. The last thing I remember was passing out in Nat's car.

I lay on my back. I carefully lifted my head, staring down at soft gray pillows and sheets, a large window to my right.

Not my room.

I blinked until my sight cleared enough to see the view outside the unadorned windows. The street below was familiar. A row of brick buildings, filled with shops and cafes, barrels of flowers dotting down the sidewalk. I saw it almost every day. It was the same view from the saloon but on the second story.

Twisting slowly around, I gripped the bed, vomit burping up my esophagus; the pain in my calf and my neck spinning my head. I'd been stripped of the bloody clothes I had been dressed in, wearing my underwear and a large navy T-shirt which wasn't mine but smelled similar to the whiskey he drank. It was almost as good as having his arms wrapped around me.

I knew exactly where I was. Everything smelled and looked like Lincoln.

I took in the open-concept loft, which stretched the same length as the bar below. A minimalist kitchen ran against the back wall, alongside doors that were likely an entrance, a closet, and bathroom. The living space took up the middle of the room and held a TV, a driftwood coffee table, and a leather sofa facing out toward the curved windows. The bedroom space stood on the other side of the room, rugs separating every space into its own. He had minimal decorations, but a few cool black-and-white photos hung on the brick walls. He used the pipes to hang things on and wooden boxes to store clothes and books.

So this was where he lived…right above my head the whole time. Easy to get in and out. Now I knew why it seemed like he never left the bar and went home. He was already home. How did I not know this? It was as if he were hiding in plain sight.

The sound of a doorknob had me moving my head around. Lincoln strolled out of the bathroom, steam billowing behind him, a towel wrapped around his waist as he rubbed his head with a smaller one.

Despite my body wracked with pain and on the verge of throwing up, I still gaped at his build, heat scurrying down my veins. He had an incredible physique. I had felt most of it, but never really taken a moment to appreciate the work of art that now stood before me. We were always half dressed and too desperate for each other to take our time and explore.

Both arms and one side of his neck were decorated with tattoos; the rest of him was a canvas waiting to be explored.

Still damp from the shower, his bare chest rippled with water, which trailed down his twelve-plus pack, disappearing along the deep V-lines starting right at the towel. I wanted to rip the towel off and lick every droplet of water off him. Okay, maybe not right this second when I still was debating if I was going to throw up or pass out again, but really, really soon. Perhaps in five minutes.

He tossed the extra towel into a basket and glanced over to me. His eyes widened. "Hey." He moved to me, holding up his hand when he saw my lips part to respond. "Don't talk. Don't strain the skin around your neck." He sat down on the bed, reaching up and brushing my knotted hair away from the bandage as he softly inspected it. "The cut was superficial, but he still nicked a few nerves. It will take a few weeks to fully heal. Same with your leg."

I stared at him, his touch ebbing the nausea, but my heart thumped at his nearness, at the musky smell of his damp skin.

"I am so sorry, Dev." His thumb rubbed my jaw, his face and throat tight as he swallowed. "My brother has always been driven by emotions, not logic, especially when he's jacked up on something, but I never thought him capable of hurting anyone. Not after the years of abuse we took from our own father."

Yeah, well, sometimes the precise thing you hate about someone is because you're so much alike.

"The moment he grabbed you?" Lincoln's eyes flicked to the far wall. "Nothing else mattered. Not going to jail, the bar, not even my brother. You. That was it. And the idea of losing you?" He let his head fall forward, his elbows on his legs, blowing out deeply.

My fingers brushed his back, sliding over his skin. His head jerked up, but he didn't look at me.

"Everything important came slamming in, and all the bullshit excuses I used to keep you away or protect my brother vanished. If I could bring my little girl back, I would, in a heartbeat, but I don't regret you, Dev. Not for a second. Both of you carved into my soul, called it home. Only one couldn't stay as long as I wanted." He turned to look at me, his voice even, but his eyes were soft. "Maybe you will."

"Fuck. Yes." My gravelly voice rolled out like sandpaper, making him burst out laughing.

He leaned forward, gently cupping my head. "I'll hold you to it…in all ways that sentence could mean."

I'd be totally okay with it…later. As if on cue, a spasm jerked the muscles in my leg, and a gurgling whine escaped my throat.

"Here." He reached into a nightstand drawer, pulling out a syringe and bottle. "Swallowing is probably painful, so this will ease your pain. Relax your muscles."

I pulled back, glaring at the needle.

"It's not anything bad. The doctor left it to ease your discomfort."

"Doc-tor?" I grunted.

"Couldn't take you to a hospital. Not if we wanted to stay off the record and keep up the pretense we were never there."

Right.

Lincoln tapped his nail on the syringe, getting the air out, then turning toward me, rubbing a sterile pad on my thigh, his touch gentle on my skin, his eyes finding mine. This would have been so sexy and hot if I wasn't about to roll in a ball and cry. He jabbed the needle in quickly, and I grabbed his shoulder, sucking in through my nose.

"There. Should kick in soon." He used the end of his towel to dab at the speck of blood the needle left. "Jail does have some perks, giving you connections to people who don't mind working under the radar. Doc was released four months before I left, wrongfully accused because the color of his skin. He had been a medic in the army. Patched me up more times than I care to remember the first couple of years. I don't know why he did it. Said he saw something in me. He was the closest I came to anyone. Good man. He was the only one I thought of when I brought you back here. No questions asked, he came."

We were quiet for a moment, so many issues from the night before stirring in my head. What happened to my uncle? Or James? What was going to happen to Lincoln? Had he spoken to Gavin? Was my sister freaking out? Was the place about to be stormed with police?

"Uncle?" I finally croaked.

"Haven't heard anything from him, but he wouldn't contact me. He'd keep all phone records clear of my name. I have no idea what is going on. It's driving me crazy. I tried to sleep after Doc left, but all I could do was either pace or watch you to make sure you were still breathing." He rubbed at his face. "I did text your sister from your phone, letting her know you wouldn't be coming home." A smirk lit his eyes. "I *might* have suggested you were staying with me for a couple of days…just can't get enough." He winked. "Which is totally true. It just sucks we're not doing what she thinks we are."

I smiled. A text like that would make Amelia crazy. But it was better than her staying up all night wondering where I was and calling the cops. I'd deal with her wrath later. I'd do anything for him.

Tilting in, I brushed my lips over his temple. The painkiller swept through me like velvet over skin, stealing away the hurt, and pulling me back toward sleep. We had so much we needed to go over, to talk about. I fought against the pull of the drug.

"Sleep." His gaze tracked mine, lacing his fingers through a few strands of hair. "You need to heal. We'll figure everything out, I promise."

I knew he needed rest as much as I did. Intertwining our fingers, I carefully turned on my side, pulling him in behind me. He didn't resist, scooting in and spooning against me. The towel rubbed the back of my bare thighs, his warm body luring me into obscurity.

"Sure…my dick pressed against your almost naked ass is totally going to let me sleep," he muttered in my ear. I smiled, taking his hand and threading it up the T-shirt, where I laid it on my bare breast. Lincoln snorted, kissing the back of my head, leaving his hand there. "Yeah, much better, Freckles. Now go to sleep."

With his warmth draping over me and the pain floating away, I sighed, feeling safe and happy. All the bad disappeared as sleep embraced me.

卌 卌 |||| 卌 卌 |||| 卌 卌 ||||

I drifted in and out of consciousness, with vague awareness of night and day. Lincoln was either cleaning my wounds or injecting me with painkillers when my whimpers woke me up. The ache running up my leg kept waking me all night. The pulse of agony grew louder until it stirred me from my slumber. Then my neck joined the agony party the instant I was awake. Nausea kept my appetite at bay, though he tried to get some lukewarm broth down my throat. Three spoonfuls felt like eating acid, and I'd roll back over and go back to sleep. I knew it would take more than a day or two to feel better, and if I slept right through it, I'd be fine with that.

When I next awoke, deep purple brushed the sky, turning black at the edges. The night encroaching on the room let me know another day was about to pass. My second here. Amelia had to be pissed by now. Besides my time with Uncle Gavin, I had never stayed away from home this long.

My brain buzzed with all that could have happened while I slept, so I forced my eyes stay to open, lifting my head to the dimly lit, quiet room. The only sounds were the distant buzz of activity in the bar below me.

Lincoln sat by the bed in a chair he pulled over from the living room. His fingers pinched the space between his eyes, his eyes pressed shut. A table next to him was stacked with bandages, cotton swabs, rubbing alcohol, and tape. I took a moment to stare at him. Unfortunately, my nurse was fully dressed in jeans and a T-shirt, but he was still so damn sexy.

"In *my* nurse fantasy…you're naked," my raspy voice cut through the silence. He jerked his head up and sprang out of the chair to me.

"Hey," he said softly. "How are you feeling?"

"Like I got shot." My voice barely rose above a whisper. "And had my throat sliced."

He sat on the bed next to me, face scrunched with worry.

"I'll be fine." I grabbed his hand. "If anything…" I swallowed with a flinch. "You should enjoy I can't yell at you now."

A wry grin lifted the side of his mouth. "But I like when you yell at me. It's fuckin' hot." He leaned his forehead against mine, his mouth lightly brushing mine.

A knock on the door lurched us both back. Lincoln jumped to his feet, his chest widening with defense. "No one knows I live here except Doc." He pressed his finger to his lips as he slunk toward the metal door.

Stabs of pain danced up my leg as I slid out of bed. I leaned heavily on my good leg. I didn't want to feel vulnerable lying in bed, no matter who was on the other side of the door.

Lincoln pressed his ear against the door, listening, his arm flexing with the tight grip of his hand on the doorknob.

"Open up." A man's low voice came through. "It's me."

"Un-cle Gav-in?" I croaked, the familiarity of his voice making me want to run to him.

Lincoln didn't look so sure but unlocked the latch and slid the rolling door open enough to peek out. His shoulders lowered, and he tugged the door all the way open, revealing my uncle on the other side.

He stepped in, then Lincoln rolled it closed behind him.

"How the hell did…?"

Uncle Gavin peered over at Lincoln, still venturing deeper into the loft. "I'm really good at my job."

Gavin's head whipped back, finding me, his brown eyes softening. "Devon…" He rushed to me, folding me gently in his arms. "Thank god you're okay. I've been so worried about you." He squeezed me to him, his voice plump with emotion. "I about lost my mind not being able to see you."

His hold was so familiar, so comforting, making me feel I was a little girl again. I dug my head into his chest, which had been a lot easier when I was younger and shorter.

"How are you?" He pulled back, his worry ran over my leg and throat.

"I'm okay," I tried to reassure him, but my raspy voice made him flinch. "Lincoln is taking really good care of me. I promise."

Gavin huffed, glowering at Lincoln, but nodded. "I figured he would."

Lincoln still stood by the door, his arms folded, watching the scene before him unfold with no reaction.

"But he is part of the reason you're hurt." Gavin placed his fist on his chest. "My entire world stopped when I saw you fall, but it also made me realize how unbelievably amazing and strong you are. You are so similar to your father. You took a bullet, Devon."

"I asked you guys to do it," I rasped. "It was the only way to get me away from James. It really is just a graze. I'll heal quickly." But hell, a graze of a bullet was like a paper cut, hurting worse than a deeper wound.

"He's certainly the reason you're in this mess." Uncle Gavin sat back to take in both Lincoln and me.

Lincoln didn't react, his attention shifting to me. "Sit down, Devon."

I realized my body was shaking with lack of energy, the little movements clenching all my muscles.

Uncle Gavin leaped into action, helping me back to the bed. I hated being weak, but I also had to give my body a break. It had gone through a traumatic experience and needed time to heal.

Once I was settled, Gavin straightened up, and the air in the room seemed to grow thick and still.

"It's been a hectic forty-eight hours, and I'm sorry it took me so long to get here." Gavin shoved his hands into his jeans, and his head snapped to the windows. "Being out of my jurisdiction took a lot more explanation and paperwork… Do you have curtains?" He motioned to the three huge arched windows across the room.

"They have a special coating on them…they look dark from the outside. No one can see in." Lincoln kept to his spot at the door. On guard. It was probably why I never considered anyone lived up here. It always looked dark and unused from the outside.

Gavin snorted, wagging his head. "Conduct of a true criminal."

I sighed, giving my uncle a look. He shifted his eyes and feet but looked unremorseful.

"My brother?" Lincoln's voice sliced in.

"He's in jail for attempted robbery and resisting arrest." Gavin stared straight at Lincoln. "Also, the hospital robbery case is being reopened as a possible link to him. It's the reason I was there the night he was caught. I was following him after a random sighting while in town for my sister-in-law's funeral."

Lincoln dropped his gaze. No one else would see it, but I noticed the slight change in him. No matter how much James/William deserved it, he was still his brother. It wasn't natural for people like Lincoln and me not to protect our siblings, even if it meant putting ourselves on the chopping block.

"As far as anyone knows, he was alone, high on coke and marijuana, and foolishly thinking he could rob a gold and silver store on his own." Uncle Gavin pulled his palms from his pockets, tugging on the bottom of his well-worn black leather jacket. My dad gave it to him the day he graduated from the police academy. "Being a captain helps, but I still have a lot to explain to the people above me. It's not something I'm proud of, but because of my rank and untarnished history, they tend to ask me few questions."

I felt a moment of guilt because my uncle, who always followed every rule by the book, was lying his ass off to his own people.

"Thank you," I whispered to him, pressing my hand to my chest.

He frowned and shifted around uncomfortably. "I always saw myself a certain way. I thought I knew how I would react in every situation…but when I saw a knife pressed to your throat?" Gavin took a step to me and stopped, staring at the ground. "I stopped breathing. Thinking. All the years of training went out the window, and in that second, when he sliced the blade into your neck, there wasn't anything I wouldn't do to save you. No law I wouldn't break, no person I wouldn't kill, to protect my family."

The lump expanded in my throat, pressing against the bandages holding me together.

"You, Amelia, Mia… You are my family. And until that moment, I didn't realize the lengths I would go too to protect all of you."

Silence descended in the moment and my uncle quickly shook himself, like it was as much emotion as he could stand, and lifted his chin to Lincoln. "I'm figuring you're smarter than this, but I will warn you again: do not attempt to visit or contact your brother. Cut all ties to him."

"Or?" Lincoln's head tipped to the side.

"As far as the station is concerned, Finn Montgomery is long gone, maybe in Mexico, and there is a recent *rumor* he might have gotten killed on a bad drug run there."

"Unlucky for Finn," Lincoln replied evenly, his attention fixed on my uncle.

"Yes, it is." Gavin didn't back down from his stare, both in a battle for dominance. "It would be stupid of him to show up and become a target again. Especially when he is better off dead."

I couldn't believe what I was hearing. Letting Lincoln slip away the other night to get me to safety was one thing, but to let an escaped convict go when he had him went against everything my uncle believed in. Some things weren't black and white. Life was gray.

"Will I be constantly looking over my shoulder?" Lincoln took one step closer.

A humorless sneer hinted on my uncle's mouth. "My niece loves you; it was easy to see it the other night. And any man who doesn't love and respect her the same *should* be looking over his shoulder. If he doesn't care enough, it's not the law he has to worry about."

"That I can respect." Lincoln's smile was genuine. "Believe me, you should have no fear of that."

"Good." My uncle dipped his head sharply. "No one will miss a guy who's already dead."

Lincoln barked out a laugh and rubbed his scruffy chin, the tension between them receding slightly.

"I'll be heading out tomorrow." Uncle Gavin turned to me, his demeanor softening as he moved closer to me. "I need to get back. If anything, Lucy is ready to kill me. Max is chewing on anything he finds. And the station does need me back."

I smiled, loving that Lucy was the first thing he thought about getting back to. I wondered if she was the reason my uncle had begun to see some rules were worth bending.

"I've tried to keep your sister from coming down here, but you know Amelia. She's not one to be pacified for long. You need to go home soon."

"But—" I motioned to my neck and leg.

"You can't keep protecting her from life, Dev. It's not your job. It's not helping her. Though, I would leave out anything about him." He tipped his head, still glowering at Lincoln. "Your sister is not known for keeping secrets, but you can't hide here for the next month. You might always have scars." He flinched at the last, wanting to undo that whole night.

He was right; I couldn't hide out forever, and I missed my niece and sister. Now was the time to treat Amelia as if she were an adult, otherwise neither of us would change. She would get a very loose version of the truth though, to protect Lincoln.

Uncle Gavin leaned over, kissing my head, quietly mumbling to me, "I love you so much."

"I love you too."

"I trust you, Devon. You have always made smart choices, and I'm going to take a huge leap here and trust you on this…" His eyes flicked in Lincoln's direction. "But know your safety and happiness come first. If it ever changes, call me. I'll be here in a second." He waited for me to nod, then kissed my forehead again and stood up, moving to the door. "I'll see you soon, okay?"

"Okay." My eyes filled with tears.

He strolled up to Lincoln, stopping at his side. "I do find one thing incredibly peculiar. What are the odds that once again your path crossed with my niece's?"

"Luck."

Gavin smirked, patting his shoulder.

"Just remember, one step out of line, a single toe dipping into your old life and I will not hesitate." The threat was unmistakable, his face hard again. "There will never be a day you can relax or stop looking over your shoulder, because I will always be watching you." Gavin smacked his palm onto his arm again, causing Lincoln to bristle, but he didn't move. Gavin glanced back at me. "Especially when you have one of the most precious things in the world to me. You got it?"

"Yeah." Lincoln didn't drop his gaze, both of them assessing the truth from the other.

"Okay." Uncle Gavin finally nodded and stepped past him. "I'll call you in a few days, Dev." He waved before sliding the door open and gliding out like a ghost. Not even his footfall could be heard going down the stairs.

Lincoln relocked the door, a heavy sigh falling from his mouth.

I stared at his back as he leaned his head onto the door, giving him a moment to regroup. I had slept through most of it, but he had likely spent the past forty-eight hours on eggshells, not knowing what happened to his brother or whether the cops were about to break down the door and drag him back to jail. It had to take a toll. He inhaled and exhaled a few times before he turned around, rubbing his head.

"You okay?" My fingers knotted into the fabric of the sheets.

A laugh barked out of him, a dazed expression sliding over his face. "Am I okay?" He chuckled, taking steps toward the bed. "I've been running from the law since I was ten, always wishing to get out, have a clean slate. But I never could, which was as much my fault as my brother's. After I escaped, I stood at my daughter's grave and promised I'd do better, be better, even if she wasn't here. I saw this place as a fresh start…to be someone else. But my brother quickly dragged me back under, making me forget my promise. You were another reminder of the life I wanted…" Lincoln stopped at the edge of the bed. "And now I have it." He gazed at me with such tenderness I wanted to hold him.

"Do I feel awful because I'm basically abandoning my brother? Yes. No one knows what we went through together, the bond it created, how it felt to be disowned by our father, to live on the streets. We only had each other. But I know my brother… When I was in jail, he didn't visit me once. And if roles were reversed now, he'd already be in Mexico. It still breaks me I have to turn my back on him. But for once I'm going to do something for me. I may not deserve it, but I don't give a shit. I want this life. I want you in it."

My lungs gulped in oxygen, staring up at him. Despite heartache, loss, tragedy, and other brutalities which had been handed to him, somehow this amazing man came out of it.

"I want you in mine too," I responded.

He sat down on the bed, moving to me.

"Though, I'll forever have a cop up my ass," he mumbled, dipping his lips to mine. "And let me say, between your uncle and your sister, holidays are going to be *so much fun*."

"Drinking's the only way I get through." My heart soared at the realization he'd already put himself into my family and my future.

"Yeah, your uncle would love that. An inebriated ex-con falling into the Christmas tree."

"Better be on your best behavior then." I bit back my laugh, knowing it would hurt and brushed my mouth against his.

"That's not how you want me."

"True."

His lips opened mine, kissing me gently, but it barely took a moment before passion built, and behind it, came the pain.

"Shit. Sorry." His fingers ran through my hair, trailing gently to the wound. "This is going to be a dreadfully long week, waiting for you to heal. Not being able to touch you?" He kissed my jaw, trailing over my lips to the other side. "Torture."

I could work around the leg, but you don't realize how much your neck is involved in the business of passion. Talking. Kissing…crying out in ecstasy.

Damn it. This *was* going to be an awfully long week. "Probably better if I go home."

Lincoln softly kissed me, cupping my face. "Tomorrow or maybe the day after."

I didn't really want to go, but I knew I had to soon. First the temptation of being this close to Lincoln would kill me and then Amelia would.

"I like having you in my bed." He grinned against my mouth, then pulled back. "But we have time to figure things out. Though I'd love you here, I think it's time we both figure out what we really want."

Grief and guilt would always haunt us, but for the first time in a long time, both of us were free. Our lives ahead of us to choose. No one held us back.

"What do you want, Freckles?" He smiled. "Besides me; that's a given."

"Obviously." I matched his smile. I wanted to go to college, but I couldn't enroll until the fall semester. I knew what I wanted, the first thing on my list. "Let's fly away."

"Fly away? Where?"

"Anywhere." I sighed dreamily and whispered, "South America, Australia, Africa… I don't care as long as it needs a passport and you are next to me."

"You know getting a passport means a background check."

"Shit. I hadn't thought of that." There was no way a man who came out of nowhere less than a year ago could get a passport. "It's a pipe dream anyway. I don't have any money to travel. Maybe a short road trip."

"Fuck that." Tugging on my hair, he leaned into me again. "We're going abroad. Whatever it takes."

"But—"

"Don't worry, Freckles, I know someone. Lincoln Kessler will get a passport."

"Already dipping your toes in, huh?"

"For you to travel? Do something that makes you happy? I will jump in with my whole body."

Damn, I loved this man. I took a deep breath, exhausted.

"Rest. We'll talk more about it later." He fluffed up my pillow, signaling me to lie down. "I'm not going anywhere."

I snuggled into the bed, his body curling around mine. "That's all I really want."

"Then call yourself lucky."

I cuddled deeper against him, his arm wrapping around me like a blanket. “I do…now.”

CHAPTER TWENTY-EIGHT

The sun shone bright and the air crisp as I entered through the back door of the saloon into the unlit hallway. A few of the kitchen staff were here. I was an hour early for work but longed for quiet and a place to concentrate. It was Amelia's day off, and I knew she would be on me the moment I went home. I wanted to be alone.

It had been two weeks since the incident, and I was still slowly healing. Frankly, it felt like forever, but I had to be patient with the fragile tissue in my calf and my throat. Similar to Lincoln, a scar marked my neck, a forever reminder of what we went through. It didn't bother me. It meant I'd survived. Had the chance to love Lincoln. Maybe I'd get a little tattoo there too.

A week earlier I returned to work, doing office work for Lincoln to keep off my leg. Tonight was my first shift back as server, an easy Wednesday night, starting slow. Even though Lincoln had been generous with my pay as bookkeeper, I was eager to get back to serving on the floor with Nat. I missed being around people, seeing regulars like Rick and Kyle, and the tips.

Also, I was going crazy from spending time at home. I needed to get out so I wasn't in jail next for homicide. Amelia's reaction to the attack bordered on neurotic. After our fight, she tried a little too hard to play the part of "I'm the older, responsible sister and I'll take care of you" and true to Amelia, she went way too far. She was driving me crazy. Hovering, texts, calls. And no shocker, she got upset every time I spent the night with Lincoln, which wasn't nearly as many as I wanted. She said it was because she missed me, but I didn't believe it entirely. She was still miffed about Lincoln not choosing her. But she'd set herself another challenge: Miguel. She claimed he was the one she liked the whole time.

Right.

When I told her what happened that night, I stuck mainly to the truth, with a few alterations. I claimed Lincoln and me were targets in a robbery gone wrong, and he saved my life and rescued me from the assailant—all true. I reassured her the robber was now behind bars and, because of his priors, it didn't look as if he'd be getting out soon. She didn't need to know about anything else.

Settling behind Lincoln's desk now, I pulled a few items from my bag, nervous and excited bubbles dancing in my stomach. Of course, I didn't regret having taken care of my mom; she had been everything to me and I missed her terribly. But I knew she'd want me to move forward, start the next chapter in my life.

Central New Mexico Community College (CNM) catalogs lay before me, a bookmark already in the section which thumped nervous energy down my legs. It had been nagging at me for weeks, something was always there, but I never really considered, which was odd given my family.

Flipping open the page, I stared at the bold header, sucking in a breath.

Criminal Justice

You are so similar to your father. Uncle Gavin's words had stuck with me, rolling over and over in my head until they switched on a light. Today when I grabbed the catalog from the college office and opened the page, I knew. It was what I wanted to do.

"Well, hello." Lincoln's deep timbre vibrated from the doorway, and my thighs trembled. I snapped up to gaze at him leaning against the doorframe, his arms folded, watching me. Every freaking time that man stepped in the room or his voice found me, my entire body reacted viscerally.

Need. Love. Lust. Desire. Yearning.

We had been unable to act on most of it. We had fooled around a little, but he was set on my recovery. Especially my neck. Even kissing was painful at times, but every day I felt better and staying away from him was becoming more excruciating than the wounds. Looking at him now made it abundantly clear.

His arms and shoulders stretched out the black T-shirt fabric perfectly. His dark jeans hung from his hips, and even though I couldn't see it, I know they curved flawlessly over his taut ass. His blue eyes glistened as he lifted an eyebrow. "You look good behind my desk, but I still think I prefer you on it. Naked."

"Don't tease unless you're ready to act on those

words." I glared at him, feeling his words slink down my spine, igniting my hormones into a bonfire.

"You don't think I can back it up?" He pushed off the door with a cocky grin, strolling toward me.

"All talk..." I stared down at the booklet pretending to be deeply engaged, but my mind wasn't reading a word, sensing the heat of his body climb over me as he leaned over.

"Is that so?" He brushed my hair to one side, his lips touching my neck skating over the skin, running shivers up the back of my head.

"Mm-hmm." I tried to pretend his mouth moving behind my ear and his teeth nipping at my sensitive spot weren't making breathing difficulty. His snicker told me I was failing miserably.

He pulled back, his head jerking above my shoulder. "What's this?" His gaze was locked on the open page, his forehead creased.

"Uh." Shit. I hadn't told him what had been batting around in my head because I had just realized it myself.

"Criminal justice?" His regard flashed from the page to me, then back. "You're joking, right?"

"Actually…" I squirmed in my seat. "It's been something I've been thinking about a lot lately."

"Becoming a cop?" A strange laugh bowled from his chest. "Seriously? You do realize you are dating a criminal?"

I chuckled, nodding.

A sharp laugh reverberated off the walls. "Shit…the irony of this."

It was not lost on me either.

He rubbed his mouth, mirth shaking his shoulders. "Jesus, Freckles. We do like walking a dangerous line, don't we?" Humor left his gaze, replaced by smoldering heat. "Am I going to have another cop on my ass?"

I stood, pushing back the chair, pressing my frame into his. "On your ass, your chest, your arms, and especially this." I reached out and rubbed him through his jeans, his length already straining the fabric. "And I thought riding the line of danger was where you liked me."

Lincoln growled deeply, his fingers digging into my hips as he slung me up on his desk, stepping between my legs. "I like it when you're riding me."

An inferno of need scorched my insides, pulling him to me. We seemed to have hit the breaking point where the craving won out.

I was healed enough.

Our mouths collided in an explosion of desire, teeth, hands, and lips, all hungry with desperation. That he had no problem with me following my dreams, even if they were in direct contrast to who he was, made me yearn for him more. I felt alive, as if my life had finally begun.

For all I knew, I would follow in my grandmother's and mother's footsteps. Alzheimer's tended to run in families, and there was a chance it was already inside me, waiting to steal me of my life. I had to live it to the fullest and not apologize. Lincoln was a huge part of this. And right now, I would take what I wanted.

Our frantic breaths turned to low moans as our hands and mouths explored each other, my fingers trying to relieve him of some of his clothes.

"Oh shit! Sorry," Nat's voice exclaimed from the doorway. Lincoln and I broke away from each other, but neither of us moved. I glanced over my shoulder to Nat half turned to leave, her eyes darting around everywhere but on us. We weren't hiding we were together, but we also didn't go out of our way to tell anyone either. Nat knew something had been going on with us for a long time but hadn't seen proof. Until now. "You *did* leave the door open."

"What'd you need, Nat?" Lincoln didn't sound fazed she had walked in on us. We still had our clothes on at least.

"Just giving you the inventory list. We're running low on tequila." She held out a piece of paper.

"Oh, that's not okay." I shook my head, my eyes wide with mock horror. When Nat learned Lincoln would not be leaving town as planned, she was adamant he put the bar back in his name. Lincoln compromised and made her co-owner, saying it was better to have one owner here at all times because he planned to take a lot more time off.

We were taking a trip to South America next month. Traveling through parts of Peru, Chile, and Argentina. When Uncle Gavin asked how Lincoln got a passport, I just smiled. He stomped out of the room saying he didn't want to know anything. I knew it was hard for him to ignore Lincoln was an ex-con, but he tried to keep Finn and Lincoln separate.

We found the cheapest flight possible, with a ridiculous number of layovers, and we would be staying in dirt-cheap Airbnbs, but we were going. I could barely contain my excitement. At one time moving to Albuquerque had felt huge, now I was ready to soar,

Lincoln and I discovering the world, experiencing different cultures, tasting strange foods.

And a lot of time to explore each other.

Then I'd come home and start classes....in criminal justice.

With a sigh only I could hear, Lincoln stepped away and took the list from Nat. "Thanks."

"No problem." She winked at me, getting over her shock at catching us. "Desk...nice."

"Bye, Nat." Lincoln waved her back toward the front.

"Remember these walls are thin," she sang as she made her way back to the front of the bar.

"Actually, I had this room soundproofed." Lincoln set the list on his desk, coming back around to me, cupping my face. "But I don't want any interruptions."

His blue eyes blazed with implication. Lincoln had prepared an explanation for when people noticed they were no longer brown. He said he was trying out colored contacts. People like Miguel and Julie totally bought it, but Nat was smarter. Her eyebrow curved up with "yeah, sure" expression, but she didn't ask. I knew she never would say anything. She understood when to leave things alone.

Lincoln grabbed my hand tugging me off the desk. "I know of this place really close by where we could go. Finish what we started."

"Oh really? Close, huh?"

"Really close."

"I better not. I have to work soon, and my boss is a real asshole about me being on time."

"He sounds like he needs to get laid." Lincoln smirked, tugging me out of the office.

"Do you think it would help him? I don't know; I think he's just a dick."

Lincoln snorted, leading me back outside, then up another set of stairs to his loft.

"Guess we'll find out, won't we?" He unlocked the sliding door, hustling me inside as he shut it behind him, turning to hungrily face me.

He stalked to me, his gaze already devouring me, my heart slamming against my ribs. He pressed against me, granting me the privilege to feel every inch of him.

"You're not just going to be late for work."

"Oh?"

"The things I have planned…you'll have to call in sick. Maybe tomorrow too. I don't think you will be able to move for a while."

"My boss will be really mad," I whispered.

"I think he'll understand." He leaned over, his words trailing down my neck as he spoke in my ear. "I am going to take my time. Taste every inch of your skin before I fuck you so deep and thorough, you won't be able to move for a week."

My lungs sputtered in response, my body reacting to his claim.

"And if your boss has a problem with that." He walked me back into the bed, stripping me of my shirt and jeans. My knees hit the edge and I fell back on it, his body crawling over mine. "Then I think you need to fuck him again, to shut him up." His lips came down, opening my mouth with a kiss so deep and intense, I didn't think I could handle slow.

I wanted him now. I ripped off his shirt, grabbing desperately for his pants.

"No, Freckles." He grabbed my arms and locked them above my head as his mouth started moving down my body, licking a path between my breasts. "I'm going to see how far I can push you until you break. Torture you." He flicked the clasp of my bra and flung it to the floor, his lips wrapping around one nipple.

"Shit." I inhaled sharply, arching my back beneath his warm tongue. I groaned as he moved to the other breast, then kissed a trail down my stomach, slipping off my underwear as he moved down my legs.

But if I thought he was kidding about torturing me, I was painfully mistaken, and I mean *excruciatingly*. Tying my hands to the bed frame, he toyed and played with me, keeping me on the crest of orgasm for what felt like hours, but not letting me go over. Nipping, licking, and sucking until I couldn't see straight, then backing off.

"Lincoln. I swear to god…." I hissed, bucking against him, my entire body shaking with desire. "Retribution will be tenfold on you."

"It's one payback I will look forward to." He winked, and slid his fingers out of me as he crawled back between my legs. "Sounds as if you are getting a little cranky."

"Asshole," I said as my legs wrapped around him, squeezing, needing to feel him. "Please…" I was not above begging.

"Say it." His thumb moved around my core, a smirk dancing on his lips as severe coiled pleasure through my body. "If you want it dirty, you need to ask for it."

The moment he smiled, I remembered almost the exact phrase coming out of his mouth the day we met. Even then, he seemed to recall exactly what made me cry out.

He dragged himself back and forth across me, creating pulsating friction that made me whimper.

"If you're gonna live out the fantasy of being with a bad boy, then tell me what you want."

"Fuck me," I demanded, almost angrily. "Now. Fuck me. *Hard*."

He grinned, untying my hands. As they dropped down, tingling from blood loss, he thrust into me, parting my lips in a full cry that clogged my throat. The pleasure of him ripped air from my lungs.

His teeth bit into the flesh of my shoulder, both of us freezing as if it were too much for our bodies to handle. Two weeks of waiting had clearly been far too long. "Fuck…" He started to roll his hips, slowly, moving over me, biting his bottom lip. "Jesus, Freckles…you feel so fuckin' unbelievable."

He picked up the pace, my desire matching his with even more need. Noises and a string of nonsensical words spouted from my mouth in between my demands for more. More of him. More of everything.

Heat started to build in my stomach, filling every limb with electricity. I didn't want it to ever end but couldn't stop the chase, the high almost in my reach.

The bed slammed against the wall, our bodies frantic as cries filled the room. Sweat dampened my skin, my eyes shutting as I felt myself tighten around him.

"Open your eyes, Freckles. Remember I prefer them on me."

I lifted my lids as he grabbed my leg, hitching it higher, plunging even deeper, hitting my G-spot. I exploded beneath him.

I clenched down, and he roared as my body greedily took from him. He thrust so hard and spilled deep inside me. Another quake rattled through my nerves, ripping me from my body. Bliss. So much, it was as if I no longer existed, where nothing could touch me but utter pleasure.

Slowly, reality seeped back around me, my chest heaving to be filled, my heart still hammering under my rib cage. Lincoln breathed heavily, his body still slumped over me. Still inside me. A dazed smile wobbled his mouth.

"Damn, Freckles." He leaned over kissing me, his voice husky. "I think I blacked out there for a moment." His lips brushed mine again. "That was…" He shook his head.

I had no words either. None of them felt worthy of what it was. If I thought it was intense and earth-shattering before…it was only getting more powerful between us. Leaning up, my mouth took his, claiming him with everything I felt. Instantly, I felt him start to harden inside me, his mouth demanding, his fingers digging into my hair.

"I warned you." He nipped my bottom lip, launching a surge of desire down my spine. "You're not only not making it into work tonight, but you might be bedridden tomorrow too." He tilted his hips forward, moving us together, and I wrapped my legs around his waist. "And damn you for giving me whatever you got."

"Do you think my boss will be okay with it?" My hips lurched with his, parting his mouth in a groan. "He might fire me."

"If he had any idea how you feel? What you feel like wrapped around his dick?" His throat was husky with desire. Lincoln set his arms on either side of my head, our tempo unhurried, but if it were possible, even deeper. "He'd demand you stay right where you are."

"Look at that, my boss does lighten up after he gets laid."

Lincoln chuckled, sending a vibration through me that twisted up to a slow building heat, clipping my breath. As his mouth commanded mine, I knew nothing else in the world mattered. Death and loss forced you to really understand what was important in life. What to hold on to. Life would always deliver ups and downs. But in this moment, being with him right now and sharing a life so full of possibilities, my heart felt free. Happy.

Chance. Fate. Whatever it was that made him walk into the bathroom on such a horrific day, I didn't care. Out of the bleakest points in my life, when I was drowning, a force brought me back to the surface. A single light in the darkness.

I had a long way to go, but it was the first time I felt real hope. A life that was mine. A future to discover. And a man to love with all my heart. I planned on doing it. A lot.

I was one of the lucky ones.

EPILOGUE

(Fifteen months later)

Puffy white clouds passed over the lowering sun, a chill running down my spine. Shadows darkened the tombstones lined out before me as my fingers brushed at the dirt collecting inside the carved letters.

Alyssa Ann Thorpe

"Happy birthday, Mom." I squatted down, laying a bundle of tulips—her favorite flower—on her grave. Tears stung the back of my lids, emotion choking the words in my throat. "Sorry, it's been a while since I've come to see you." I cleared my throat, blinking up at the darkening sky. "But I doubt you're here anyway." I believed deeply in Chief Lee's sentiment that Dad and Mom were together somewhere, soaring like eagles, pieces of their souls finding each other.

Amelia, Mia, and I had visited her grave a few times after she first passed, but my schedule was crazy lately, and our visits became more infrequent. Amelia didn't mind; she hated cemeteries. "Mom isn't even there," she'd argue.

Without thinking, I'd driven here today, needing to talk to my mom. Even if she wasn't really here, I wanted to be close to her. Share my news. Somedays the ache of missing her was so much I could hardly breathe. Both Mom and Dad should be here. Dad would especially be proud.

"So much has changed." I wiped my eyes, sitting down cross-legged on the ground. "Amelia is doing so well. She and Mia are living in a small place near the salon; it's cute and safe. Amelia's one of the most popular stylists at the salon now and is actually dating a guy I like. He treats her well but doesn't put up with her shit, which is exactly what she needs. He absolutely adores Mia, which is nice because Zak, that worthless piece of crap, refused to help out. Amelia sued for sole custody. He didn't even try and fight. Mia may want to know him down the road, but for now he's out of her life. Mia has grown so much. Smartest girl in second grade. Stubborn and so freaking inquisitive. She looks so much like Dad, especially when she gets mad." I laughed at the memory of Amelia and me cracking up when Mia's face pinched identically to Dad's. "She has tons of friends, and scarily, a boyfriend or two. There she takes after Amelia."

I zipped up my coat against the particularly chilly day.

"You'd also be so thrilled to know Lucy has moved in with Uncle Gavin. He's still Uncle Gav, and tight lipped about his feelings, but I've never seen him smile so much. He's *really* happy, and Lucy is the best thing that ever happened to him. After Lisa, we know how much he deserves it." My uncle told me at Christmas when they came to see us, Lucy had officially moved in with him and Max, even though unofficially she pretty much had been since the summer. To watch them together, his eyes tracking her with overflowing love, burst my heart with happiness. And as I thought, no one at the precinct cared they were an item.

"And me…" A smile tugged at my mouth.

So much in my life had changed. I had South American stamps in my passport and was already planning to put European ones in it later in the summer. But school and the police academy had pretty much taken every waking minute of my time. I lived an apartment with other students for the summer, taking classes, going to a few parties, meeting new people, but it didn't take long to realize it wasn't for me. I had never been a party girl, but the freedom of not worrying about everyone's bills was refreshing. My roommate probably wouldn't consider me "living" in the dorms, since most nights I was curled in someone's bed across town. When my roommate first met Lincoln, she told me, "Girl, if I ever see you here, I will be disappointed in you. I would never leave that man's bed." Some days it was a tempting idea.

"I never imagined I'd be here, but now that I am…I can't imagine doing anything else." I shook my head in awe. "I know it's going to be so much work, and I'll think about quitting a hundred times a day at first, but I made it this far. I survived the academy. Top of my class." My voice went soft. "I think you and Dad would be proud."

The police academy had been twenty-one weeks of hell. Every muscle and bone were in agony all the time, I cried more times than I'd care to admit, and had obtained so many "war" wounds, I had to take ice baths. It was brutal and unforgiving. Physically and mentally it broke you. But I kept my dad's image in my head, hearing his encouraging words, pushing me forward, knowing I had the strength and stubbornness to make it through. And this was easy compared to what was ahead of me.

"I start field training tomorrow." I gulped, my nerves bundling in my stomach, recalling stories from my dad and uncle about how hard a field training officer could be on rookies. Today, I had a walk-through and met the captain and the rest of the station. My FTO gave me a gift, which I had to wear every day for two weeks, no matter the weather. Let the hazing begin.

"Can you believe it? I'm a rookie cop." Uncle Gavin has been such a help with all my questions. He put in a good word for me at the Albuquerque station, where I was starting tomorrow. It would be a lot of grunt work, but everyone had to start at the bottom and work their way up. Eventually I wanted to be a detective, but it was years down the line.

My cell buzzed in my pocket, and I tugged it out of my coat, a smile spreading my mouth into a goofy grin.

Get your ass home now, Freckles. Lincoln's text lit up my screen. *I have plans for you before work.*

Heat rapidly filled my limbs. Standing, I brushed the dirt off my pants.

Home.

After the summer, I had moved in with Lincoln. He said it would help me save money because I had to quit the bar, focusing on school and the academy, but we both knew the truth. Besides me being there all the time anyway, we couldn't get enough of each other. At the end of the day, I wanted to crawl into bed with him. Our time was sparse recently, and neither of us wanted to waste it playing games. Well, not those kinds of games. If my mother's disease and my father's death taught me anything, it was to go after what you want. Life could take it all from you in a moment. I didn't want to live in fear of Alzheimer's or being shot on the job and not enjoy the time I had. Life was unforgiving and cruel, so when it gave you something wonderful, you had to grab it.

"Happy birthday, Mom. I'll be back soon. I love you. Tell Dad I love and miss him so much too." I touched her headstone and turned back to Lincoln's Bronco, which he'd let me borrow, climbed in, and raced home to the man I loved.

Jogging up the stairs to my loft, all the metal dangling off my uniform pants clicked together. One light was on in the living room, giving the room a shadowy glow.

"Lincoln?" I zipped off my jacket, hanging it on an exposed pipe we used for a coatrack.

"Officer Thorpe…" His gravelly voice came from the other side of the room. I turned toward the bathroom. He leaned against the frame, water dripping off him, only wrapped in a towel, displaying every inch of hard muscle. "Just barging in here? I hope you have a warrant." He rubbed his beard, raising one eyebrow.

My tongue slid over my lip, desire roasting every nerve. "I don't. But it's your word against mine. Who do you think they'll believe? A cop or an ex-criminal?

"Wow." He shoved off the wall, stalking up to me, his gaze roving me hungrily. "I see I'm dealing with a dirty cop. Maybe I can offer something then. A *bribe,* maybe?"

Need coiled through my body. The subtle note of reality, the line we were walking, the truth that penetrated the game, blurred the lines of fiction beneath the game and made my blood sizzle.

"I'm not that kind of cop."

"Oh, I think you are." He stepped up to me, smelling fresh from the shower. His fingers tugged at the bottom of my shirt, his eyes rolling over the gift I was given today at the station, a T-shirt. Over my heart was printed: *Albuquerque Police Department.* In bold giant letters on the back was: *Rookie.* All of us newbies had them on today, and I didn't doubt we would be wearing them until we proved ourselves.

"Barely a rookie and already *so dirty.*" He leaned in so close his breath slunk down my neck. "What can I do for you to look the other way, officer?" His mouth skimmed my throat, slamming desire through me.

I gripped the metal hanging from my belt, curling my fingers around the handcuffs. "You know I can arrest you for bribing an officer."

"I haven't even gotten to the enticing part…but those will definitely be part of it." He pointed at the handcuffs then tugged at his towel, letting it drop to the floor.

At the feeling of his bare skin, his erection pulsing against my hip, I could no longer think, raw craving taking over.

Using a maneuver I learned at the academy, I grabbed his arms, stepped my foot between his, and twisted us around. With a shove he fell back on the bed, fire igniting his blue eyes as I climbed on him, straddling his legs.

"Damn! That was hot." His hands knotted into my hair, yanking me down until our mouths collided. My blue police slacks and sweatshirt itched against my skin. I unbuttoned my pants, sliding them off with my shoes and socks, then stripping my shirt over my head. He pressed his hands to my hips, grinding me against him, the thin fabric of my underwear the only thing keeping him from entering me.

"I may not be the good cop, but I'm not so easily paid off." I snatched the cuffs from my pants, looming over him. "And I'm kind of into torture."

Lincoln's eyebrows raised. "Whatever I need to do to wipe my slate clean, officer." He grinned.

"Oh, that's going to take decades." I grabbed his wrists, and in a blink cuffed them both to the bed. "So we better start making a dent… We'll be here for a while."

He throbbed and twitched underneath me, his pupils dilating with need, intensifying my own for him. I planned to be exceptionally merciless.

"You know when I said retribution would be tenfold on you?" A leer twisted my mouth as I unlatched my bra, letting it drop, knowing he couldn't touch me. "I'm going to see how far I can push you until you break. Torture you."

He groaned as I slide my tongue down his body. I would probably cave before he did, but for now I was going to torment the hell out of him. It was only fair.

I had no idea what was ahead of us, what curveballs life would toss out, but now I found it exciting. As long as Lincoln was by my side, we would overcome anything.

The cop and the ex-con.

Sometimes life had a funny way of breaking you into tiny pieces and putting you back together. Handing you something you never thought you wanted, which turned out to be the exact thing you needed.

Turning the unlucky to the lucky.

The about to *get* lucky….

Thank you to all my readers. Your opinion really matters to me and helps others decide if they want to purchase my book. If you enjoyed this book, please consider leaving a review on the site where you purchased it. It would mean a lot. Thank you.

Also check out Stacey Marie Brown's other Contemporary Romance and Paranormal Romance novels listed in the front of this book.

Acknowledgements

I really fell in love with these characters, and I knew I wanted to keep going with their story but was unsure if readers would feel the same. I am so happy you did! And also demanding Stevie's story. I still don't want to let go of them. Who knows, I might find more of these delicious characters to write about!

I couldn't so this alone. A massive thanks to:

Mom- Every book exists because of your help. Thank you.

Kiki at Next Step P.R- Thank you for all your hard work! https://thenextsteppr.org/

Colleen- Thank you for having my back and helping me with it all! You are awesome.

Jordan- Every book is better because of you. I have your voice constantly in my head as I write. http://jordanrosenfeld.net/

Hollie "the editor"- Always wonderful, supportive, and a dream to work with. http://www.hollietheeditor.com/.

Hang Le Designs- For being so kind and doing such a beautiful cover! http://www.byhangle.com/

To Judi at http://www.formatting4u.com/: Thank you!

To all the readers who have supported me: My gratitude is for all you do and how much you help indie authors out of the pure love of reading.

To all the indie/hybrid authors out there who inspire, challenge, support, and push me to be better: I love you!

And to anyone who has picked up an indie book and given an unknown author a chance. THANK YOU!

About the Author

Stacey Marie Brown is a lover of hot fictional bad boys and sarcastic heroines who kick butt. She also enjoys books, travel, TV shows, hiking, writing, design, and archery. Stacey swears she is part gypsy, being lucky enough to live and travel all over the world.

She grew up in Northern California, where she ran around on her family's farm, raising animals, riding horses, playing flashlight tag, and turning hay bales into cool forts.

When she's not writing she's out hiking, spending time with friends, and traveling. She also volunteers helping animals and is eco-friendly. She feels all animals, people, and the environment should be treated kindly.

To learn more about Stacey or her books, visit her at:

Author website & Newsletter:
www.staceymariebrown.com

Facebook Author page:
www.facebook.com/SMBauthorpage

Pinterest: www.pinterest.com/s.mariebrown

Twitter: @S_MarieBrown

Instagram: www.instagram.com/staceymariebrown/

Twitter: https://twitter.com/S_MarieBrown

Amazon page: www.amazon.com/Stacey-Marie-Brown/e/B00BFWHB9U

Goodreads: www.goodreads.com/author/show/6938728.Stacey_Marie_Brown

Her Facebook group: www.facebook.com/groups/1648368945376239/

Bookbub: www.bookbub.com/authors/stacey-marie-brown

Made in the USA
Columbia, SC
21 July 2019